MISS, I NEVER

Jill Heller

Acknowledgements.

How 'Miss, I Never' came about: In my book 'You Can't, But I Could', the heroine is writing a novel. Some of the passages she's working on appear in the text. Gabriel Davies said, 'You should write that one.'

I'd like to thank Simon Davies for his meticulous editing, and Julie Phillipson for her cover, which has so perfectly captured the spirit of Class 3M.

My thanks to Adrian Parker for proofreading.

I'm grateful to the members of 'Testing the Water' writing group for their help and encouragement.

There are too many people to name, who unknowingly contributed to 'Miss, I Never'. If I say thank you to 'the dream team' at Grimsdyke First and Middle School, way back then … you know who you are.

And lastly, my thanks to the hundreds of children who taught me so much.

This is for Sophie, who will soon be answering to Miss, and Gabriel, who persuaded me to write it.

Ten minutes until the bell. Just ten minutes before twenty-three children would come through that door and her life would never be the same again.

Lauren surveyed the classroom: spotless floor, cupboards, spare desks up against the wall, three rows of four double desks in front of her, walls and windowsill stark and bare. The only sign of life was the maidenhair fern on her desk. Lauren's hands were sweating and she wished she had another half hour to try to remember something, anything to help her survive this first day.

Her thoughts shattered at the sound of the bell. 'Ouch', was it always going to be that loud, that shrill? Was there any way of turning the volume down?

The classroom door opened. Twenty-three children trooped in and sat down. They had been allocated their desks last July and by some miracle remembered where to sit.

'Good morning children. My name is Miss Massey. I'll take the register, then I'll tell you what we're going to do this morning.'

Twenty-three faces looked up expectantly.

Lauren picked up a biro and glanced at the register. 'Charmaine Abbot.'

'Yes Miss.'

A hand in the second row shot up, 'Miss, I don' wanna to sit next to Col. He's smelly.'

'What's your name?'

'Bradley, Miss.'

'Bradley. That is not a very kind thing to say.'

Lauren realised that unkind it may be, but it was also true. Col, Colin was decidedly smelly and on the first day of the school year, too. That did not bode well for the future of the class ambience. Lauren could not recall anything in any lecture or book that addressed the topic of smelly children.

'For the time being come and sit up here in this empty desk.'

Giving Col a dirty look Bradley did as he was told.

Lauren returned to the register.

'Spencer Baxter.'

'Yes Miss,' in a surprisingly deep voice.

'Graham Collins.'

'Yes Miss'.

'Kylie Fletcher.'

'Yes Miss.'

'Kirsty Fraser.'

Silence.

'Kirsty Fraser. Is Kirsty not here?'

A voice near the front said, 'Kirsty is here Miss, only she, like, she speaks soft, like.'

'Oh, I see. Kirsty put your hand up, please.'

A small hand, attached to someone in the back row, reached tentatively heavenward.

'Thank you Kirsty.'

On automatic, Lauren got to the end of the register. It had never occurred to her that taking a class register could be anything but simple and straightforward, yet here she was about half an hour into her teaching career with the problems of the malodorous Col and inaudible Kirsty.

Lauren looked down the list of names, remembering the oft-repeated advice, 'get to know their names as soon as you can – a little *aide-mémoire* can help.'

Obviously some surnames were not English. Thank goodness for Chang. Lauren had identified him at once, and Ashok and Pritti were clearly recognisable. But which one was Ignacio? Lauren realised that her knowledge of Spanish might come in handy one day. Was Inga Karlsson the girl with the blonde plaits or was that Suzanna Kowalski?

'Now,' Lauren said, 'I'll try to learn your names as soon as I can. I have got twenty-three to learn. You have only got one. It's polite for you to call me Miss Massey.'

Bradley's head had disappeared behind the lid of his desk.

'Do you understand, Bradley?'

The lid went down with a thump. 'Yes Miss.'

'Miss who?'

'Miss you, Miss.'

'Yes, but what is my name?'

Bradley's mouth fell open and his head tilted slightly to the left.

'Tell Bradley what my name is children.'

A chorus of 'Miss Massey' arose from the class.

'It is polite,' Lauren said, 'to call people by their name. You calling me "Miss" is the same as me calling you "boy" or "girl", and that's not very nice, is it?'

A chorus of 'No Miss' arose from the class with one or two 'Massey's' trailing away as the hiss of the Miss faded away.

Lauren sighed and decided to leave the 'Miss' business for another day … another week …

The next hour or so was spent writing names on exercise books and allocating reading books. Lauren had been entrusted with a large chart indicating where each child was on the reading scheme. It occurred to her that the chart on a jumbo jet, or ship circumnavigating the globe

3

might be simpler to understand.

Their labours were interrupted by the far-too-loud bell.

'It's playtime, Miss,' Colin shouted.

'You will line up one row at a time and go out quietly.'

Lauren found her way to the staffroom. Fiona, a young woman, a few years older than herself was waiting for her.

'Are you surviving? It is Lauren, isn't it? It gets easier, I promise you.'

At that moment another teacher butted in wanting to talk to Fiona.

Lauren found herself in a corner of the staffroom, cradling a mug of coffee, searching her mind for some nugget of advice that would help her get through the day.

She had been surprised at the advice just about every teacher she came across doled out to her. Lauren had decided to keep a scrapbook of 'little hints and tips' or 'advice to probationary teachers.'

There was the deputy head who said, 'You'll not be short of that, not of advice you won't. Everyone's been to school, so everyone reckons they know how to teach and the first thing they'll tell you is that you're getting it all wrong. Just remember this, young Lauren, if their child is happy the parents will tell all and sundry you're a good teacher. Child not happy you're the lowest of the low. So if we sat on our behinds dishing out Mars Bars all day the entire teaching profession would be pronounced brilliant.'

Then there was the dithery teacher who looked as if she had straws in her hair and who'd said, 'shh shh' to her class all the time to no effect whatsoever. She'd told Lauren 'Just three things to remember: never sit in the deputy head's favourite chair in the staffroom, find out where you're supposed to park and don't upset the caretaker. Remember that and you'll be all right.'

A young teacher, probably still smarting from her mistake said, 'Bring your own mug to the staffroom, not one with some clever motto on it. That can grate after a while. Never, ever, use anyone else's mug but don't make a fuss if someone uses yours.'

One school seemed to have very odd priorities. 'Find out what the really important things are, like where the head likes children to put the date when they're writing essays. Heads can get seriously tetchy if you get that wrong.'

Lauren hoped she'd never have to teach a class beginning to do 'joined-up' writing. She'd done a teaching practice where a class was doing just that. The class teacher had said, 'With joined up writing lower case R's are the minefield. With most children the R just disappears altogether, goes underground, drives headteachers bananas. And watch your lower case F's. Do they have a tail and go below the line? If so how far?'

There was a lot more in the same vein. Several teachers had taken Lauren to one side and said, 'A lot of what they teach you in college is a load of nonsense. Do what I tell you and you'll be fine.' One had said, 'Trust me, I've had thirty years' experience.'

Lauren remembered what her favourite lecturer had said about the thirty years' experience. 'Sometimes it's just one year's experience thirty times over.'

Two pieces of advice had made Lauren wonder whether she'd chosen the right profession. 'Don't make empty threats, but sarcasm is fine. It's lost on the children, but it will make you feel a whole lot better.' That one was only marginally better than, 'Don't smile at them until half term or they'll think you're a soft touch.'

Lauren had been left in no doubt that the enemy was out there somewhere. For some teachers it was the children, for others it was parents, the head and deputy head also ranked high on some lists.

Just for the moment Lauren couldn't recall anything remotely helpful.

Fiona came back to join her. 'As it's the beginning of term it will be Assembly after break. After Assembly I'm going to get my class to tell each other about the best day of the holiday. That will take us nicely to lunchtime and you can catch your breath then.'

'Thanks. I think I'll do that, too. I had lesson plans...'

'So had I. But they never work on the first day back. I've learnt just to survive the day and start with lesson plans tomorrow.'

Chapter 2

Dropping her bag, Lauren slumped into the saggy, baggy easy chair in her flat. She'd have to do something about the chair one day. The seat cushion dipped to the left, pitching her sideways. To make herself more comfortable Lauren went to fetch a pillow from her bed, kicking her shoes off on the way.

Cradling a cup of tea, Lauren leant back in the now overstuffed chair, closed her eyes and went over the events of the day.

A sea of small faces bobbed in front of her closed eyes. Could she put names to them?

Lauren had made a copy of her class register to keep at home, so she could learn the children's names quickly. Better do that soon, she thought, while she still remembered some of them. Picking up a biro she began writing beside the names.

Charmaine Abbot – easy, front row left

Spencer Baxter – deep voice. Meerkat … or was that Mark Murray?

Graham Collins – red hair,

Kylie Fletcher – not sure … curly hair?

Kirsty Fraser – the silent one

Adam Gregory – eyelashes, longer than any male had a right to

Robert Harding – ears, like sails, recommend stands sideways in a high wind

Bradley Hawkins – yes, image firmly imprinted

Ignacio Hernandez – not sure

Louisa Hughes – the freckled, motherly one?

Inga Karlsson – Swedish but dark, hiding behind much too

long fringe
Suzanna Kowalski – blonde plaits
Chang Liu – thank goodness for Chang
Arabella Miller – the one with eyes like raisins?
Mark Murray – long neck, small head looks like meerkat or is that Spencer?
Sally Newman – not sure
Ashok Patel - Yes
Pritti Patel - Yes
Colin Riley – Noisome. Funny ... you can be noisome and absolutely silent
Maria Stewart – now there's a name to conjure with, but who is she?
Joanna Taylor – too large trainers, looks like a rag doll?
George Webb – solemn, plump, pudding basin haircut, looks like very small monk
Jonathan Wheeler – can't picture him.

Lauren checked the yesses and gave herself a pass mark.

The biggest plus from the day had been Fiona. Lauren felt she could go to Fiona for help. Most of the rest of the staff seemed quite a bit older. They had been kind ... almost soothing. There was a hint of 'there, there' to their welcoming remarks. Lauren had felt as if she was being patted.

As for the deputy head, Hugo Preston, he looked like someone from another era, wearing a suit complete with waistcoat. But for the short hair standing straight up, toothbrush fashion, he could have been Mr. Pickwick. A large man, somehow he didn't look solid. The visible flesh looked like well risen dough. Lauren had the impression that if she poked her finger into his cheek there would be a dimple which would, only very slowly, disappear. Hugo Preston moved in waves, rising on his toes before lurching forward. Lauren found herself thinking of a perambulating duvet.

Mr. Preston had been polishing his glasses when he drifted over at break time. He squinted at Lauren through half-closed eyes. She reckoned he thought he was twinkling at her – which was what Mr. Pickwick would have done. Mr. P continued polishing his specs when he addressed her.

'It is Lauren, isn't it? Welcome to Springmeadow. Spectacles have to be kept clean, my dear. You can't be optimistic with a misty optic.'

Lauren gave herself an invisible pat on the back for managing to squeeze out a smile.

And that Assembly after break... At the beginning of a school year you'd think that Mrs. Montgomery would be up-beat, positive …. welcoming.
But no, Mrs. M made it clear that everyone was to behave themselves, work hard at all times and there was to be no chewing gum. She went on something alarming about chewing gum. Try as she might Lauren couldn't remember anything else about this morning's sermon.

She did remember the first time she saw Mrs. Montgomery...

It was at her job interview. Lauren on one side of the table, a bundle of nerves held together by her best, not-too-short skirt and jacket. Lauren remembered hoping the panel couldn't see her shaking legs.

The three people on the other side of the table were bored stiff and not making a very good job of hiding it. The man, leaning back with one arm on the back of his chair, looked round the room searching for something more interesting than Lauren. The woman, to the right of the head teacher was doodling in large circles, with a red biro, on the pad in front of her. These people clearly had better things to do. Mrs. Montgomery, just glared, the two lines above her nose deepening as she frowned. Mrs. Montgomery's appearance was a gift to a cartoonist. Her face, round as a soup plate, had a surprisingly sharp nose in the middle of it. On the nose were balanced completely round, dark-rimmed glasses. Her hair, almost flat on the top had a raised bit either side. Lauren couldn't decide whether Mrs. Montgomery looked more like the owl or the pussycat.

Looking down at the application form in front of her Mrs. Montgomery said, 'I see you studied Spanish, Miss er … er... Massey. Why was that?'

'My maternal grandmother is Spanish.'

'I see.'

This was followed by a long silence. Then, looking down at the application form, Mrs. Montgomery was suddenly alert. She came to life.

'I see you have Grade 8 on the piano. Do you still play?'

'Yes, I'm a little rusty but …'

'Would you be able to play the hymns for assemblies?'

'Yes, I could do that.'

The atmosphere in the room changed. Something that could have been a smile appeared on Mrs. Montgomery's face. She nodded at the people either side of her. They too, perked up sensing that their ordeal might soon be over.

'The person appointed today will be taking a class of seven and eight year olds in September. Would you be willing to do that?'

'Yes, I did one teaching practice with that age group.'

'Thank you, Miss Massey. Would you please wait with the other candidates. We hope to make an appointment this afternoon.'

Lauren had gone back to sit with the other four candidates: young women of roughly her age, all doing their best not to look hopeful, trying to look cool.

By the way Mrs. Montgomery had reacted when she discovered that she could play the piano, Lauren reckoned she was in with a chance. Her heart sank when she recalled the dreary chords of the hymns they'd sung at school and the way the children's voices swooped from one note to the other. Hymns were not exactly Rachmaninoff's piano concerto, but if she got the job and was expected to play the hymns, perhaps she'd be allowed to come in early to practice.

Lauren hugged herself as she remembered the moment when the door of the interview room opened and the man from the panel said, 'Miss Massey, would you please join us.'

She'd got the job and now she'd survived the first day.

Tomorrow Lauren was to find Mrs. Graham. When Mrs. Montgomery told Lauren that Mrs. Graham would be handing over 'the responsibility for hymns' Lauren found herself hoping the hymns would behave themselves. And tomorrow Lauren would also unveil the careful lesson plans. She hoped the lessons would, somehow, find their way into Bradley and Col. Ah, yes … Col. She'd remember to take some perfume to school tomorrow.

Mum and Dad would want to know how her day had gone. Lauren visualised them waiting for the phone to ring.

She had a pretty good idea what each of them would say.

With the phone passed from one to the other, Lauren assured her mother and father that her flat was absolutely fine and all was well. Her Dad finished with, 'All right for money, are you, Lauren, love?' Her mother said, 'You are eating properly, aren't you dear? It's so important to keep up your strength. Remember not to skip meals, lots of fruit and vegetables and don't forget the protein.'

With her fingers tightly crossed, Lauren assured her mother that she was eating good healthy food.

Putting the phone down she headed straight for the bumper pack of mini pork pies sitting on the top shelf of the fridge with only a bottle of Prosecco for company.

Chapter 3

Friday, the end of the first week: as Lauren waited for the children to troop in she smiled to herself. She knew all their names and quite a bit more about them. Academically Pritti and Adam were streets ahead of the rest of the children. Ignacio, who had been completely silent on the first day, started talking on day two and hadn't stopped, his accent so strong he could have been imitating Manuel from Fawlty Towers. Mark Murray, the dead ringer for a meerkat, had a liquid, infectious giggle – and once he got giggling, so did everyone else, including Lauren.

Kirsty Fraser was a shy wee thing. It took a lot to get a smile from her, but when the smile appeared, it lit up the room. Not only was Kirsty's voice turned down to minimal decibels, her Scots accent was almost impenetrable. She and Arabella were inseparable, which was handy as Arabella often chipped in as interpreter for Kirsty. Kirsty's spelling leaned heavily towards the creative side. Lauren had been puzzling over Kirsty's story following the adventures of a dining sore. The truth only revealed itself when Arabella whispered 'like a brontosaurus' in Lauren's ear.

Lauren decided that if she had to describe her class she would have said they were a jolly lot. Most of them smiled most of the time, they laughed at Lauren's jokes and Sally Newman was always singing. She'd come in after break warbling about a faithless lover, which sounded a tad odd coming from the lips of a seven year old. But faithless lover or not, singing was singing and as Lauren's dad too often said, 'because it is so good a thing, I wish all men would learn to sing.'

As for her own status and importance, Lauren was

now in sole charge of the hymns. She would dearly like to have those particular hymns pensioned off and sent away to enjoy a peaceful retirement, which was what they deserved, having given uncomplaining service for many centuries. She'd wait a bit before asking Mrs. M if she might introduce some new ones and perhaps even have the occasional hymn practice.

Fiona told Lauren to choose her moment if she was going to ask Mrs. M anything. 'Most people go to Mrs. Graham for advice,' Fiona said, 'she's been here forever.' Mrs. Graham was one of those frizzy haired, cardiganed women who looked as if they have been knitted. She had handed over the onerous burden of hymns to Lauren with undisguised relief.

Lauren felt she was beginning to make headway. Most of the children added Massey after Miss when they addressed her. Lauren realised she'd have to steel herself against one or two catch phrases.

When Suzanna complained that Bradley had taken her pencil sharpener, her special one, shaped like a panda with an orange bow over one ear, Bradley reacted with indignation – righteous or otherwise.

'Miss, I never.' This was Bradley's default reply whenever he was addressed.

After playtime the panda with the orange bow in its ear, attached to a pencil sharpener, mysteriously reappeared on Suzanna's desk.

And there was that episode with the noo-noo.

Searching for a missing library book, Lauren had found a rather grubby, possibly-once-pink corner of a blanket in one of the spare desks. A piece of blanket it clearly was, two sides of the square were finished with a deep satin binding, now seriously fraying.

Lauren held it up and asked the class.

'Does anyone know what this is?'

She gazed down at a sea of curious, speculating expressions.

'It looks like a noo-noo,' Sally said.

'A what?' Lauren asked.

'A noo-noo. My little brother's got one. He won't go anywhere without it, he won't go to sleep without it. My Mum says he'll be clutching it when he walks up the aisle on his wedding day. He's already three year's old.'

'Is this his noo-noo?'

'No, Miss Massey. Our Billy's noo-noo is much better chewed than that.'

'So no one knows who this belongs to?' Lauren asked.

On a whim she carefully put the noo-noo back in the empty desk where she'd found it, letting the children see her do it.

Which one of them still wanted that scrap of comfort blanket close by?

By the following morning the noo-noo had disappeared.

Alas, Col was still oderiferous. Lauren had perfected a technique for not breathing in when Col approached her desk to ask how to spell something, but that didn't solve the problem, which was clearly a tricky one.

Should she ask Mrs. Montgomery's advice? Was today a good day?

You could always tell what mood Mrs. Montgomery was in by the position of her bosom. If her ample frontage was well corseted and worn high – watch out. Should the corseting be less stringent, allowing the bosom to relax just a little, then Mrs. Montgomery was in a mellower mood. This mellowness was relative, but if a request was to be made or advice asked, it was essential to note the whereabouts of the bosom.

Today it sat perilously near her chin. No, Lauren decided, today was not the day to ask Mrs. M for advice.

Mrs. Montgomery's given name was Norma, but no one ever called her that. Lauren wondered whether her husband ever ventured, 'Norma, my dear ...' It was easier to imagine the scene at their breakfast table with Mr. M saying, 'Mrs. Montgomery, may I trouble you for the toast?'

It was no good asking Hugo Preston, either. The deputy head was counting the minutes to his retirement. He tried to turn everything into a joke and Lauren knew that on this occasion it would be only too easy.

Had the Col problem got worse? It was certainly no better. Lauren wondered if there was such a thing as an odorometer, a gauge to identify the intensity of a scent. Her own liberal daily dabbings of perfume wore off too quickly to make any difference.

Bradley still sat where Lauren had placed him on the first day. Bradley turned to glare at Col at regular intervals. There was some kind of vendetta between the boys. She'd seen them on the playground, squaring up to each other, standing – all four foot nothing of them – legs apart, baby faces doing their best to look menacing. They reminded her of puppies trying to growl.

Lauren glanced down at a pink form on her desk headed, 'Medicals.' Below that was written, 'children for whom you may have cause for concern.' It asked for 'name, date of birth of any child you may think is in need of medical attention. Please also state the cause for your concern.'

Lauren had a light bulb moment: malodorous child – over to you doctor. She looked up Col's date of birth and under 'cause for concern' wrote, 'a delicate matter.' Let them think it was something to do with his waterworks and her prissiness and inexperience. No way was she going to write, 'this child smells to high heaven.'

Charmaine's non-stop coughing needed attention. Lauren reckoned it could just be nerves, but better be sure. She added the name of Chang who needed to have his hearing tested. Lauren noticed that when the carefully chosen, (by her), classical music was played, as the children left assembly, Chang covered his ears with his hands. There was definitely something wrong with Chang's hearing.

The children trooped in. They seemed exceptionally happy. Perhaps they, too, had that Friday afternoon feeling. Lauren had planned a quiet, peaceful end to the week: some silent reading, then finishing off uncompleted tasks. She'd end the day by introducing the class to 'Charlie and the Chocolate Factory.' They would love the book so much that, should they misbehave, Lauren reckoned the class could be brought to heel by the mere threat of no 'Charlie today.'

Ignacio began chatting to his neighbour three minutes into silent reading time. A reprimand was only effective for a further few minutes.

Lauren decided that the moment to pounce at him in Spanish had arrived. Taking a deep breath she said, 'Ignacio, por amor de Dios, cállate la boca.' It was perilously close to telling him to shut up, but was probably allowable, being foreign and therefore educational.

Ignacio looked stunned, did a double take and

stopped talking.

Feeling just a tad smug Lauren revelled in Ignacio's silence.

'Charlie and the Chocolate Factory' was every bit as popular as Lauren had hoped.

At the end of the day the children filed out saying, 'Goodbye', with the majority adding, 'Miss Massey.'

Adam added, 'I hope you have a lovely weekend.'

Ignacio was the last to leave. As he reached Lauren he said, 'Mees, you don't speak Spanish so good.'

Chapter 4

It was really warm for early September. The two rooms Lauren called her flat were getting stuffy and there was no way of encouraging a breeze to run through it. She'd go to the park with a book and a sandwich, go for a stroll under the trees and do the shopping on the way home, perhaps even remember her mother's advice and buy something healthy.

Feeling virtuous, Lauren finished the marking first.

In the park she found a comfortable bench, and getting out her book, put her lunch, which was in a paper bag, on the ground beside her. The glare from the sun on the white pages made her eyes itch, so, putting the book down Lauren closed her eyes and leant back.

She sat up with a start. There was something wet and furry round her ankles. Looking down she saw a cocker spaniel pick up her lunch bag in its mouth and race off with it. Furious, Lauren stood up and was about to give chase when a man appeared from nowhere. He started running after the dog, shouting, 'Come back, Goldie, come back.'

Lauren watched in horror as the dog, clearly enjoying the game, stopped and lay down full length on top of the bag. Catching up with it, the man said, 'Come on, Goldie, give it to me.' But the dog wasn't done yet and continued sitting on it, panting with its tongue lolling inches away from the bag.

The man made a grab for the bag which resulted in a very brief tug of war. The bag tore, spilling the contents over the grass. The man looked down, then over to where Lauren was standing, hands on hips.

He walked over to her, 'Was that your lunch?'

'Yes, it was,' she said, too loudly, 'you really ought to keep your dog under control.'

'I'm so sorry. She's never done that before. I will, of course, pay for your lunch. Would you like me to go and get a replacement for you?'

At that moment two children appeared and stood beside the man. Lauren realised, with something like horror, that the boy was...Adam, Adam in her class. Fiona had told her about him, how Adam and his little sister were being brought up by Dad, a widower.

Adam looked up with an angelic smile and said, 'Hello, Miss Massey.'

'Hello, Adam.'

Lauren turned to the man. 'Thank you, it won't be necessary to replace my lunch.'

Grabbing her book Lauren hoped she was making a dignified exit. But she had to walk past the scattered contents of her paper bag: one burger, a very large, sugary doughnut and a Mars Bar.

Only yesterday morning Adam had been listening to her extolling the virtues of healthy eating.

On Monday morning Lauren dreaded Adam's arrival but she need not have worried. He greeted her with his usual angelic smile.

She had intended to ask the children to write about their pets, or a pet they would really like, but the memory of Goldie running off with her mega-calorific lunch changed her mind. They would write about their favourite toy or a toy they'd like.

At break Lauren told Fiona about the lunch bag incident. Fiona laughed, 'I love it. WHAT did you say was in the bag?' Fiona giggled. 'The lunch is beside the point Lauren. What about Mr. Gregory? Dishy or what?'

'I didn't really notice,' Lauren said and was rewarded with an unbelieving look from Fiona.

On Tuesday Adam arrived barely visible behind a huge bunch of flowers. He had difficulty holding them in one arm. The spare hand was clutching a letter. Hard behind Adam loomed Mrs. Montgomery, glaring at the flowers, then at Lauren, then at the letter. Only Adam was spared.

'Miss Massey, please see me at first break,' whereupon Mrs. Montgomery sneezed several times and dabbed her generous nose with a tissue. Lauren had been told that Mrs. Montgomery was allergic to pollen, perfume, polish, shampoo ... the list was endless. This meant that her nose was permanently moist. She shed tissues in her wake. Mrs. Montgomery reminded Lauren of the story of Hansel and Gretel, dropping crumbs to find their way home. Mrs. Montgomery's whereabouts could be pinpointed by following the trail of tissues around the school.

At break time Lauren knocked timidly on Mrs. Montgomery's door.

'Come. Sit.' She glared at Lauren.

'Miss Massey, I will not have romantic liaisons conducted on the school premises, do I make myself clear?'

'This is not a romantic liaison, Mrs. Montgomery. (Lauren had not had time to read the note.) I expect Adam's father sent the flowers to apologise.'

'Apologise? Apologise for what, may I ask?'

'His dog ate my lunch.' This was not strictly accurate but Lauren was not about to describe the scene.

'And where did this happen?'

21

'In the local park.'

'Miss Massey, I am seriously disappointed in you. You have been with us a matter of days and already you are conducting a liaison with a parent. This is unwise, extremely unwise. Frivolity and discipline do not mix. No good can come of this, I assure you. I urge you to terminate this ... this liaison immediately.'

'Mrs. Montgomery. I was in the park, on my own, reading. Adam's dog just came up to me and stole my lunch. I had never even seen Mr. Gregory before.'

Mrs. Montgomery continued to glare.

'Well, if that is the true story, the bouquet Mr. Gregory sent by way of apology is, shall we say, unnecessarily luxurious. That will be all, Miss Massey.'

Lauren didn't have time to read the note until her lunch break.

'Dear Miss Massey,

Please accept these flowers as an abject apology for what happened on Saturday. I should have sent them yesterday, but could only find petrol station ones and they were so dull they hardly deserved to be called flowers.

This seems a very inadequate way to apologise. Would you allow me to take you for a meal one evening?

Sincerely.

Greg (Michael Gregory)'

Oh, no, no. That was not going to happen. Lauren could visualise the scene if the restaurant Mr. Gregory chose happened to have Mr. and Mrs. Montgomery at the next table. Mrs. M would have conniptions, steam coming out of her ears. She might even spontaneously combust.

Lauren looked at the flowers, now resting in a bucket that Fiona had found somewhere. Bucket and flowers took up the best part of her desk. One thing Mrs. M was right about; by way of apology the bouquet was unnecessarily luxurious. It was just too ... too much, over the top: several long-stemmed roses of the deepest possible red, spiky dahlias, pale yellow or ridiculously golden, exotic frondy, pale green leaves ... No wonder Adam, struggling behind them, could barely see his way into the classroom. What was Mr. Gregory thinking of? There was such a thing as proportion ... appropriateness and this bunch was quite simply ... outrageous.

The children would be coming in soon. Lauren looked at her visual aid for the afternoon's lesson. The children were going to be introduced to maps and the rules of map-making. She had borrowed a large square garden tray from Sarah, her landlady, and some sand and toys from the infants' classroom. And here laid out in front of her was a miniature farm, with barn and outhouses, a road, a path and some fences.

'Don't touch, please, we need this for our lesson.' Col's hand froze inches above the barn.

To explain how things worked Lauren had made a map of the school grounds: the entrance, caretaker's house, canteen and school building.

'We just need to know the amount of space it takes up on the ground. You can use the wooden blocks to draw round, if you want to, or just use your rulers. And only put on your map things that aren't going to wander away. You can decide what your farm is called.'

'No cows, then?' said Arabella.

'Not the farmer, neither,' Spencer rumbled.

'Quite right,' Lauren said. 'Do you think you can manage it?'

Lauren noticed that the first thing Adam did was to make his large piece of paper square. The farm was laid out on a square tray.

The lesson was the kind Lauren liked best. The children all busy, and she could walk around and talk to them about what they were doing.

Before they'd even started on the maps, several of the children's papers had signposts or notices indicating that this was 'Old MacDonald's Farm.'

But for the interlude in the morning with Mrs. M, accusing her of a 'liaison', the day had gone well. Most of the children had definitely got the hang of map making. True there was the odd cow, pinned for all eternity to a particular spot, but once finished the maps would be displayed, filling up at least one of the gaping, empty classroom walls.

Sitting in her wonky chair, now permanently over-stuffed with a pillow, Lauren tackled the day's marking.

Kirsty's idiosyncratic spelling took a bit of decoding. Lauren hoped that when her shyness had worn off a bit Kirsty would come and ask how to spell a word.

Bradley never asked. He had an enviable confidence in his ability to communicate. Lauren had to admit there was a certain direct, raw energy in Bradley's way with words that might have got him a job with an up-to-the-minute company trying desperately to appeal to teenagers.

The snappy replies, 'I never,' 'It never' were clear and to the point.

Here he had written about a birthday meal for his sister – at McDonald's.

'Tracey dussunt like bergers so she wantid sum fink kelse.'

It was the two K's that struck Lauren most forcefully. Two C's certainly wouldn't have done the trick.

Lying in bed that night Lauren found herself wondering what kind of creatures finks and kelses might be. Finks had to be smooth, slinky and upright with tiny little pink legs. Kelse's? Little beady eyes, flat-ish, fluffy, woollier, timid ... perhaps nocturnal...

Chapter 5

The term bumbled along nicely. The visit from the probationer's supervisor was perfunctory but, seemingly satisfactory. Lauren and Fiona had begun spending time outside school together. Lauren could report to her parents, in all honesty, that everything was fine, and with, perhaps marginally less honesty, that she was eating sensibly.

Lauren was getting used to playground duty. You had to get onto the playground early so that, if there was an accident and you were on the playground, the school didn't get sued. No teacher on the playground when the knee got grazed – school got sued. So you hotfooted it onto the playground and hoped someone would remember to bring you a cup of coffee.

Looking round Lauren noticed a group of boys from her class in a huddle on the corner of the playground. Usually it was girls in a huddle, boys racing around.

What on earth were they doing? As Lauren got closer she realised they were peering down each other's trousers. Oh, she thought, please don't let them be comparing …'

She glanced at her watch. Thank goodness it was time to blow the whistle.

The school doctor had offered to give every class a health and hygiene talk and she'd be coming to Class 3M today. Lauren looked forward to meeting this miracle worker.

Col's medical had been last Friday. The following Monday he'd come up to her desk to ask how to spell a word and there was something missing. Lauren had managed, up till then, not to inhale when Col was in close proximity, but … she took a tentative breath. Nothing. Col

26

was an odour free zone.

The doctor was already in the classroom when Lauren came in. Doctor Ryan-Jones was pleasingly plump and wonderfully Welsh. The lilt in her voice and the way she huung on to a syllable here and there so fascinated Lauren she found it hard to concentrate on what the Doctor was actually saying.

'I'm glad to meet you, it is Lauren isn't it?'

'And I'm glad to meet you, Doctor Ryan-Jones.'

'Della, please. You were a bit worried about Charmaine's cough. You were right to mention it. I'll keep an eye on her. It's nerves, bless her, and she should grow out of it.'

The doctor glanced at her notes, 'Now, about Chang's hearing. I think I know what the problem is. Have you ever heard Chinese music, Lauren?'

'Yes, it's awful, like tin cans and out-of-tune bellows.'

'Well, I think that's what Western music sounds like to Chang. As far as he's concerned he can hear it only too well.'

'Oh. What should I do about it?'

'There's nothing anyone can do about it. Chang will get used to it. It's painful to him but it's not doing him any harm.'

'And Col, Colin?' Lauren asked.

On the day of Col's medical a nurse had been sent by the doctor to ask the precise nature of Col's problem. Lauren had whispered the answer.

'Well, I examined him and managed to find a little rash. I did my best to look solemn and I said to his Mum "with delicate skin like Colin's I'm afraid you'll have to keep him extra clean and change his underwear every day.

27

We don't want the rash to turn nasty, do we?" I could see Mum liked the "delicate" bit, so I said, "I expect you've got the delicate skin, too." She nodded and smiled, then she said, "I told his Dad our Col was delicate, but he wouldn't 'ave it ..." Sometimes a bit of diplomacy is called for. Mothers have enough guilt to contend with without me adding to it.'

The children came trooping in looking curiously at the doctor.

Lauren introduced Doctor Ryan-Jones to the class. Thanking Lauren the doctor began.

'I'm going to talk to you this afternoon about keeping healthy and happy, because no one is happy when they're poorly, are they?'

A dutiful chorus of 'no' came from the class.

'And afterwards you can ask me any questions that come up.'

Bradley's hand shot up.

'All right, just this one question now, but the other questions will have to wait until I've finished.'

Looking at Bradley the doctor said, 'What did you want to ask?'

'You know belly buttons, Miss?'

'Yes, I know belly buttons.'

'My Dad he says that's where the canningbull puts the salt. Is that true, Miss?'

'No, that is not true. Let's get on, shall we?'

Without putting his hand up Bradley said, 'Wass a canningbull?'

The doctor sighed. 'Do you believe in monsters?'

A chorus of 'yes' arose from the class.

'Now, there's a pity,' the doctor said, 'and your teacher

it is full of tellys. I can see them if I stand on my brother push chair.'

Lauren put the exercise book down. Open Evening was coming up. Bradley's Dad would see this and might punish Bradley for disclosing the secret. And if she was aware of someone harbouring stolen goods and didn't say anything, did that make her an accomplice?

Lauren wondered if there was anyone on the staff she could ask. She'd ask Fiona. Anyway did teachers always believe everything children wrote? Just to be on the safe side, sadly, Bradley's exercise book would have to go missing on Open Evening.

The last book was Adam's. 'My dad has a special room just for his work stuff. Its called a studio. There is a desk with a big board on it and hundreds of pens and things. My dad is an illustrator, that means he is a drawer.'

Oh, Lauren thought, Adam's dad is a drawer and Bradley's dad is a fence. Is there a wardrobe somewhere?

'My dad is a drawer. He has a special room just for his drawing stuff.'

'My dad,' Michael Gregory ... an illustrator. It hadn't occurred to Lauren before. The illustrator of those books about a daft cocker spaniel was called – yes – Michael Gregory. Surely there couldn't possibly be two illustrators called Michael Gregory. And if she remembered rightly, the cocker spaniel in the books was the image of the thieving Goldie.

She would find one of the Michael Gregory books first thing tomorrow and check.

As soon as she got to school, Lauren headed for the library. There were a few books by Michael Gregory, most of them about a daft spaniel with a lopsided tongue. The dog's name was Barker. The boy and girl in the illustrations bore striking resemblances to Adam and his sister.

At playtime Lauren called Adam, 'Don't go just yet I want to ask you something. Did your Dad write this book?'

'Yes.'

'And is this dog Goldie?'

'No, that's Barker, Goldie's Daddy. Goldie is a bitch.'

Absolutely anatomically the correct term, Lauren thought, but it did sound odd coming from the mouth of a seven year old.

'I gave Barker his name. Dad gave mum a cocker spaniel for her birthday. When it arrived the dog started making noises and mum said, "Why did you buy such a terrible barker?"'

'Was it very loud?'

'No. Mum said it sounded more like a seagull. Then someone asked me what our dog's name was and I said, "terrible barker." I was only small then. Dad laughed and said, "Barker it is," so the name stuck.'

'Where does your dad get his ideas for the books from?'

'It's things that really happen, Miss Massey. Goldie is always getting into trouble. She steals things.'

Lauren remembered Michael Gregory saying, 'She's never done anything like that before' as she watched Goldie disappear with her lunch.

'Goldie steals things?'

'Oh yes, all the time.'

'Thank you Adam, you can go out now. There's still plenty of playtime left.'

Lauren was beginning to dislike Michael Gregory intensely. He'd already got her into trouble with Mrs.

Montgomery with a ridiculously large bouquet by way of an apology. Now Lauren was sure it was only a matter of time before she'd star in one of his books. Her mega calorie lunch, painted in full technicolor, would be seen strewn across the pages of a book for all the world to see.

Lauren wondered whether she should ask him, very nicely, not to do it, and decided against it.

She would be meeting Michael Gregory, all too soon, at Open Evening. The governors of Springmeadow School or Mrs. Montgomery or someone, had decided that there were to be two opening evenings each year. One very early in the school year and one at the end. Lauren would ask Fiona to tell her how Open Evenings worked.

After receiving the huge bouquet, Lauren had sent Adam home with a brief, very brief, letter for his father. 'Thank you very much for the flowers. I assure you there was no need for you to send them.' She had decided to simply ignore his invitation to a meal. He'd get the message.

Still ... he'd be sitting here, beside her, in this room, presumably, with a vivid picture in his mind of her lunch strewn across the park, just itching to commit the whole thing to paper and sell the book. It would be hilarious. Of course it would. Lauren felt herself getting angry.

Then there was Adam. Adam was ... well behaved, bright, sunny, cheerful, considerate. A class full of Adams would be complete bliss to teach. Lauren vowed she wouldn't let her dislike of Michael Gregory affect Adam.

Lauren's musings were brought to an abrupt halt by a sudden commotion outside her room. Fiona appeared holding the back of Bradley's collar in one hand and the back of Col's collar in the other.

'Miss Massey, I'm very sorry to have to tell you that I caught these boys fighting along the corridor. I don't know what they were doing inside the school building at playtime. May I leave them with you to deal with?'

'Of course, Miss Bates.'

Col and Bradley stood in front of Lauren's desk, their expressions a mixture of anger and shame.

'Now, what's all this about?' Lauren asked.

Bradley sniffed and clenched his fists.

'Come on, who started it?'

'I hit him back first 'cause he was going to,' Bradley said, glaring at Col.

'Were you?'

'Yes I were,' Col replied.

Lauren realised that the conversation had hit a buffer. She was half tempted to congratulate Bradley on his perfect definition of a pre-emptive strike, but decided it was time for decisive action.

'I've a good mind to send you to Mrs. Montgomery, unless …'

Both boys looked up hopefully.

'Unless you shake hands and say sorry. Now go on, go on, … shake hands.'

'Sorry Col.'

'Sorry Brazza.'

Brazza, Lauren though, where had that come from?

'And you'll have to stay in at playtime this afternoon and write about, "Why I must not fight." Now go and sit down and think about how silly you've been.'

As person-in-charge-of-playing-hymns Lauren had to sit at the piano, as impassively as she could, while Mrs.

Montgomery took a rehearsal for Harvest Festival. The hymn singing had to be perfect because the vicar, The Rev. Palmer, was coming to take the service. Mrs. M's idea of rehearsing was to say, 'Sing it again, only do it better this time.' The children interpreted 'better' as louder, so having got it 'better' three times in a row the result was verging on raucous. The hymns, Lauren was sure, were the ones her grandmother had sung. Lauren wondered whether the children had the faintest idea what they were warbling about.

On harvest festival day, with the stage covered in offerings from the parents, mainly tins of baked beans, the children sang that they had ploughed the fields and scattered, and assured the assembled company that all was safely gathered in.

When the vicar asked the children what the harvest festival was all about, a small girl in the front row put her hand up. 'It's about mice,' she offered. 'I saw a picture of a harvest mouse. It was tiny, tiny.' She put her hand up and indicated on her little finger just how tiny the mouse was.

Completely unfazed, the vicar said, 'Quite right, quite right. I expect the mice, together with all God's creatures, are grateful for the harvest too, and are even now raising their voices in praise.'

Chapter 7

Relishing their Saturday morning, Fiona and Lauren sat in the window of the Apollo Cafe, shopping bags at their feet.

Lauren carefully hoovered up the last remaining crumbs of a slice of lemon drizzle cake with her index finger, making sure she captured every last bit of icing.

'I think the father of one of the children in my class is keeping stolen goods. Should I do anything about it?'

'Are you talking about Bradley Hawkins?' Fiona asked.

'How did you know?' Lauren's crumb covered finger stopped half way to her mouth.

'He's been inside more than once. But I think Mr. Hawkins is more a rogue than a villain and he's an absolute charmer. I've met him. I had Wayne, Bradley's older brother, in my class. Just wait till you meet him. He'd try to sell snowballs to eskimos.'

'So how come he gets into trouble?'

'Overconfidence I guess. And perhaps not the sharpest knife in the box.'

'Bradley's written about what I assume are stolen goods in his dad's garage. His dad will see it on open day, which could get Bradley into big trouble. What should I do?'

Fiona thought for a minute. 'You could ignore it, and hide the exercise book. You could tell Mrs. M – no, scrub that one. I know! You could tell Mr. Hawkins you know what he's been up to and you want a cut to keep quiet and not go to the fuzz.'

'How much of a cut?' Lauren asked. 'It would have to be worth my while.'

'Ten percent sounds reasonable, not too greedy.'

'How do I go about it? You'll come with me, Fiona? I suppose we'd have to sidle up to him one dark night and say, "We know everything and I do mean everything. What's it worth for us to keep shtum?"'

'We'll do it,' Fiona nodded, 'we'll stand there, arms crossed, eyes narrowed. And if he's done something a whole lot worse than hiding stolen goods and he thinks we know, we could make a real killing.'

Lauren leant back in her chair.

'My mum suggested I do a bit of coaching or give piano lessons to supplement my income, but I think a visit to Mr. Hawkins would be a great deal more lucrative. O.K. I'll mislay Bradley's exercise book on Open Evening.'

'Ah yes, Open Evening. I want to get you properly genned up on that. Our two Open Evenings are strategically spaced for a purpose; there is a formula to be followed. The one near the beginning of the year, next week's one, is so that we can tell the parents that everyone in the class is badly behaved and thick as porridge...

'But ...' Lauren interrupted.

'Hear me out, girl. You phrase it differently for each child, of course; this one is behind the rest of the class in this or that subject, that one doesn't seem to grasp basic mathematics, comprehension needs attention ... struggles a little to express herself, lacks confidence, doesn't contribute, laziest creature on God's good earth ... if you need more phrases of a similar nature I can provide them. The point is that these children right now are miserably backward, inadequate in every way, so that by the end of the year you can tell their parents that they are all now absolutely brilliant thanks to your incomparable teaching.'

'That's all very well, but what happens next September, if by the end of this school year they're all brilliant?' Lauren asked.

'Every child goes completely to pieces over the summer holidays, forgets everything he ever knew. So that next September they will all …'

'I get it,' Lauren said, 'once again will be thick as two short …'

'You're a quick learner, girl.' Fiona said.

'Hmm.' Lauren wondered how she could possibly tell the dreadful Michael Gregory that Adam was deficient in any way – or Pritti, or a great many of the other children.

'Oh, and if any parent says they'd like to see Mrs. Montgomery for any reason, smile sweetly and say, "by all means." There's not a bat's chance in hell that they'll get to see her, but you needn't tell them that. Mrs. Montgomery is absolutely terrified of parents. You know those lights outside her office – the red and green one?'

Lauren nodded.

'There will be four chairs outside Mrs. M's office on Open Evening, supposedly for parents, but the red light will never go off. New parents sit there forever, willing someone to come out so the green light will go on. Old stagers know it's not going to happen.

Have you noticed that Mrs. M puts the red light on at 3 o'clock and hides in her office every day? Horror of horrors, this is the time of day when a parent might actually stray into the school. There's always the danger that Mrs. M might meet one face to face.'

Fiona laughed before she continued.

'We had a staff meeting last term when someone from the office came down and suggested we start a Parent

Teacher Association. He said several of the other schools in the borough had them. Mrs. M's face was a picture. It got redder, her cheeks puffed out, she shuffled in her chair. I think there was steam coming out of her ears. After the chap had gone she said, "That's not going to happen on my watch. We'd be making rods for our own backs, give them an inch ... they'd start questioning everything." By the way is your class all bright and sparkly for Open Evening?'

'Not really. I have maps on one wall, self portraits with a lot of drippy paint on another, but one wall is still rather dreary.' Lauren recalled the sheets of writing with meagre pencil drawings and wishy washy colouring.

'Tell you what,' Fiona said, 'follow my recipe for instant sunshine and the "phwow" factor. I'll come and help you. We make a template of a seven-year-old-size t-shirt – two dimensional, of course. Then we cut these t-shirts out of sugar paper in a variety of bright colours. On the pale coloured ones the children can paint their design and on the darker ones they cut out and stick things on. Suggest things like ice cream cones, sunglasses and buckets and spades. It doesn't really matter what you suggest, you'll get footballs and kittens. You can label it "holiday memories" if you like. I promise you it will solve the dreary-wall-blues at a stroke.'

'Good idea, thanks Fiona. The thing I'm dreading most about Open Evening is seeing Mr. Gregory again. You remember I told you about meeting him in the park, his wretched dog stealing my lunch, and the oversized apology bouquet? I have a horrible feeling he's going to put the whole episode in one of his books.'

'Then you'll be famous!'

'No I won't, Fiona. I'll look a complete eejit and he'll

make mega bucks out of it.'

Chapter 8

The day after the Open Evening letters went out, Charmaine came up to Lauren's desk and, shifting from one foot to the other, said, 'Miss Massey, my mum can't come on Open Evening. She'll be looking after Maisie and Billy. Can she come in when she fetches me, in the afternoon, like?'

Lauren had planned to go home, shower, change, eat … but with an appointment immediately after school it would hardly be worth going home – even if it was doable.

'Of course', Lauren said, 'tell her that's fine.'

During the day the children made a huge performance of tidying their desks. Dramatic use was made of yellow dusters. Then they wrote notes to tuck away for their parents to find.

Charmaine stayed behind when the other children filed out. She waved at someone just outside the door.

Mrs. Abbot came into the classroom: a large woman with a mass of black wavy hair cascading over her shoulders and down her back. She held a very small girl by the hand. The child had a be-ribbonned tuft of hair sticking straight up, making her look like a pixie.

Seeing Charmaine the toddler beamed and ran towards her.

'This must be Maisie,' Lauren said.

'Yes, Miss Massey. Can Maisie do colouring?'

Charmaine had somehow, picked the child up, and was now on the receiving end of a shower of very wet kisses.

Fetching crayons and scrap paper, Charmaine placed Maisie firmly on her knee and handed her a crayon.

Lauren watched, enthralled. Charmaine was so capable. Lauren thought then, if she had any children she'd happily leave them in Charmaine's care.

Charmaine suddenly got up, took Maisie's hand and left the room swiftly, calling over her shoulder, 'Maisie needs a wee.'

Having assured Mrs. Abbot that Charmaine hardly coughed at all now, was well behaved and working hard, Mrs. Abbot's face fell. She said, 'She does worry about her joins.'

'Her joins?'

'Yes, writing joins. Someone told our Charlie she wrote babyish, like. She was ever so upset.'

Lauren felt herself bristle. How dare anyone, ANYONE criticize Charmaine's writing.

'If there's a booklet, thingey - you know showing the right way to do joins, her Auntie Ivy will help her. Sid and me aren't too hot when it comes to writing.'

When Mrs. Abbot, Charmaine and Maisie – who had insisted on planting a very wet kiss on Lauren's cheek – left, Lauren headed for the staffroom.

Lauren wondered why someone who had gone to the trouble of christening their daughter Charmaine, was now calling her Charlie.

The staffroom was deserted. Everyone else had the sense to go home. Biting into a pork pie Lauren realised she had no idea how she could tell parents their children were dense, uncooperative and lazy, which was what Fiona had counselled. Or had she? Perhaps Fiona just meant Lauren should tone down the praise a bit.

Washed, combed, changed, powdered and shaking like the proverbial jelly, Lauren went back to the classroom.

It had never looked so tidy and she had to admit the multi-coloured t-shirts did make a … an impact. Lauren hoped Mrs. M wouldn't look too closely at some of the slogans, but the overall effect was certainly lively.

A couple had entered the room.

No wonder Mark Murray looked like a meerkat. His dad was a dead ringer for Vladimir Putin, that Russian politician, who everyone knew was leader, emperor of all meerkats. Mark's mum, small and smiley, came towards Lauren, hand outstretched. 'Miss Massey, at last, I've been so looking forward to meeting you.'

Lauren could have hugged her. She very nearly did.

Once again, Lauren failed miserably. How could she criticise Mark?

While she was talking to the Murrays another pair came in. This was how it was going to be for the next couple of hours. Lauren had a sheet of paper on her desk, she'd jotted down 'handwriting' beside Charmaine's name. For the ten minutes or so that she talked to parents, she could concentrate on the child they were talking about, but when they'd gone … Lauren hoped she'd never bump in to any of them in the street. She would be bound to attach them to the wrong child.

An extremely glamorous, bejewelled woman entered the room, preceded by a cloud of perfume. Lauren wondered who she could be. She tried not to look surprised when the vision turned out to be Mrs. Webb, mother of George, the small, round, solemn monk.

A man and woman stopped at the classroom door. The man swaggered around the classroom, occasionally glancing at the walls. It couldn't have been easy to swagger in such a short space, but he managed it – shoulders swaying from side to side. The woman beside him had on an egg-yolk yellow satin blouse, exactly matching her hair.

When the chairs beside her desk were free, swaggerer plus blonde mate approached Lauren's desk and sat down.

'Miss Massey. Bradley says you don' have a car? Is it true?'

He leaned forward, getting his head a little too close to Lauren's, and smiled slowly at her.

'That's terrible. Lovely young lady like you needs a car. I can find you a nice little mini, one careful owner, not a scratch on it, rock bottom price. Cherry red'd suit you. What do you say, Glaw?' Mr. Hawkins shot a perfunctory glance in his wife's direction then turned his full attention back to Lauren.

'If it's driving lessons you're needin', my brother does it, special rates for friends. Now what do you say? I could get you the whole package – drivin' lessons, nice little runabout, guarantee you pass yer test first time round.'

Lauren thanked him as politely as she could manage and muttered that she didn't need a car at the moment.

'Well, when you do decide to get your own wheels – and you will, you will – you know where to come, Miss. Winter's comin' and it will be a whole lot easier for you, safer. And helfier. We can't have our Miss getting wet in a bus queue, and getting poorly, now can we?'

There was more of the same. Anything she needed, ask Mr. Hawkins.

As they left Mrs. Hawkins said, 'Bradley doing all right is he?'

'He's doing well, Mrs. Hawkins.'

Lauren sighed. And she'd spent hours worrying about the incriminating exercise book, now lying at the back of her desk drawer.

Lauren was suddenly conscious of two men studying the display of t-shirts. They were laughing. When they turned round she realised that here was the dreaded Michael Gregory with an older man.

And suddenly there was Fiona.

She came in quickly and put a mug of coffee on Lauren's desk. 'I forgot to remind you to bring a flask. You'll need it. All the talking ... I've got plenty.'
Then she was gone.

It was their turn: Michael Gregory and the older man. They sat down. Michael Gregory's eyelashes were even longer than Adam's, and the pale green polo-necked shirt and navy blazer were exactly right.

'Good evening, Miss Massey,' Michael Gregory said. 'This is my father, Alan, he helps me look after the children, so he usually comes to Open Evenings. I hope that's all right.'

'Of course,' Lauren said, and smiled pointedly at Adam's grandfather.

'Has Adam been behaving himself?' Michael Gregory asked.

'Good as gold,' Lauren said and instantly wished she hadn't. Gold was much too near the name of the thieving Goldie.

Lauren was waiting for the stolen lunch scenario to be brought up so they could get it over with.

'Adam can be a bit lazy, Miss Massey. He'll do as little as he thinks he can get away with.' Michael Gregory was staring at her with a smile playing around his lips.

Stare away, Lauren thought, I bet he's trying to memorise my features for his wretched book.

47

The older Mr. Gregory said, 'You do realise, Miss Massey, that you are the oracle, the fount of all knowledge. At every meal time Adam comes out with, "Miss Massey says ..."'

'How awful!' Lauren exclaimed, racking her brain for every daft thing she'd ever said.

'Not at all,' Michael Gregory said. 'Until this year Adam never told us anything. If we asked him what he'd done at school, the answer was always "nothing." Now every evening we get a minute by minute report.'

Lauren felt herself blushing. How ghastly. Now – by proxy – this awful man would know absolutely everything that happened in the classroom.

Alan Gregory stood up. 'I think we've taken up enough of your time. I'm so glad to have met you at last, Miss Massey. Keep up the good work and don't let anyone bully you. You're doing a grand job.'

The younger Mr. Gregory didn't move. He seemed reluctant to go.

Another couple hovered. Mr. and Mrs. Riley, Col's mum and dad.

'We're ever so grateful to you Miss Massey,' Mrs. Riley, gushed. 'Last year we couldn't get our Col to come to school. He said his teacher picked on him. Comes like a lamb, now he does. I hope he's not quarrelling with the Hawkins boy. My mum says those two are like a red rag and a bull. An' I know which one is the bull.'

There weren't many questions to answer about Col. Mrs. Riley was only too happy to explain the family's history and problems, including the delicate, complicated and explosive state of her mother-in-law's digestion. Mr. Riley sat beside her in stoic silence.

Then everyone had gone.

Lauren could hear voices coming from the room next door and footsteps.

Feeling completely drained Lauren put her arms on her desk, followed by her head and closed her eyes.

'You O.K.? How did it go?'

It was Fiona.

'Thanks for the coffee. It was a life-saver. I think the evening was all right. Ask me tomorrow, when I've digested it. Anyway, I survived. It's over. How about you?'

'Better than expected. I'd been warned about some parents who nitpick over every detail, but forewarned … Didn't I time my coffee rescue well? Michael Gregory is film star gorgeous.'

'Is he? I hate him. He's going to make a fool of me, I know he is. Anyway how do you know him?'

'How do I know him? Lauren, any warm-blooded female setting eyes on Michael Gregory will want to know who he is. I spotted him at sports day last year.'

'I like Adam's grandpa. He said something a bit odd. He said, "don't let anyone bully you." What could he mean?'

'Ah … Rumour has it that Michael Gregory once had a run-in with Mrs. Montgomery. I don't know the details, but that could explain it.'

'How did he manage to get close enough to Mrs. M to have a run in with her?'

'No idea. Come on Lauren, you look done in. I'll give you a lift home. We can't have you getting poorly, now, can we?'

Chapter 9

Although exhausted, Lauren couldn't get to sleep that night. When she shut her eyes parents' faces swam into view. Some faces stayed long enough for her to focus on them – others floated away before she could pin them down.

Had she written down all the comments? All the requests for help? There was absolutely no hope for Kirsty's spelling. Mrs. Fraser, with an accent as heavy as Kirsty's but with a slightly louder voice, confessed that she had never quite got the hang of spelling.

And after Louisa Hughes' extolling the virtues of her mother's new boyfriend's wonderful bottom-warming car, Lauren was surprised to discover there was a Mr. Hughes seemingly firmly still attached to Mrs. Hughes.

Chang's parents had been shy and grateful. Lauren had felt a fraud. Grateful for what? She was bumbling her way through and just about getting by. Ignacio's parents hadn't turned up. Now that was a worry.

And the wretched Michael Gregory. He'd studied her face carefully. Oh yes, she'd noticed that all right, and he didn't mention the episode in the park. Sneaky that – if he had told her she was going to be in his next book Lauren could have asked him not to do it. The fact that he didn't say anything was proof … proof, absolute positive proof that he was writing the book and even now was doing the preliminary drawings. And what was worse, everything she said in class would be repeated, by Adam, at tea time or breakfast, or whenever, to Michael and Alan Gregory.

Lauren put the pillow over her head to shut out … everything.

She managed to blot out the sea of faces but there was still something lurking in the corner. Kirsty had written that she'd had 'a nuff.' This nuff was keeping Lauren awake. It was an airy creature like an empty potato skin, only pink. Lauren fell asleep to a vision of the nuff wandering aimlessly around the classroom in the company of the slinky finks and fluffy kelses.

Dragging herself into school the following morning Lauren found the sheet of notes on her desk where she'd left it. Some of her scribble was illegible. In the margin she had written 'flour pots' perfectly legibly, but the words meant nothing to her. What did loobiks mean? Libibibooks might be library books. Yes, that rang a faint bell.

Was there such a condition as brain-ache? Lauren was having a bad attack and hoped no one would say anything remotely intelligent for at least a week, as she would not be able to process it.

Fiona came breezing in. 'Need an aspirin?'

Lauren groaned, 'I didn't sleep a wink. All those faces …'

'Don't worry. Today I suggest a long session of silent reading, then silent learning of tables and a bit of quiet colouring, then let your two best readers read the story. By the way, don't forget it's fire drill, just before afternoon playtime. Grab the register, line them up and proceed to your post.'

During silent reading Lauren called Ignacio up to her desk.

'Ignacio, are your parents ill? They didn't come to see me yesterday.'

'My mum she O.K., my dad, he O.K. They don't speak English so good.'

'Ignacio. You know I can speak Spanish … a bit. I really would like to meet your mum and dad.'

Lauren waited for Ignacio to contradict her assertion that she could speak Spanish. He studied her for a moment, then said. 'O.K. Miss. I tell 'em.'

Lauren looked down at last night's sheet again. She had written something lengthy and incomprehensible beside Adam's name.

By lunchtime Lauren had a splitting headache. She kept telling herself she only had to get through the afternoon then it would be half term, she'd go home and sleep and sleep and …

Ten minutes before afternoon playtime the fire bell rang. The playtime bell was loud enough. The fire bell was so loud it loosened your teeth and Lauren had a sudden funny sensation round her tummy. Could the maximum decibels be test-stressing the elastic in her underwear? Lauren was surprised to see that the window panes were still intact.

Grabbing her register Lauren said, 'Adam at the front of the line, line up, that's right, one row at a time. Pritti, I want you at the end. Make sure everyone stays in front of you.'

Children streamed out of the building in surprisingly orderly lines, finishing up in rows at the far end of the playground facing the school.

Hugo Preston, the deputy head, was clearly in charge. One class was told to shuffle two inches to the left and everyone was to 'stand up straight.'

For the life of her Lauren couldn't think why.

Teachers began taking the roll call. Lauren wondered if she should have brought a biro with her. Surely just counting the children would have done the trick, wouldn't it?

Lauren called the register – everyone here except Maria who was recovering from an appendix operation.

'Quiet everyone,' Napoleon Preston walked up and down, one arm behind his back surveying his troops. He stopped in front of Bradley.

'What's the matter with your leg, boy?'

'Nothing, Mr. Preston.'

'Well there soon will be if you don't stop annoying the boy in front of you.'

There seemed to be a mild commotion going on two lines to the left of Lauren's class. Mrs. Graham was in deep conversation with the girl at the head of her line.

'All present and correct then?' Mr. Preston boomed.

'No, Mr. Preston. I'm afraid Emily is missing,' Mrs. Graham said.

'Missing? What do you mean, missing?'

'Not here, Mr. Preston.'

'Send someone to find her then send her to me. This behaviour will not be tolerated.'

Two children from Mrs. Graham's class were sent in to search for Emily.

That's right, Lauren thought. Brave Napoleon sends two helpless children into the burning building.

After a few minutes the two children reappeared shaking their heads.

'I'm sure she was here this morning,' Mrs. Graham said. 'I took the register myself. You had my class for games this afternoon, Mr. Preston.'

'Indeed I did and your class took far too long getting changed, Mrs. Graham.'

A girl in Mrs. Graham's class put her hand up.

'Please Mrs. Graham, Emily's little brother is in Miss Scott's class.'

A small boy was fetched. He had a short-back-and-sides haircut and short trousers that were far too long for him. He stared up at Mr. Preston.

'What's your name?'

'Leo.'

Lauren thought that anything looking less like a lion would be hard to imagine, but the lad, unflinching, was gazing up at the bulk that was Hugo Preston.

'You are Emily's brother?'

'Yes.'

'Did she come to school this morning?'

'Yes.'

Consternation filled the silence that followed. Leo continued looking up at Mr. Preston, chin held high. Lauren thought that with his old-fashioned haircut, Leo looked like a miniature … tailor, no haberdasher. She could just imagine him measuring out yards of ribbon.

Someone from Mrs. Graham's class said she didn't see Emily at lunchtime.

Mr. Preston addressed Leo.

'Did your mother come to take Emily home at lunchtime?'

'No.'

'Did your daddy come to take Emily home at lunchtime?'

'No.'

'Does Emily go home on her own?'

'No.'

Lauren began to wonder if she'd ever get her cup of

tea. The children were beginning to fidget.

Another long silence.

Mrs. Graham addressed Leo.

'Did anyone come to take Emily home at lunchtime?'

'No. She went to the dentist.'

'Who fetched her?'

'Granny."

'Did Emily bring a letter?'

'Yes.'

'Who did she give it to?'

'Mrs. Montgomery.'

The relief was palpable. Lauren decided that tea was now a distinct possibility. There was no sign of Mrs. Montgomery. Fire drills were clearly beneath her. By now she would be burnt to a large greasy crisp.

With several harsh words letting all and sundry know he was not best pleased with their behaviour, Mr. Preston dismissed the classes one by one to go to their playgrounds.

Lauren staggered up to the staffroom, hanging on to the thought that after a cup of tea it would be just over an hour until half term.

Chapter 10

Lauren dozed as the train crawled towards Moreton-in-Marsh. Every time she opened her eyes she fancied the bricks on the houses were getting yellower, more golden, nearer to the colour of Cotswold stone. Dad would be meeting her.

There he was, glasses glinting in the sun, wearing his weekend uniform: turquoise tweed jacket with leather elbow patches. Enfolding Lauren in a polar-bear strength hug, he said, 'Let me have a look at you.'

Stepping back he said, 'I do believe you're thinner. Beware, your mum is determined to fatten you up and she hasn't even seen you yet.'

Lauren slid her arm through her father's as he wheeled her case to the car park. There was the cream coloured Morris Traveller her dad had so lovingly restored.

Lauren felt herself relax. 'Mum O.K.?'

'She'll be all the better for seeing you, love. Her big news is that she's joined the golf club and is having lessons.'

'Really? What brought that on?'

'Good question. The official reason is to keep fit and your mum decided it's better to do it in the open air rather than indoors in a stuffy old gym. The real reason is that Edna has taken up golf and persuaded Sarita that it's a good thing to do.'

'What made Auntie Edna join?'

'Official reason?'

'Real reason, Dad.'

'Edna has got the hots for the golf pro.'

Lauren laughed. 'So Mum goes along as chaperone?'

'Gooseberry more like.'

'What happens if said golf pro prefers Mum to Auntie Edna.'

'End of beautiful friendship, I expect.'

They drove the rest of the way in silence, Lauren drinking in the familiar places, noticing that the broken stile at the bottom of the lane was still broken.

And there was Mum. Once again Lauren disappeared into a voluminous hug.

'Let me have a look at you.'

Sarita stepped back. 'You've lost weight. Have you been eating properly? You can't have been. Oh you poor love I hope you haven't been too tired to eat. They're not overworking you are they?'

'Mum I'm fine, and no, they're not overworking me.'

Lauren decided she should publish her newly discovered slimming diet consisting of pork pies, sausage rolls and Prosecco. She'd get an endorsement from Prosecco, of course, and make megabucks.

Lauren wondered why her bedroom looked smaller and quite so absurdly clean.

It was eleven o'clock before she surfaced on Sunday morning. Dishing out scrambled eggs, her mother said, 'Grandma's coming to lunch. She can't wait to see you; roast lamb, roast potatoes, all the trimmings and apple crumble for afters.'

'Custard or cream?' Lauren asked.

'Both.'

'Perfect,' Lauren sighed.

'Mum, there's a Spanish boy in my class but he doesn't think much of my Spanish.'

'There's nothing wrong with your Spanish, dear. I

expect he's from Catalonia. The Catalans think they're speaking Spanish but when I hear them I'm reminded of a gobbledegook we spoke at school. We called it Pig Latin.'

Grandma Massey arrived: yet another hug.

'Let me have a look at you. You've lost weight Lauren. Don't overdo it, dear. I know you youngsters like to be slim, but whatever they say, men prefer a good armful. No man wants to get into bed with a bag of bones. Look at the women in the Rubens paintings, all pink curves and dimpled flesh, delicious, absolutely gorgeous. The models nowadays, they all look alike to me; stick insects with bosoms. What do they call them nowadays? Boobs, that's it. Stick insects with boobs, not womanly at all. And you want to go in at the waist,' here her grandmother demonstrated the 'in' bit with her hands, 'and out above and below, like a cello. I know they're uncomfortable, but there's a lot to be said for corsets, accentuating the in and out, curvy … voluptuous.'

Rubens's women always reminded Lauren of lard. Mum swore lard made the best pastry.

'Grandma,' Lauren said, 'can you give me one good reason why I should mind if a man likes a bag of bones or not?'

'Oh, piff, Lauren, you've not come all over feminist have you? You can't fight nature – and why would you want to? Find yourself a lovely man, my dear.'

The period before lunch was spent sipping sherry, reminiscing and catching up with the local news. The smell of roasting lamb made Lauren question her addiction to pork pies.

Over lunch Lauren found herself telling her family, with only the merest soupçon of exaggeration, just how awful the head and deputy head of Springmeadow were.

'Mr. Preston, Hugo Preston, can hardly open his mouth without some dire pun escaping it. Last week he sidled up to me in the staffroom and said, "What's the difference between a stoat and a weasel?" I must have muttered something because he then said, "a weasel is weasily distinguished and a stoat is stotally different."

'What did you say?' her mother asked.

'Nothing. I just wanted to go and lie down in a dark room.'

'Is he worse than your grandpa?' her father asked.

'Much worse.'

'That bad, eh?' Her father sighed. 'You could always flummox him with Mrs. Bigger. Remember Mrs. Bigger? Who is bigger, Mrs. Bigger or Mrs. Bigger's baby? Answer: Mrs. Bigger's baby is a little Bigger.'

Her father tackled an exceptionally crispy roast potato.

'Come to think of it, it's a wonder anyone ever learns to speak English. We have a Portuguese driver who gets into a tizzy over the weather forecast. He'll hear "with outbreaks of rain" then he asks me, "sir, is gonna rain or no?"

You said the head is terrifying. In what way? Does she growl?'

'She looms, she disapproves, tuts. Nothing is ever quite right or good enough. I'm playing the hymns now, their old ones were dreary, lifeless. Mrs. M had to scrutinize every song I wanted to introduce. "The Magic Penny", an innocuous little piece about spreading love around, very nearly got the thumbs down because Mrs. M said "magic and hocus pocus have no place in a Christian Assembly."'

'When I was at boarding school,' her father said, 'the sports master frightened the living daylights out of me. My father told me to imagine what he'd look like in the bath. He told me to try to visualise this master squeezing water out of a sponge onto a rubber duck. So try to visualise her, Mrs. Montgomery is it? Getting out of a bath – a rather too hot one.'

Lauren got the picture and wished she hadn't. Mrs. M was not so much fat, as solid. She occupied space, seeming to be immovable even when she was processing forward. Lauren tried to remove the vision of Mrs. M's back – yards of bright pink flesh, a behind, and ample thighs, from her mind. She tried to concentrate on the rubber duck but it was invisible behind a mountain of bubbles.

Shaking away the image Lauren said, 'Mum, dad tells me you're taking up golf.'

As was her habit, her grandmother had collected all the crispiest, juiciest tidbits of the meal at the side of her plate, to enjoy at the end. Taking her concentration off her plate for a moment she said, 'Very good for the waist, is golf, and the bust.' Fork in hand she demonstrated her version of the golf swing, 'it's that twist – and all the walking, providing you keep your shoulders back, of course.'

Her grandmother's waist was now rather like the equator; an imaginary line around a solid sphere, with a black belt indicating where it would be if it did exist.

When Lauren and her dad set out for a walk Mum said, 'Mind you're back by four. Edna's popping in for tea.'

Lauren couldn't understand why people found autumn sad. It was such a restful time. The fields looked as if they'd been lovingly stroked. The sun picked out little specks of gold in the tubes of hay that could have been a giant's cotton reels.

Gaining Brownie points, Lauren and her father were back home well before four.

Auntie Edna was already there. She had a new hairdo and hair in a new colour and … one ear now had two piercings, so two ears, three little hoops.

No hugs this time, just a thorough up and down, then up again, appraisal.

'O.K. What's your secret? You've lost a couple or four pounds. What's the secret?'

'Pork pies and Prosecco.'

'Ha, ha, very funny Lauren. I expect you toy with a lettuce leaf.'

'Yes, Auntie Edna, and for a very special treat I allow myself a wafer thin slice of cucumber.'

'Hmm. I think you should stop calling me Auntie. "Auntie" adds ten years to anyone's life and "aunt" piles on another five.'

For the rest of the week Lauren luxuriated in doing very little. Some days, when her mother was on her receptionist's shift at the Medical Centre, Lauren wandered into the village. The shopkeepers were genuinely pleased to see her. Two of them asked if she still saw 'the young Hooper boy'. 'The two of you used to come in together.' The young Hooper boy, Cameron, now ancient history, was in Australia on an enormous sheep farm. Mrs. Manning from the post office said, 'I always hoped the two of you would get together.'

Lauren wondered why people either wanted to fatten her up or marry her off or both.

One evening after tea, her mother said, 'You are happy

at Springmeadow, aren't you? You don't think you've made a mistake, there's nothing worrying you, is there?'

Nothing, Lauren thought, apart from the fact that I'm going to be exposed as a prize idiot in a widely circulated children's book.

'No Mum, it's just there's such a lot to get used to.'

'And it doesn't sound as if you've exactly hit on the management dream team. But you have made a friend?'

'Yes, Fiona. She's invited me to go to hers on Friday night, stay with her on Saturday and she'll drive us both back on Sunday. I can get the train.'

'Where does she live?' her father asked.

'Abingdon.'

'Well, if you can wait till I get home from work I can drive you there. It's no great distance.'

'Dad that would be wonderful. In that case I'll take my guitar back with me.'

Saying goodbye to her mother Lauren felt a ridiculous tickle in her throat. She would only be a matter of hours away and would be coming home at Christmas, even before Christmas. She'd come home for a weekend in November.

Case, guitar and a carrier bag, full of nourishment from her mother, were tucked into the boot. Lauren climbed into the car beside her father.

'Lovely of you to do this, Dad.'

'Not at all. It's my cunning way of getting you to myself for a bit.'

'You'd like Fiona, Dad. Good banter.'

With Lauren checking the address, her father stopped in front of a detached house set back from the road. On one side of the lawn stood a post with a length of elastic hanging down. On the end of it dangled a moth-eaten tennis ball. A tangle of bicycles leant up against the house.

'Fiona has four brothers,' Lauren said.

'Ah …' Her father took a twenty pound note out of the pocket of his jacket, tucked it into Lauren's pocket, and giving it a little pat said, 'Do something daft with that or buy something highly unsuitable to eat. I won't come in with you. Keep writing those letters, and take care of yourself.'

And he was gone.

With her case, guitar and bag of provisions, Lauren headed up the path.

Chapter 11

The building in front of her, square and solid, with a roof-shaped roof and just as many windows as you could fit on it and still leave room for the front door, looked exactly like the illustration you'd find in a children's book under H for house.

And there was Fiona, bouncing down the steps; wearing faded dungarees and hair tied back with a scarf. She looked like a teenager.

'You're here, brilliant. Dump your stuff in the hall and come through to the garden. We've just had a breakthrough. Joe has got the water thingey, the water feature going.'

They walked through the house into the garden where three of Fiona's brothers stood contemplating a terra cotta fountain, which poured water from one jug to another. They had to be her brothers. They all had her light brown, verging-onto-ginger-but-not-quite, hair. The youngest's was wavy like Fiona's.

'She's here,' Fiona called out, 'and Lauren, this,' she pointed at the youngest brother, who looked about 15, 'is Joe, inventor and scientific genius who has got this amazing contraption to bring forth water.'

Joe took a bow.

Fiona pointed at a brother who must be 17 or 18, 'And this one is Harry, financial wizard and the family's hope for a future of obscene riches.'

'Good to meet you Lauren,' Harry said.

'And here, we have William, entrepreneur extraordinaire.'

'It sounds as if the three of you should go into business

together,' Lauren said.

William surveyed his brothers for a moment, then said, 'We'd kill each other.'

'Not if Miles was around you wouldn't,' Fiona put an arm around William. 'Miles, the peacemaker is brother number four, no, actually he's number one. You might see him tomorrow, that is if you don't blink. He's coming to fetch some stuff, one of his whirlwind visits. Miles works for an advertising agency. He's the artistic member of the family and widely acknowledged to be the sanest.'

'Who's doing food?' Joe asked.

'I am,' Fiona said, ' and yes I did remember to get the bolognese sauce out of the freezer and no, I haven't put garlic in the salad and the celery is in a separate bowl and, worry not, there will be seconds for dessert. Mum will be back by seven so if you lot can hang on till then ... oh and Mum said, don't touch the biscuits on the top shelf, her book group is coming on Monday. Come on Lauren, I'll show you where you're sleeping.'

They collected Lauren's case, guitar and carrier bag. Lauren followed Fiona up a wide, well-trodden wooden staircase and was shown into a small room overlooking the garden. On the single bed there was an enormous green plastic laundry basket full of men's underpants.

'Whoops,' Fiona picked up the basket. 'I forgot about this. Not one pair of these has ever seen the inside of a drawer. They get washed and put in this basket. No one knows or cares whose is which. In the morning the boys come in here and grab a pair – so first up gets the Calvin Klein underpants.'

Downstairs, Fiona's mother had arrived: a small, slight woman, much darker than Lauren had imagined she'd be.

How could this little lady have produced those three strapping sons? There was no mention of a Mr. Bates, who must have been the original owner of the light brown hair. Fiona had never mentioned her father – and at first glance there were no photographs of him on view.

'It's lovely to meet you, Mrs. Bates.'

'Please call me Susan. Lauren, I'm really glad Fiona has a friend at work, and so glad you could come.'

Lauren couldn't believe the size of the saucepan the pasta was cooked in, nor the industrial quantities of spaghetti, poured out of a catering-sized bag into the pan. The huge bowl of spaghetti bolognese that appeared on the table could, successfully, have stood in for a washing up bowl.

'Manners,' Susan said, 'we have a guest.'

Lauren was reminded of Snow White and the Seven Dwarves, only in this case the dwarves towered over Snow White. There was nothing wrong with the young men's manners, but the pasta was vacuumed up at an alarming rate.

'Good grief,' Harry said, 'you must be important, Lauren. We've got bought dessert. Wow.'

From a cupboard Fiona produced three Marks and Spencer's pavlovas. Three! Lauren imagined herself standing in front of her class asking how much each of them would get: six people, three large pavlovas.

Not knowing the house rules, and to be on the safe side, Lauren said, 'Just a small piece for me, please.'

Joe stared at her, 'Really?'

Susan stood up and waved the cake slice in the general direction of Lauren.

'If I cut it too small, you'll just get a plate full of

crumbs.' She made a cut then placed the implement a few inches to the left.

'Is that all right for you, Lauren?'

'Yes, thank you, Susan. Perfect.'

There followed a disorganised but effective apportioning of pavlovas. A second one had been attacked with a knife and was being passed round anti-clockwise. Meeting pavlova number one halfway round the table, it retraced its steps. Lauren hoped she wasn't staring. There was a large chunk missing from pavlova number three. All too soon, all the pavlovas were just sweet memories and crumbs.

Almost on automatic Harry began filling the dishwasher.

That night Lauren slept under a duvet cover over which Superman and his many clones flew, intent on saving the world, their blue cloaks spread wide, like wings. Supermen seemed appropriate to Lauren. Untroubled by parents, finks, kelses or nuffs she slept well.

'O.K. if we go in to Oxford?' Fiona asked. 'I need some tops for school. We can do some sightseeing if you like, and I know a great little place for lunch.'

They explored shops, had coffee and lunch. Remembering her unexpected twenty pound windfall, Lauren bought herself a new, pale cream blouse. Home and school seemed miles away – somewhere in a different universe.

Back at Fiona's house an elderly green Jaguar blocked the garage.

'Ah, Miles is here. Come and say hello. I expect he's about to leave.'

Miles was admiring the water feature. He seemed to

be the tallest of the brothers and Lauren could already see he was by far the best looking.

Joe looked up. 'Oh good. Miles was just going. He's been forced to admit that I'm bloody brilliant.'

Miles looked up, spotted Lauren, and stared.

'Lauren, Miles; Miles, Lauren,' Fiona said. 'Can I at least have a hug from my big brother before you set off again.'

Not taking his eyes off Lauren, Miles said, 'Lovely to meet you Lauren. Actually, Fee, I'm not in that much of a hurry. I had thought of staying tonight. I might ... take some photographs of the ... the.. old barn tomorrow morning. You weren't expecting me to stay, I know. So, Fee, why don't I take you and Lauren to the Dog and Doughnut for a bite?'

After a short ride in the green Jaguar they reached the pub. Before entering Miles stopped and stared up at the inn sign, swinging, and whining a little in the wind.

'O-O here we go again,' Fiona said. 'Miles doesn't approve of that sign.'

Lauren studied it. At first glance it looked like a dog jumping through a wide hoop. She looked a little longer.

'Well, if the dog is meant to be jumping through a doughnut, the doughnut is a bit ... mingy and wouldn't the dog mind all that sticky sugar on its coat?'

Miles glanced approvingly at Lauren. 'Precisely. No self-respecting hound could ever be persuaded to jump through a giant, even if mingy, doughnut.'

Seated in a corner they studied the menus.

'The sausage and mash with onion gravy is really good,' Fiona said.

Remembering the gigantic helpings from last night

Lauren asked, 'How many sausages?'

'Four, usually,' Fiona replied, 'but I expect, as a special favour they'd let you have two.'

'Yes, two sausages and mash sounds good,' Lauren said.

Looking at the menu again Fiona said, 'I'll have three – four for you, Miles?'

Miles shook his head. 'I'll have the beef and ale pie. My company is doing a massive promotion on sausages at the moment and I've overdosed on everything to do with them. We've researched sausages, tasted them and done hours-long brainstorming sessions, and all to decide on maybe half a dozen words to promote a company's differently-flavoured bangers. What, ladies, is the collective noun for sausages?'

'A sizzle,' Fiona said.

'Adequate but not original enough. What do you think Lauren?'

'A song of sausages. A symphony. No. A song.'

'Sing a song of sausages,' Miles said. 'Hmm. That can go somewhere in the "perhaps" file.'

During the meal they searched for sausage superlatives and a better design for the inn sign. They decided the best picture would be of a dog running off with a string of doughnuts which had been baked joined together in a chain, like a paper chain. How this culinary feat was to be achieved was, according to Miles, 'a mere detail.'

'Why don't I drive you two back tomorrow?' Miles asked.

'Because, brother dear, I shall want my car to get me to work.'

'Of course. I sometimes forget you've been let loose behind the wheel of a car.'

Fiona and Lauren decided to leave early on Sunday morning. Joe had to be got out of bed, and joined in the farewells in pyjamas.

Once they were out of sight Fiona began laughing.

'What's so funny?'

'Miles. He's smitten. I've never seen him really smitten before. If it was any of the others, I'd tease them, but Miles is quite a sensitive soul and I wouldn't like to frighten him off.'

Lauren had to admit that the same thought had occurred to her. Miles definitely passed muster, but she was having a long rest from complicated attachments.

'I like your brothers, all of them.'

'Miles keeps popping back. He's always got an excuse but he really comes to check that everyone's O.K. When I said Harry was a financial wizard I wasn't joking. His very enlightened maths teacher got his class interested in the stock market. They have a notional portfolio which they follow in class. What said maths teacher doesn't know, is that one of the boys has an uncle who is playing the stock market for them for real. Harry's problem is going to be how he tells mum where all his money has come from.'

For the rest of their journey Fiona filled Lauren in about what would be happening in the run-up to Christmas. The reception class always put on the Nativity play and all the other classes had a slot in which to do something Christmassy. The only liaison that took place was to ensure that two classes weren't doing exactly the same thing, which, apparently, had happened once.

'Things get very fraught,' Fiona said, 'there are

tantrums and tears – and that's only the teachers.'

After they'd driven in silence for a while Fiona asked, 'How do you feel about going back tomorrow?'

'Absolutely fine,' Lauren said. And found that she really meant it.

Chapter 12

Back in her flat thoughts of school took over. Maria had been away far too long after an appendix operation. Surely she would be back tomorrow.

Lauren hoped that some of the illegible notes she'd written on Open Evening were not matters of vital importance. She'd managed to decipher most of them but the remainder could have been written by a desperate spider fleeing from an inkwell; the squiggles and lurches didn't even resemble letters. 'Flour pots', although legible, remained a mystery. Her plans for the second half of the term were fairly well under way, but now there was Class 3M's slot at the Christmas performance to consider.

Fiona had advised her to keep it simple. One or two Christmas songs should do it, with a little, a very little, dressing up. The class liked singing and there were too few opportunities.

Arriving early Lauren got a little frisson of … what was it? Pride? Something … something definitely on the positive side of the line, when she walked into her classroom. One or two of the t-shirts on the wall were coming adrift, but apart from that it looked … exactly as a classroom should look. And it was hers.

Fiona put her head round the door. 'Been up to the staffroom yet?'

'No, why?'

'Staff meeting at lunchtime. It will be about Christmas. I could give you the script now, word for word. I won't see you till then, I'm on playground duty.'

The ghastly bell rang. Funny it wasn't nearly as bad as Lauren remembered it.

The children came in. There were a great many 'Masseys' after the 'good morning, Miss.' Progress was being made.

And there was Maria, smiling shyly, perhaps a little pale, handing her a letter.

'It's lovely to have everyone here today. I hope you've all enjoyed your holiday because we've got a busy time ahead of us.'

Lauren realised she sounded like a cartoon teacher, and decided she was absolutely fine with that. To start the day, the children were going to take it in turns to tell the class what they'd done over half term.

Sally's little brother spoiled the family's outing to Windsor Castle by being sick, 'a lot of times,' Ashok and Pritti, (who Lauren had worked out were cousins) had attended a boring wedding along with, according to Ashok, 'at least a million people,' Louisa's Mum's boyfriend 'can't drive his new car any more because he speeded too many times and a camera thing caught him and took a picture,' and Robert Harding's little sister got lost in one of those huge shops. 'It took hours and hours to find her, and there she was, fast asleep in a big comfy chair. She cried when they woke her up.' Col's cat had kittens and he was sad because his dad gave them all away, all of them.

So a good time had been had by all.

At lunch time the staff assembled. The most comfortable easy chair, usually Hugo Preston's perch, now awaited Mrs. Montgomery. The second most comfortable chair, Mrs. Graham's by virtue of seniority, now bore Hugo Preston's bulk. Lauren was only too aware of staffroom chair-hierarchy.

The wait was long enough for Mrs. Montgomery to

make a proper entrance. There should have been a fanfare – or at least a piping aboard like they did in the navy, with those feeble, nasally-shrill whistles, when someone important arrived. Lauren decided that the nasal whistles would be more appropriate for Mrs. M. Battleships came to mind. If you approached Mrs. M with a question or a request you had to be armed for confrontation. The thinks bubble above her head always read, 'I am not going to like this.'

What would happen, Lauren wondered, if one day a chink appeared in her armour, or the shield was accidentally lowered … what if something came along that, while Mrs. M hadn't been giving the world her full attention, that actually pleased her and she found she liked what she was hearing or seeing? How would she cope?

And there she was. Even her worst enemy couldn't deny that Mrs. M had presence.

'I hope you are all well rested because, as you know, we have a busy time ahead of us. If everyone plays their part things will run smoothly. We have a tried and tested programme from which it is unnecessary, and indeed it would be foolish, to deviate. Christmas festivities here at Springmeadow are run on traditional lines, and none the worse for that. It is what our parents expect.

Our traditional approach to festivities causes the minimum amount of disruption to the children's lessons and does not encourage indiscipline. New-fangled Christmas jingles are unnecessary. You know my views on Santa Claus. Letters to Santa Claus only encourage greed. We, at Springmeadow, do not align ourselves with those who see Christmas merely as a commercial opportunity.

I shall, as usual, put up a timetable that will enable

you to rehearse your contributions in the hall. These will not commence before November 15th.

Mr. Preston will take Miss Massey's class while she accompanies the reception class rehearsals for their Nativity production.'

Lauren didn't hear any more. She felt herself bristling. Mr. Preston take her class! Never! He'd terrify Kirsty and Maria and he wouldn't give George time to get there. George always did get there, in the end, if you gave him time, and Mr. P was not known for his patience. He'd already labelled Col and Bradley 'villains' and would be too hard on them even before they opened their mouths. O.K., Lauren thought, she was playing the hymns so she was official accompanist, but there were ways of letting people know what was going to happen ... perhaps you might even ask them. Would it be asking too much to be asked?

Lauren looked over at Hugo Preston. His expression hovered somewhere between boredom and a scowl. With one thumb tucked into his armpits, he looked as if he was about to twang his braces.

Fiona caught up with Lauren as they left the staffroom.

'Don't tell me she didn't ask you before,' Fiona said.

'This is the first I've heard of it. I don't mind playing for the Nativity. I just can't imagine Mr. P taking my class. I'll have to strengthen them up for the onslaught, get them doing press-ups first thing in the morning and give them all doses of a strong tonic.'

'Or you could teach them karate,' Fiona added. 'Just telling you like that is a bit ... much, even for Mrs. M.'

During the next few days Lauren felt herself getting

braver. There was a definite stiffening in her spine. She'd planned to teach her children a song which mentioned … Shock! Horror! Santa Claus, and now she was determined to do it. She would, single handedly, sneak Santa Claus into Springmeadow's Christmas concert. Lauren decided that she would present Mrs. M with the ungreedy words of the song, and tell Mrs. M that her class had set their hearts on singing it. This was not true at the moment, but Lauren would make sure it was when the time came to approach Mrs. M.

The weather was getting colder and children began coming in their winter uniforms. The pale green and white striped dresses and pale green polo shirts, began to give way to bottle-green sweatshirts with the school crest on them. It made the classroom look different, more sober.

One afternoon, just before home time, Lauren asked the class, 'How many of you know the song "Santa Claus is coming to town"?' Nearly all the hands shot up. 'Do you like it?' This was followed by a chorus of 'yes'.

Sally began singing it. Well in tune, too, Lauren thought smugly.

'Good', Lauren said, 'because I thought we might do that for the Christmas concert. Would you like that?'

They would. They most definitely would.

So Mrs. M would to be approached by Lauren, one day very soon, when she felt brave enough. Mrs. M would, no doubt consider it insolence, or a word to that effect, that, after what she had said at the staff meeting, Lauren could even contemplate such a song. Mrs. M might, possibly, put it down to Lauren's inexperience, but would she actually ban it, veto it, consign the song to outer darkness? Lauren had always wondered where the outer darkness was and what went on there. Considering the sort of things that had been sent to outer darkness, it could only be a jolly place.

When Lauren told Fiona what she was planning Fiona's first reaction was disbelief. 'You wouldn't!' A little later the comment turned into, 'Go for it, gal. Good luck.'

There was still a day or two before Lauren would have to request an audience with Mrs M. She would rehearse her speech.

Just now there was pile of marking to get through. Was it possible the children had already improved after only a couple of months of her brilliant teaching, Lauren wondered.

She was getting better at deciphering handwriting and spelling, especially Kirsty's. Lauren always left Kirsty's written work till last. After tackling it Lauren knew she would need a cup of tea, at the very least. Perhaps even something stronger.

And here it was, a whole page of it. 'Grandma wants too be fin like a modul. Sum days she only eats grate froot.'

A definite improvement, Lauren thought. Several words were spelt in an entirely orthodox way and there was no doubt what the thrust of the sentence was; a grandma wanting to be thin like a model. She was doing it by … A light bulb popped up above Lauren's head: for 'grate,' read 'great', fruit is clear enough – grapefruit! Quite right Kirsty, that huge yellow sphere has nothing to do with grapes. Great fruit was entirely logical.

Progress was definitely being made.

Chapter 13

The thought of it was making Lauren twitchy. She couldn't put it off forever.

A notice had already appeared on the staffroom notice board asking teachers to let the school secretary know what their class would be performing in the Christmas Concert, 'to enable us to produce a balanced programme.' Yes, Lauren thought, and so Mrs. M can veto anything deemed unsuitable.

As she recalled the 'balanced' bit Lauren stood on one leg and wondered how her class doing a high wire act would go down. Perhaps wondering how it might be received was better than wondering how it might go down.

She had tried a few style options in front of a mirror. The grovelling innocent approach had been discarded as unconvincing, even with a bit of hand-wringing added; the direct approach only marginally better, standing tall, head held high, shoulders back. 'Mrs. Montgomery I am here to tell you that my class will ...' but every time she got to the word 'tell' her shoulders drooped, automatically, of their own accord. Her shoulders knew something.

Fiona was no help. She'd, half-seriously, suggested Lauren write Mrs. M a letter. Lauren just hoped a solution would present itself.

After one or two highly dramatic narratives at news time, the class's expectations were raised. It was hard to compete with a fire two doors away from Jonathan Wheeler's house, which caused two fire engines and an ambulance to roll up all doing the nee-naw nee-naw, ever so loud. Fortunately no one was hurt, but Mrs. Evans, whose house it was, cried anyway because she said she'd never get the smell of smoke out of her curtains. And Inga had been at the shopping centre when two policemen put a man in their car and then pushed his head down just like they do on the telly.

After that, 'I went to see my grandma on Sunday,' just didn't cut it any more.

One morning at news time Adam put his and up.

'Miss Massey. My grandpa taught me a poem. May I say it?'

'Of course you may, Adam. Come up to the front of the class.'

'It's called "The Pudding Song".' Adam launched forth:

'Oh who would be a puddin'
A puddin' in a pot
A puddin' wot is stood on
A fire which is hot?
Oh sad indeed the lot
Of puddin's in a pot.

I would'n be a puddin'
If I could be a bird.
If I could be a wooden
Doll I would'n say a word.
Yes, I have often heard.
It's grand to be a bird.

But as I am a puddin'
A puddin' in a pot
I hope you get a stomach ache
For eating me a lot.

I hope you get it hot
You puddin'-eating lot.'

When he finished, Bradley called out, 'That's neat. Say it again, man.'

Sally said, 'Can he say it again, Miss Massey?'

'Of course. Off you go, Adam.'

As Adam reached the last verse the door opened and Mrs. Montgomery stood, framed in the doorway. Her look darkened as Adam, in full ham actor mode, uttered, 'I hope you get a stomach ache ...'

Adam finished reciting the poem, put one arm over his tummy, bowed and went back to his desk.

For a moment there was complete silence. The children's eyes were on Mrs. Montgomery, Lauren's eyes were on Mrs. Montgomery. Mrs. Montgomery's eyes were popping out of her head. The piece of paper in her hand swayed to and fro.

Eventually she said, 'Miss Massey, come and see me at break time.'

Once again Adam, through no fault of his own, had got her into trouble.

Lauren waited for the 'come' before entering. The 'sit' came immediately afterwards. Mrs. M hardly waited for Lauren to reach the chair before she launched into her tirade.

Lauren noticed that Mrs. M's bosom was neither very high nor at its most relaxed. Behind shiny maroon satin, the bosom lay in neutral position.

'Miss Massey, while I applaud any endeavours to encourage children to learn to recite poetry by heart, your choice of poem, in this instance was most unsuitable. It appeared to be encouraging vengeance if I heard it aright.'

'Mrs. Montgomery. I had not heard it before. Adam simply asked if he could recite a poem. The poem is written by a pudding.'

'Written by a pudding?' Mrs. M stared.

'Yes. It's meant to be funny … humorous.'

'Humorous?'

'Yes. Shall I give you a copy?'

'That will not be necessary, Miss Massey. Ah … you have the music for the Nativity?'

'Yes. Mrs. Graham has given it to me.' You might have asked, said something about it, Lauren thought. Her mild anger stiffening her resolve.

'Mrs. Montgomery, I would like to discuss my class's contribution to the concert.'

'Yes?'

'I'm afraid that before I knew of your views on Santa Claus my class had set their hearts on singing "Santa Claus is coming to Town".'

'Indeed.' Mrs. Montgomery stared at Lauren. 'Indeed,' she repeated.

'There is no hint of greed in the song. It's a simple ditty reminding children that they should behave themselves.'

Mrs. Montgomery still said nothing. Lauren thought she was making headway, either that or she was about to sink without a bubble. With her fingers tightly crossed, Lauren continued.

'It's a jolly little song, my uncle, the vicar, allowed it to be sung in church.'

Mrs. Montgomery sat back in her chair. Her eyes widened.

'Your uncle is a vicar?'

Lauren hoped Mrs. M wouldn't notice her blushing.

81

She must remember to inform her father that he had acquired a brother, a brother who had taken holy orders.

'Yes, we don't see him very often. He's in Australia.'

'This, this song, mentioning Santa Claus was sung in a church, you say?'

Lauren nodded and wondered what particular circle of hell awaited people who told porkie pies about vicars.

Mrs. M's mood had changed. It had most definitely shifted.

'Miss Massey, I dare say you have a favourite carol.'

Lauren nodded, wondering where this was heading.

'I most certainly do. "Ding, dong, merrily on high" has been my favourite ever since I was a gel. I have mentioned it to Mrs. Graham. She, of course knows more about these things than I do, but Mrs. Graham suggested that the notes are not suitable for children's voices. I wonder … do you think your class could manage …'

Ah, thought Lauren, it will be yes to Santa if my class will also ding dong.

'Mrs. Montgomery. I think that's a wonderful idea. May I take it that class 3M's contribution will be "Ding, dong, merrily on high" and "Santa Claus is coming to Town?"'

'Yes, Miss Massey, you may.'

The look on Mrs. Montgomery's face did not quite stretch to a smile, but there was something a little wistful around the eyes.

Lauren realised that her victory had come at a price. It was hard to imagine Col, Bradley and Spencer, her miniature basso profundo, singing 'glo-o-o-oria'. She'd have to find a way round the 'orias'.

When Lauren told Fiona that it was now official, her

class would be singing about Santa, Fiona was impressed.

'I'm not sure why I was so determined to get Mrs. M to accept the song,' Lauren said. 'My dad reckoned I was never too good at choosing my battles. But once I decided to go for it …' Lauren stopped speaking, took a deep breath and remembered that confession was supposed to be good for the soul. She told Fiona about the fabricated vicar and the song said imaginary vicar had allowed to be sung in church.

Fiona laughed, 'A hanging offence, blasphemy at the very least. I love it – and if ever I get into trouble I know who to come to to argue my case.'

Ignacio's parents had been delighted to speak to Lauren in Spanish. They asked her to be sure to let them know when Ignacio didn't behave himself. The following day a beaming Ignacio arrived with a large tupperware box, smelling of garlic, full of genuine Spanish paella.

Chapter 14

Set in stone, the 15th of November – the day Springmeadow School was allowed to begin Christmas rehearsals – arrived, inconveniently, on a Saturday. So the 'rehearsal schedule' appeared on the staffroom notice board, on Monday 17th. Each class was allocated hall time and, 'in order to ensure the continuity of the children's education, rehearsals should not be undertaken at any other time.'

Beside each of the times allocated to the reception class there was a star. Following the star down the page Lauren found her name:

Miss Massey/Mr. Preston. How odd it looked: Miss Massey stroke Mr. Preston.

At home time on Tuesday Lauren addressed her class.

'Tomorrow morning Mr. Preston will be coming to teach you.'

Kylie's eyes widened. 'Forever?' she asked dramatically.

Col crossed his arms and stuck out his lower lip. Arabella put her arm around Kirsty.

'No, only at the times I'm playing the piano for the little ones' Nativity play. I want you to be very polite to Mr. Preston and do your best work.'

Mr. P had asked Lauren what her class would be doing. She had prepared the lessons; he would be childminding.

The first few, reasonably civilized reception class rehearsals were for learning the songs. The children sat on the floor and Mrs. Graham sang them one line at a time. 'Away in a Manger' was a must and Lauren thought 'Little Donkey' absolutely right. 'Three Kings' was probably necessary to accompany the miniature procession but why not have a recording, with a lush and lovely arrangement?

Fortunately, the next class up, and sometimes the audience, would be joining in with the singing. Lauren played as softly as she could so as not to drown the small, hesitant voices.

When rehearsals moved up a notch and the children began to be told how and when they would be coming in, and where they would stop, everything changed.

Rehearsals became a combination of herding, riot control and looking out for plaited legs or a quivering lower lip. It was essential to reach the owner of the lip swiftly and make soothing noises before a loud wail emanated from behind it.

Only two or three years younger than her class, the children looked so small. Lauren could sympathise. They had only just begun to get used to this huge, strange place called school, when the teachers started to behave very oddly: putting them into lines saying, 'walk', 'stop', 'sing', 'not now', 'stand over there Johnnie, no, over there, no not facing the wall'. Lauren could see that it was all too much for some of them.

Casting, Lauren decided, had been done entirely on the basis of the degree of general bewilderment or aplomb. The three kings, as yet very small beings, had aplomb in spades. They were already self-assured, taking the presence of subservient pages completely for granted. Here, Lauren could see three future captains of industry. Joseph, a round, perpetually smiling boy, would surely become a diplomat. He was already the peacemaker when one of the pages, misunderstanding an instruction, sat heavily on top of one of the kings. Amelia, Adam's little sister was to be

Mary. With blonde hair, big eyes and the Gregory eyelashes, she was perfectly cast. Lauren could see that Amelia was nervous, but she was going to do it anyway.

The baby Jesus was causing a few problems. There seemed to be a severe shortage of baby dolls. The Barbie doll offered by one of the children didn't make the grade. 'Thank you dear, she's lovely, but not quite right, just now.'

The doll currently standing in for the Holy Child had once belonged to one of Mrs. Graham's daughters. Unfortunately it had a problem with its eyes. One of them was permanently shut and the other eyelid had worn loose, causing it to wink frantically at the slightest touch. This gave the doll a rakish air. It appeared to be leering. Amelia was mesmerised. She couldn't take her eyes off it. Lauren heard her confide to one of the teachers. 'I don't like that doll very much.'

In one of the many pauses, when Lauren waited idly at the piano, she wondered how Michael Gregory's latest book was coming on, wondered if Adam and Amelia ever saw the drafts. Although she knew nothing about publishing, Lauren thought it unlikely that the book, featuring Goldie and a greedy teacher in the park, could be out by Christmas. Perhaps that was something to be thankful for.

Lauren's class, always delighted to have her back, were surviving Mr. Preston's ministrations with some heartfelt complaints. 'Mr. Preston never lets us go out to play as soon as the bell goes.' 'He makes us wait.' 'For no reason.' 'Always.' 'On purpose.' 'He made Col stand in the corner and he hadn't done nuffink.' Lauren thought that standing in the corner had gone out of fashion when Dickens died. She looked over at Col who, drawing his forefinger slowly towards his nose, was practising crossing his eyes. Clearly Col had not suffered too much from his enforced study of the classroom wall.

Lauren realised that Hugo Preston would be looking for reasons to find fault with her teaching, classroom management … he'd find something.

In the staffroom, coming to the end of a seemingly pointless story about a bus conductor and an irate passenger, Hugo Preston turned to Lauren and asked. 'Who's the lad in your class uses words of 12 syllables? He sounds as if he's swallowed a dictionary. How old is he? Seven? Eight? Do you know what he said?' Hugo Preston waited until he had everyone's attention. 'He said, "Under the circumstances perhaps I should leave that word out. Under the circumstances" … did you ever?'

'That will be Adam Gregory,' Lauren said.

'His father's an author,' Mrs. Graham added.

So he is, Lauren thought, but she was pretty sure Adam's vocabulary came largely from his grandfather. Old-fashioned sayings frequently popped out of Adam's mouth. On one occasion, when the class had been talking about wasting money, Adam said, 'Ah yes, a fool and his money are soon parted.'

Realising he still had the floor, Hugo Preston continued, 'And who's the plankatious little chap?'

'Plankatious?' Lauren asked.

'Yes, as in thick as two short planks – little round chap … fringe …'

'I can't think who you're describing,' Lauren said, managing to smile but wanting to scream, this man shouldn't be allowed within 20 miles of a class of children.

Trooping her class in for a designated one hour's

rehearsal, Lauren thought the exercise entirely pointless. It was only hall time because there was a piano and a stage; forget the piano, she'd use her guitar. It would at least be something different. She'd stick to rehearsal times but in her own classroom.

In a light bulb moment Lauren decided to borrow some tuned bells from the Borough's music store. Her class's version of Ding Dong would have an introduction. The first two notes of Ding Dong would be played three times on bells.

The guitar was an unqualified success with the class.

'Wow, can you do proper pop, Miss Massey?' Jonathan asked.

'My brother used to call it a "yeah, yeah",' Graham said, vigorously demonstrating air guitar as he sang 'yeah, yeah, yeah'. Ah, Lauren thought, an echo of the Beatles.

There were, as Lauren had anticipated, one or two problems: the 'orias', two or three children who couldn't keep a tune at all and Spencer's deep, deep voice whose range did not include any musical notes. And Col, when he tried to sing made an odd noise. It sounded as if something unfortunate was happening in the water pipes – something between a growl and a gurgle. Right, Spencer and Col would star as bell ringers. For a second a twinge of doubt surfaced. Could she trust Col as a bell ringer? Lauren decided she would.

Some of the children had sweet, clear treble voices. Sally's voice was probably helped by all the practice she'd had singing about her false lovers. Sally could sing a verse on her own. Mark, who seemed to have the strongest lungs, could do some of the 'orias' solo. Two or three children could sing a verse together.

Lauren slowed the Santa song down considerably and it was none the worse for that. After the first session, with the class in fits of giggles as Lauren demonstrated, making faces, just how carefully and precisely she wanted them to enunciate every word, rehearsals went well.

Lauren would be playing the piano for carols when the whole school would be singing. In spite of people constantly changing their minds about the order of the programme, and Mrs M dithering around in a permanent tizzy, Lauren felt reasonably confident that she knew what she was doing. If the worst came to the worst, she would improvise.

Fiona's class were to perform a play about the shepherds seeing a star and following it round and round the stage all the way to Bethlehem. The play included talking sheep. These had caused no problem at all, but Fiona told Lauren that on first seeing the star the child told to say 'Lo' had instead said, 'Hello', which they both agreed seemed perfectly logical.

Signs of Christmas hit the shops long before they ventured into Springmeadow. On the first of December a small tree appeared in the entrance hall. Making a big production of the process, Mrs. Montgomery and Mrs Graham decorated it with red baubles. The caretaker put branches of holly along the windowsills. Paper chains, held in place with hefty blobs of Blu Tack, hung between the windows in what looked like an attempt to join them together, holding hands in a window dance.

On a low table, slap bang in the middle of the entrance hall, impeding anyone wanting to walk in a straight line, was the Nativity scene: a knitted Nativity scene. Rumour had it that it had been created, many years ago, by Mrs. M and Mrs. Graham. The brightly coloured kings, leaning, only very slightly in different directions, held tiny gifts. The shepherds, in more sober colours, stood beside Mary and Joseph and the knitted crib. The sheep were the least successful creatures; all four of them appeared to be doing the splits.

The knitted figures gave Lauren an idea. For the performance her class would wear their anoraks and woolly hats, the brighter the better.

Consulting Fiona regarding any Springmeadow Christmas rituals she might not know about, Lauren learnt that, 'You'll get loads of cards, chocolates and probably some soap. And there's the staff lunch. The dinner ladies supervise the children and the staff sit down to Christmas dinner, with all the trimmings, in the staff room.'

'Do we fit?'

'Just. It's not too bad, apart from the food being stone cold by the time it reaches us.'

'Do I send a Christmas card to Mrs. M and Mr. P?'

'Definitely, but no gushing: brief, snappy and to the point.'

Lauren didn't ask whether it was done or not, she'd already decided to make every child in her class a card.

Chapter 15

Dear Mum and Dad,

How lovely to get a real old-fashioned letter with messages from both of you and Gran. Please tell her I am eating properly and I can't have lost any more weight as my skirts and trousers are staying up nicely.

Thank you for forwarding the letter from Cameron. You said that when you saw his Mum she was working up to asking you if I was attached, if there was anybody. Thanks for hinting that there might be. You're a star, Mum.

Cameron was never very good at coming to the point either. In his letter he says he's coming back from Australia for good and hopes he'll be seeing me at Christmas. He asked if the New Year bash was still going on at the tennis club. I expect it is, but I won't be going. Fiona has invited me to stay with her family in Abingdon over the New Year. You won't mind, will you? I'll be with you for the rest of the holidays.

Cameron is a bit vague about his plans, but I think he wants to pick up where we left off. Well, that's not going to happen.

It will be obvious why I have to write you a proper letter in return. I couldn't wait for you to see my class photo. I don't know why Hugo Preston decided to plant himself in the picture on the opposite side to me. He muttered something about symmetry. I discovered that he is in <u>all</u> the class photos. Fiona reckons Mr. P has been in every class photo since he arrived at the school aeons ago. Why? Can it be sheer vanity? There must be hundreds of school photos gathering dust in attics all over the country. If someone picks one up they'll be wondering who on earth the roly-poly man with the toothbrush haircut can be. As well they might. Clearly Mr. P is not, as Grandpa used to say, 'the full shilling'.

I've traced round the children and put their names in their silhouettes. Remember when you taught me how to do that, Dad? That old family photo?

The run-up to Christmas is keeping me busy as I am accompanist-in-chief. Well, accompanist-in-only, really. I wish you could hear my class singing. I'll see if I can find a way of making a recording. A video would be even better. If I could do that I could video Fiona's class play too. It's a bit wooden and verges on the ridiculous, but somehow becomes oddly moving when the shepherds finally reach the stable.

I do hope it snows on Christmas Eve. Do you think Mr. Miller will bring a sheep into church again? I know we loved it, but I reckon the sheep didn't think much of it.

You said we'll be five for Christmas dinner: us four and … who is number five?

I'll phone and let you know which train I'll be coming on.

Give my love to Gran. I've got a copy of the class photo for her, too.

Much love and I can't wait to be with you.

Lauren

Chapter 16

There were to be three performances, three days running: an afternoon one for the reception class's parents and guardians to see the Nativity play, and one afternoon and one evening performance for the contributions from all the other classes.

The evening performance had been hard won. Three years ago parents and teachers, pointing out that not many fathers could get to an afternoon show, petitioned Mrs. M, who, after much grumbling, and muttering about 'the thin end of the wedge', reluctantly agreed to opening up the school 'of an evening'.

Once again Mr. Preston would be taking Lauren's class on the afternoon of the reception class's performance. Her class, giving a collective sigh, was now resigned to the ordeal knowing it would be over soon.

The short December days dawned, grey and drizzly, with little hope of colour outdoors. Inside school, in spite of the rigidly restricted rehearsal times and Mrs. M's insistence on the continuity of the children's education, the atmosphere positively fizzed. The whole idea of performing was exciting, of course, but one of the performances was going to happen … at night, starting at seven o'clock. They would be coming to school in the dark and going home 'ever so late.'

'You'll probably be going home at about half-past eight,' Lauren told her class, 'it will be dark and very cold.'

'Will there be ghosties about?' Kirsty asked, barely audibly.

'Yes, an' robbers,' Bradley added, 'with guns big as this.' He opened his arms.

'What a pity,' Lauren said. 'It looks as if somebody isn't sensible enough to be out at night time. You will have grownups with you. Ignacio, will your parents be able to come?'

'Yes Miss. Dad comes afternoon. Mum she come night time.'

Lauren had managed to communicate with Mr. and Mrs. Hernandez but they hadn't sent back the form asking when parents would be attending the performances.

'It's this way,' Ignacio explained, leaning on Lauren's desk. 'Depends on a sifts.'

'Sifts?'

'Yes Miss. If my mum she do first sift, dad he do evening sift, no problem.'

'Oh. I think you mean shifts.'

'Yes Miss, sifts.'

On Nativity performance day Lauren wore one of her sober dresses; navy with pale blue piping and a necklace exactly the same shade as the piping. Lauren thought the dark dress would help her blend in with the piano and perhaps make her disappear a little.

She had no idea how the performance would go. But fearing the worst Mrs. Graham's hair got frizzier by the hour and Mrs. M's bosom, hoisted ever higher, finished perilously near her chin.

The dress rehearsal had been a total disaster. One of the kings, having been away for two days but now returned, had been temporarily replaced by a page, who in turn had been replaced by a shepherd. Replacement places had been taken to heart by the new cast – page turned king still defiantly donning the crown. Unwinding the new cast and putting the original king back on his throne caused total bewilderment, involved another king wailing 'It's not fay yah.' It was not clear exactly what he was protesting about, but no one had time to find out.

Mary, Amelia Gregory, had, unusually for her, been quite tearful, averting her eyes from the winking doll. One of the shepherds lumbered clumsily in all directions, feeling his way around the stage, as he was having trouble seeing. His tea towel headdress kept slipping over his face.

Lauren wondered why Mrs. M and Mrs. Graham were getting into such a tizzy. The parents would think the children wonderful, whatever they did.

She glanced at the classroom clock. The performance would start in ten minutes. Predictably, Hugo Preston arrived at five to two, only just giving Lauren time to get to the hall, but there was definitely no time for a loo break.

The hall was already full of chattering parents when Lauren slid onto the piano stool. There, right at the end of the third row, furthest away from her, sat Michael and Alan Gregory.

Resplendent in green velvet, Mrs. Montgomery perched bang centre of the front row, between two worthies, one bejowelled, the other bejewelled, who Lauren recognised as school governors.

In spite of the chattering in the hall Lauren could hear shushing and the occasional, 'not now dear' and 'I need a wee', coming from behind the curtain.

Glancing at her watch Mrs. M stood up and faced the audience.

'Good afternoon and welcome to Springmeadow's Nativity play. I'm sure you are all aware that a great deal of work by all the teachers goes into these productions. When the performance is over may I ask you to remain seated so we can get the children changed and ready for you to take them home. The children will come and find you. I am sure you will enjoy the performance.'

Mrs. Montgomery nodded pointedly at Lauren, but that was not the signal for her to begin. Mrs. M sat down and glared at Lauren. The glare got sterner, the face redder. Lauren's signal to begin playing 'Silent Night' was the little handbell Mrs. Graham would ring from behind the curtain. For a moment Lauren panicked; what if she couldn't hear the bell? She did her best to ignore the staring glare on Mrs. Montgomery's increasingly reddening face.

There it was ... a little tinkling sound finding its way through the curtain. Lauren began playing, the older children sitting along the sides of the auditorium began singing and the curtains opened slowly revealing a clutch of shepherds who, on spotting their parents, reacted with delight. Several of them even remembered not to wave. The shepherd on the far end of the stage stuck her tummy out and wedged her thumb firmly into her mouth.

Words were spoken. The shepherds moved off leaving one to 'keep watch'. The watching shepherd made her way to the 'rock' at the edge of the stage, sat down heavily on it and began picking her nose.

The performance was proceeding as it should. The moment for Mary and Joseph's appearance had arrived. Lauren began playing 'Little Donkey.' There was no donkey but, hand in hand, Mary and Joseph made their way to the stable on the side of the stage. The shepherd, now having a good scratch, kept watch on the other side.

The baby, already hidden in a box of hay, would be revealed during the singing of 'Away in a Manger.' Fiona told Lauren that the Nativity production was always exactly the same, note for note, possible tricky spots ironed out.

Glancing at the audience, Lauren could see that every parent's eyes were glued to one child.

As Lauren began playing 'Away in a Manger,' Amelia reached into the box of hay and produced … a bright orange teddy bear.

There was a brief gasp from the audience and some embarrassed laughter. Michael Gregory was biting his lip trying not to laugh. Gregory senior, Alan, held a handkerchief to his face, his shoulders shook.

Clearly Amelia had had enough of the leering doll and had substituted it for the friendlier teddy bear.

Mrs. Graham appeared from stage left, snatched up the teddy bear and put the doll in Amelia's lap.

Amelia looked up and with a sigh of resignation grabbed the doll and held it, upside down, by its foot.

The kings were to come up the central aisle and climb to the stage by special steps. A teacher would be holding them back, opening the door at the precise moment they should appear … and here they came. They approached, their journey barely impeded by the page who gave his gran a smacking kiss as he passed her. Members of the audience knew the drill and positioned themselves accordingly.

Then there they were, all assembled on the stage in the tableau: kings, shepherds, Mary, Joseph, several restless sheep, (as they surely would be, Lauren thought.) The 'look out' shepherd, now thoroughly bored, slid off the 'rock' and was now sitting on the stage chewing the end of her sleeve.

Now for the finale, the children on the stage, the youngest would sing one verse of 'Away in the Manger' on their own. Lauren played as softly as she could. From the corner of her eye she could see handkerchiefs and tissues emerging from pockets and handbags.

She put her hands in her lap. The performance was over. After a few seconds' silence the audience burst into applause. Cries of 'well done' and 'lovely' came from the audience. The children beamed. Mrs. Graham appeared and ushered the reluctant children off the stage.

Lauren wondered what to do. She hadn't planned her escape. People were obediently staying in their seats waiting for their children. She couldn't sit at the piano forever, nor could she be first person to make a move.

Gradually people in the audience stood up and went over to talk to friends. Lauren decided to wait for a bit more mingling before heading for the door.

As she stood up, she realised that the two Mr. Gregorys were heading her way. She had to admit that, rotten book or not, Michael Gregory was decidedly dishy.

'Well done, Miss Massey,' he said, 'Congratulations on being solo accompanist.'

'You should have been given an honourable mention at the very least.' Alan Gregory added. 'Someone asked me who you were.'

'Oh dear,' Michael Gregory said, 'Perhaps I shouldn't have let Amelia bring her teddy bear to school this morning. She was a bit tearful. I had no idea what she was planning.'

Lauren laughed, 'Good for her. That baby doll is seriously scary, the stuff of nightmares. Amelia shouldn't get into trouble. Full marks for using her initiative – solving the problem on her own.'

Lauren did wonder how Amelia had managed to

make the switch.

Michael Gregory seemed to be studying her face.
Lauren remembered THE BOOK. in which she would star.

'Do forgive me,' she said, 'I really must be going.'

Feeling a bit deflated and not knowing quite why,
Lauren went back to her classroom. She'd forgotten to
remind the children to bring their woolly hats tomorrow.

For once, Hugo Preston had dismissed the children on
time. The classroom was empty.

Chapter 17

Lauren slept fitfully that night. The incident with the teddy bear would make the 1975 production of the Nativity memorable. But it had gone well. The parents loved it. Lauren wondered why she was feeling so ... so flat.

Somehow her class got through the following morning with lots of extra requests to go to the toilet, and squeaks of delight breaking out at the least provocation. Excitement hummed in the air. Lauren wondered what would happen if she lit a match.

There were spare woolly hats, so everyone would be hatted. Both Kirsty and Arabella had acquired oversized mittens. George would also be wearing a very long, inexpertly hand-knitted scarf. The scarf reminded Lauren of one her grandmother had knitted during a power cut. Apparently there had been no instruction on the pattern to stop knitting. Lauren had used the resulting yards to wrap round all of her soft toys at once. In order to ensure that George didn't trip over his scarf and launch himself onto the audience, Lauren tried wrapping it round him several times. The result was, woolly hat, scarf, anorak, trousers. George had disappeared. Watching intently Charmaine asked, 'Can we all wear scarfs, Miss Massey?'

'If you like, but you all look absolutely fine just as you are.'

At the dress rehearsal the classes had seen each others' contributions. 3M would be following Fiona's class.

Shifting from one foot to the other, shushing each other and giggling with nerves, 3M waited in the corridor for their turn to go on.

To the sound of applause from the hall, Fiona rushed

past Lauren as her class left the stage. 'I think my chief shepherd is about to throw up. Good luck.'

Lauren's class filed onto the stage clutching their musical instruments. Lauren holding her very recently tuned guitar. At the children's request she, too, was wearing a woolly hat, a red one with a pompom.

Hugo Preston was in charge of the curtain. This entailed, from time to time, hovering onto the stage in full view of the audience to make sure everyone knew who was performing this vital task.

'Thank you Mr. Preston,' Lauren said. And, somewhat jerkily, the curtains opened; the jerks just about masking Col's sudden explosive belch.

Adam stepped forward and, as instructed, waited for complete silence. In a clear voice he said, 'Class 3M will be performing two songs, accompanied by Miss Massey on the guitar.' Lauren hadn't told him to say that and guessed that must be Alan Gregory's addition. 'First we will sing "Ding Dong Merrily on High", then we'll sing "Santa Claus is Coming to Town."

Back in his place Adam tapped Col on the shoulder. Col rang the 'ding' bell which was answered by Spencer with the 'dong' bell. This happened three times. The children waited for the last 'dong' to die away. Lauren played a chord and the children began singing. The 'orias', though by no means smooth, were not too bad. A vigorous round of applause followed.

'Santa Claus' was accompanied by two reasonably subdued drums and untuned jingly bells, whenever the chorus was sung.

When the song finished the audience erupted into applause and cheering. The children bowed.

Someone, Lauren was pretty sure it was Michael Gregory, shouted 'encore'. But the curtains were drawn.

Back in the classroom euphoria reigned.

'I think they liked us, Miss Massey,' Mark said.

'You did very well,' Lauren said, 'I'm really proud of you.'

'We were the best,' Jonathan said, 'My brother saw the rehearsal. He said we were definitely the best.'

'I reckon we're going to be on telly,' Bradley said. 'We're better than anyone. We're the best, we're the best, we're the best.'

'This isn't a competition,' Lauren said. 'Every class is the best in a different way.'

'They're boring,' Bradley said. 'We're the best.'

Lauren decided to change the subject and reminded the class to bring a carrier bag or something to take their possessions home with them at the end of term.

The following morning Adam arrived with a letter.

'Dear Miss Massey,

I really must congratulate you on your class's performance. Unusually, I could hear every word the children sang and I know they enjoyed performing. The guitar accompaniment was a master stroke, blending so well with the young voices. The bells, too, were most effective.

My father and sister-in-law are coming to the evening performance. I really wish I was coming with them so I could see it again.

Yours sincerely,

Greg (Michael Gregory).'

Lovely, Lauren thought, if slightly on the over-effusive side, rather like the too big bouquet.

There were other appreciative notes from parents and lots of 'My mum said we were the best.'

The day dragged. The hands of the clock seemed to be stuck.

Lauren knew class 3M's contribution to the Christmas festivities had gone down well and there was every reason to think tonight's performance would be as good – or was she having the merest hint of a doubt?

She was, temporarily, at least, in Mrs. M's good books, agreeing to perform her favourite carol. And Lauren had noticed a shift in her own status in the staffroom. Fiona told her that the other teachers wondered how Lauren had managed to get round Mrs. M's dislike of Santa. Let them wonder. Only Lauren and Fiona knew about the 'Ding Dong' 'Santa' deal … and the phantom vicar.

While the children experimented with Christmas card designs, Lauren got on with some marking.

She had decided to challenge herself and decipher Kirsty's spelling, however long it took. Asking Kirsty or Arabella would simply be giving in. So far, to her smug satisfaction, Lauren had succeeded.

Although a mere wisp of a child, food ranked highly in Kirsty's world. She recorded her grandmother's string of increasingly spartan diets in minute detail and her uncle's love of 'muscles in whine'. Lauren's own fault, she acknowledged when, for once, Kirsty had come to ask how to spell a word - 'muscle.'

But now Lauren was completely stumped. At the bottom of an otherwise decipherable page about the weekend's happenings, was a word that might as well have been written in Sanskrit. Perhaps it was.

Kirsty had written, 'My mum likes the chuknbra.'

'The' Lauren mused, so a noun. Could her mother like a new kind of bra? Something to do with the diet? No. The diet was grandma. Wasn't there some uniquely Scottish sport that had something to do with a chukka? Or was that polo and a pukka?

And there was Kirsty, sitting a few yards away, but Lauren was not going to give in and ask her to decipher.

She glanced at the clock. The hands were moving after all.

'All right, you can pack away now. What are you going to do when you come to school this evening?'

A sea of hands went up.

'Tell me Col.'

'We come 'ere. Nomumsndads. Just us.'

Yes,' Lauren added, 'grownups in the hall.'

'And to be nice and fresh for tonight,' Lauren said, 'if you can manage it, have a little rest this afternoon.'

'Like my gran does?' Louisa asked.

The children giggled. Clearly there were not going to be many rests.

Chapter 18

Fiona had invited Lauren to go back with her for a cup of tea and 'a flop for an hour or so' before the evening performance.

Fiona's poorly shepherd had not turned up and she told Lauren that the contingency plans were decidedly shaky.

'Jason leads them. They've got to walk round the stage at a certain pace and Jason is the only child who doesn't see everything as a race. It's going to be a complete disaster. I think we both need a generous slug of Prosecco in lieu of tea.'

Lauren was not going to argue with that.

Stretched out full length on Fiona's sofa, Lauren closed her eyes. It would be bliss just to stay there, top up the wine, borrow a blanket …

'Hey, don't make yourself too comfortable, we've got to return to the fray, remember? We can't have you arrested and accused of being drunk in charge of a guitar. I can just picture it. Hefty policeman asks, "Do you have a licence for this, madam? In the wrong hands it could be a lethal weapon."'

Lauren had a sudden vision of herself beating Hugo Preston around the head with her guitar.

'If I wanted to be dangerous, a brass instrument would be far more effective.'

Reaching into her handbag, Lauren took out a notebook and biro. She wrote, 'the chuknbra.'

'Fee, do you know what this means?'

Fiona studied the word. 'No, give up. What is it?

'I haven't the faintest idea. Kirsty wrote it in her news

book.'

Fiona looked at it again. 'Kirsty? The wee Scots lassie?'
'Aye,' Lauren said.

They'd agreed on scrambled eggs on toast, but as she changed into her performance gear, Lauren wondered if the eggs had been such a good idea. They didn't seem to be going down the way they should. The eggs were hovering.

Back in her classroom, with the wall clock showing 6:25, a time she'd only seen on its face on Open Evening, Lauren tuned her guitar.

The children began trickling in, some running to their desks, sliding into their seats, panting dramatically.

Yesterday's modest carol-singers costumes had been embellished: gone up more than a notch or two. Inga wore a large fur hat with bits of string hanging down either side of her face. As the strings were very thin and the bobbles on the end of them not entirely round, it looked as if a pair of mice had taken up residence either side of her pale blue coat. Pritti and Ashok had acquired new anoraks, large, shiny, puffy and red. They beamed at Lauren with satisfaction. Not to be outdone by the children who were sporting mittens, Bradley had on what looked like his father's driving gloves, possibly a pair from a dodgily acquired job lot. And Sally was definitely wearing lipstick.

But worst of all were the scarves. Kylie and Louisa wore day-glo scarves: one magenta, one lime green – both were frilly and sparkly; lying oddly against their sensible fawn anoraks. The boys wore a sprinkling of Chelsea scarves, with here and there some red ones emblazoned 'Arsenal.' The reds and blues glared at each other, muttering. Yesterday 3M had looked like a group of children about to go carol singing. Now they looked like a miniature football crowd on the point of erupting.

Lauren sighed. There was nothing she could do about it now.

'Remember,' she said, 'when you get on to the stage, put your hands together and breathe in very slowly, three times. There's still a bit of time so, just to keep us all lovely and calm I'll read you a story.'

Making sure that the well-wrapped-up children were all paying attention Lauren said, 'This is the story of Pinocchio.'

Ignacio began giggling. 'Mees that a very funny name. My auntie she marries Italian guy. He tells me in his language eye is occhio, so the story is about someone 'as pineyes.'

'Pin eyes. Teeny tiny pin eyes ... ' Mark started giggling setting everyone else off.

So, much Lauren thought, for a nice quiet story to calm everyone down.

'Actually, Ignacio, the story is not about pin eyes. Pinocchio was a puppet. You know, a doll with strings. Well ... Pinocchio was a wooden puppet, but the man who made him wanted him to become a real boy.'

Lauren read on. Just as the class was properly settled, she glanced at her watch.

'Right, line up in order.'

It felt strange walking along the silent, dimly lit corridor. The moonless night rendered every window pane pitch black.

Almost bursting with excitement, they waited at the stage entrance.

They heard the applause.

Fiona emerged, beaming. 'Heaven be praised,' she

said, 'Jason turned up.' Her class rushed down the corridor heading for their classroom.

Class 3M made their way on to the stage. Hugo Preston had placed Lauren's chair slap bang in the middle of the stage. She moved it over to the side.

Tonight Hugo Preston sported a black bow tie and maroon velvet smoking jacket. He had done something to his hair, so that instead of each hair standing up individually, the hairs had united, forming little groups. The effect was now more hairbrush than toothbrush.

'Thank you Mr. Preston.'

The curtains opened in a series of jerks. This time the auditorium was in darkness; the sea of faces just a blur of white circles.

Blinking a few times, Adam stepped forward, made his announcement, then tapped Col on the shoulder.

Col 'dinged,' Spencer 'donged.'

Oh, no. Somewhat carried away Col dinged a fourth time. Without missing a beat, Spencer donged. Like a true pro Lauren thought.

Everything else went exactly as it was supposed to go.

At the end of the performance, unexpectedly, Hugo Preston appeared on stage and applauded, before retreating to attend to the curtain. Lauren wondered if he'd done that to show appreciation of their performance or to properly display his velvet jacket and bow tie.

Back in the classroom, waiting for the whole show to be over, Lauren said, 'I want you to think about the Christmas story because you're going to be writing about it tomorrow. Think about the details. Remember when we talked about details? Things like what the shepherds were wearing, what the stables looked like ...'

'What kind of sandwiches Joseph had,' Jonathan suggested.

'Do you think the baby Jesus had a proper bib, like?' Charmaine asked. 'Mum says the new sort are useless. You need bibs that catch things, s'well as mopping.'

From the general buzz coming from the auditorium, Lauren concluded that the performance was over.

This time parents were allowed to fetch the children from their classrooms.

A tangle of hugs, 'Well done,' and 'It was lovely' ensued. Beaming, the parents thanked Lauren and bid her goodnight.

And then there was just Alan, (the older Mr. Gregory), a slight blonde woman and Adam left in the classroom.

'We won't keep you, Miss Massey,' Alan Gregory said, 'but Rebecca, Adam's aunt, very much wanted to meet you.'

'I've heard so much about you,' Rebecca said. 'That's such a cliché, but it's true. I just had to put a face to the Miss Massey Adam talks about. I loved the performance.' She smiled at Lauren, 'It was … absolutely … exactly right.'

'Thank you,' Lauren said, warming to her, knowing what she meant. 'The children worked really hard.'

Rebecca was ruffling Adam's hair.

'Come on, Sausage, it's time we got you home.'

Alone in the classroom Lauren smiled. It hadn't mattered one jot that the children had made daft additions to their costumes. They sang so well. She must remember to praise Spencer for adding the fourth unexpected 'dong' so promptly.

Turning off the classroom light Lauren smiled to herself. She had just survived her first Christmas Concert. That could only be a plus.

Chapter 19

The mood in the classroom the morning after the performance was one of intense satisfaction. An unkind person might have described it as ill-concealed smugness. Praise had been heaped on class 3M and they had lapped it up. Remembering the additions to their costumes, Lauren decided that as a group this lot never did things by halves. They were ... the word 'wholesale' sprang to mind.

Sally hadn't quite removed last night's lipstick.

Lauren knew there would have to be a debriefing before the class could get down to work. Everyone's mum, dad or nan had said they were ever so good. Lauren stopped them when the critics got going on comparisons with other classes.

'Now before we do our Christmas writing, I want to thank Spencer for something. Can anyone guess what that can be?'

Spencer looked as puzzled as everyone else.

'Was he kind to someone?' Ashok enquired.

'I'm sure he was,' Lauren said, 'but that's not what I'm thinking about just now.'

Silence.

'It was something that happened while we were on the stage yesterday evening.'

Everyone looked puzzled.

'Didn't anyone notice that instead of doing three "dings" with his bell, Col did four and Spencer answered, straight away, with a "dong", even though he didn't know it was coming. Well done, Spencer.'

Spencer beamed. Col joined in and beamed, too, basking in the 'ding, dong' glory.

'Now. If we're going to be writing the Christmas story are there any difficult words we're going to need?'

Adam's hand shot up. 'Frankincense and myrrh, Miss Massey. At breakfast time my dad and granddad were arguing about where the aitch goes in myrrh. Usually Granddad is a better speller than dad.'

Lauren was prepared; the words duly written on the blackboard.

'Well done, Adam, any others?'

'Bethlehem, Miss,' Pritti said.

'Can we put hotel instead of inn it's the same thing isn't it and anyway lots of people don't know what a inn is I never heard of a inn before and you said it's always best to write so people can understand what we're writing about.' Louisa eventually paused for breath.

'We stayed in a motel once.' Graham contributed. 'It was smelly.'

'Could they stay in a caravan park instead, Miss Massey, they're ever so nice.' Arabella was trying to be helpful.

Clutching at straws, Lauren said. 'Well ... there is an inn on our High Street. Haven't you noticed?'

It was impossible to miss. Next door to the bookmaker's, the shop's name, shone out, day and night in sickly green neon lights 'DONUT INN'. Lauren had been sorely tempted to stick the word 'go' between donut and inn.

Lauren wished she hadn't mentioned the inn. It was only going to muddy the already very muddy waters even further.

'Any more words?' Lauren asked.

'Harold,' Spencer's bass voice boomed out.

'What do you mean, Harold?'

'King Harold. The nasty one who told the soldiers to kill all the babies so he was sure to get Jesus.'

Harold had just been demoted. Lauren had distinctly heard the child nearest her, parroting The Lord's Prayer,' lead by the vicar, say 'Harold be thy name.' Last week Harold was God. Today he was merely a Judean King.

Left to her own devices Lauren would have left Herod out of the picture altogether. But the local vicar, the Reverend Palmer, invited by Mrs. M to come and speak to the children, had started his narrative with an overview of the political situation in Judea in the year 37 BC. He didn't seem to notice that a sprinkling of six year olds in the front row had fallen asleep. The Reception class had been spared that particular treat.

Rolling the names of the kings elaborately round his mouth, enunciating every syllable, the vicar then proclaimed that these three worthies, if they had existed at all, would not have been kings, but men of science, wise men, who went to pay homage to a new prophet.

After that session, back in the classroom, Jonathan had confessed to being muddled. Mrs. M had decreed that all the children should write down the Christmas story. Lauren had given them her version. Now she could only hope for the best.

She walked round the classroom, watching as the children settled. Maria pulled out her sequinned pencil case and carefully studied the choice of writing implements before deciding on a pencil with a kewpie doll stuck onto the end of it.

Several children were already scribbling away.

Back at her desk Lauren looked, for the umpteenth

time at what Kirsty had written. She was going to have to admit defeat.

Lauren glanced at her watch.

'It's nearly playtime, so you can stop now. You can carry on after play. I would like this writing finished today.'

The bell shrilled. The children lined up. Adam hung back.

'Miss Massey I think I should explain why my Aunt Becky calls me Sausage. You see, when I was small I couldn't say it. I don't mind her calling me that at home, but once in a restaurant Aunt Becky called me Sausage and actually we were ordering fish and chips so the waiter got confused.'

'Does your Aunt Becky live with you?'

'No, she lives with Uncle Matthew and my cousins. Aunt Becky is my mum's sister. She does the girlie things with Millie, Amelia, buys her clothes, things like that.'

'I liked your Aunt Becky,' Lauren said.

'She likes you Miss Massey, so does granddad and dad.'

'Thank you Adam. Off you go. You don't want to miss all your play time.'

So Michael Gregory liked her, Lauren thought. As well he might if she was to be, unasked, starring in his latest book.

The Christmas story writing continued for the best part of the day. Lauren was sure that there would be two, perhaps three that would finish with the unanswerable flourish 'and then they all went home to tea.' This always happened, no matter what the topic in hand. It was an ending of sorts, and possibly no worse than the 'once upon a time' beginning, but didn't quite cut it with adventures in impenetrable jungles or on distant planets.

With all the exercise books in, Lauren took out Pinocchio.

Kylie put her hand up. Her lip trembled.

'It isn't going to be sad is it? Pinocchio isn't going to die, is he?'

'He can't die, 'e's already dead,' Bradley said, 'very, very, very dead.'

Kylie's lip continued to tremble.

'He's a doll, a puppet,' Lauren said smiling at Kylie, 'and … in the end, if you listen carefully, you'll find it isn't a sad story at all.'

Col always feigned boredom during story time, elbows on the table head cupped in his hands. Lauren wasn't fooled.

Charmaine put her hand up.

'Miss Massey. I don't understand something. It's not about Pinocchio, it's about baby Jesus. How could baby Jesus who got born at Christmas, like, manage to do all the miracley things, the bread and fishes ones … when he died at Easter. He must have been ever so small when he died.'

The bell rang.

'I'll explain tomorrow, Charmaine. You can line up now. Kirsty, I'd like a quick word before you go, dear.'

The 'dear' was vital to indicate all was well and that Kirsty was not in trouble.

Arabella hung back with Kirsty.

'I'm not sure what you mean by this word.' Lauren pointed at 'the chuknbra.'

Kirsty looked at Lauren in disbelief, clearly indicating

114

that surely everyone knew …

'It's that man married to Mrs. Queen: the Chook a N brough.'

Fortunately, for the most part, the children had adopted Lauren's version of the Christmas story, Charmaine going on at some length about baby Jesus's inadequate attire. Adam made use of something he'd seen on television and went to town on the three kings' return journey. 'As they didn't want to give away the secret of where the baby was, they went home a different way and dodged into doorways with their camels if they saw anyone looking suspicious.'

Pritti commented on the odd presents the men had brought for the baby.

Mrs. M had insisted that all the children should write the Christmas story, and they had – most of them got the gist of it pretty well. Mrs. M could hardly quarrel with the endings Lauren had anticipated, with everyone going home to tea. One or two had everyone living happily ever after, including the camels, Lauren supposed.

Charmaine's puzzlement about Jesus being born at Christmas and dying at Easter proved a tad tricky to explain.

'It wasn't the first Easter that Jesus died,' Lauren said. 'He lived through lots of Easters just as you have.' This didn't make any sense at all, but Lauren didn't feel strong enough to try to explain that there hadn't actually been any Easters to live through until …

Lauren fervently hoped that the Rev. Palmer would not be wheeled in to explain Easter, or to explain anything, ever again.

After the concerts the fizz went out of the term and the last few days just tricked feebly away.

The forced merriment of the staff lunch was only just

on the right side of painful. Mrs. M declined to sport a paper hat, which were all in either orange or purple: and all slightly-too-large crowns. The cracker jokes were uniformly terrible, not improved by being read out by Hugo Preston in what he probably thought was a Santa Clausish 'ho, ho' voice. The effect was further spoilt when he got a bad attack of hiccoughs.

As Fiona had predicted, the meal was stone cold. Lauren wondered if the one sprout she had felt obliged to take, had even been defrosted.

Any serious work was out of the question, so the last two days of term were taken up with drawing Christmas cards, tidying up and making paper chains. The children had a collective 'Eureka' moment when Lauren showed them how to assemble a paper chain. The class went to it with something like a frenzy, forming a ragged assembly line of cutters and pasters. Some heated discussion broke out concerning the order of colours when Col raced on, obviously only concerned with speed, not wanting to be held up by aesthetic considerations. Pritt sticks were used with abandon and discarded like so many husks.

Once again Class M was not doing things by halves. The resulting chain, covering the whole of the back wall, became an object of immense pride. Brothers and sisters from other classes were brought in to admire it.

'How did you get it so long?'

'You make lots of little ones first then put them together.'

'You shouldn't of told. It was our secret.'

An unexpected problem arose. Who was going to take the magnificent paper chain home?

'You all know how to make them now – you can use

any paper, paper from magazines is fine, you'd have lots of colours. You can all make your own.'

The words 'lead balloon' came to mind as Lauren regarded the reaction to her suggestion: blanket disapproval.

'You could share it – a little bit each.'

'Nah,' Bradley said, 'no fun.'

'Draw lots?' Maria suggested.

'That's a really good idea, Maria. You each write your name on a piece of paper, we put them in … this box, we shake it up, draw out a name and that person gets the whole paper chain. Does everyone agree?'

A chorus of 'yes' went up.

Names written, papers folded, placed in box, shaken, stirred and … twenty three children leant forward as Lauren picked out a name. The eager anticipation was tangible.

Lauren unfolded the paper. 'Chang,' she announced.

Chang smiled shyly. There was more than a hint of bewilderment in his expression.

Decision made, incident over, the other 22 children accepted their lot with a collective shrug.

Two older children appeared at the door with a large box of lost property, holding up each item for inspection. A sock with a strange name tag was claimed by Graham, 'It's my cousin's name.'

Two very small pairs of underpants caused a lot of giggling, set off by Mark. After a great deal of turning the item over and over and, 'I think it's mine, it looks like mine, I think so,' Kylie claimed a cardigan.

On the morning of the last day of term, beaming children came in bearing gifts for Lauren. There were chocolates, a tin of M & S chocolate biscuits, soap, hand cream, two poinsettias, (which Lauren loathed with a passion), a box of mince pies from Adam, 'made by my granddad' and a pen from George.

All cards had been put in the class 'post box' lavishly decorated with cotton wool snow. The cards from Lauren were already in the box: a simple collage of a tree with a parcel underneath it, the parcel labelled with the child's name. Lauren needn't have worried about anyone being left out. Adam arrived with a carrier bag full of cards and Louisa's mum had also made sure everyone got a card.

Graham and Ignacio acted as postmen, rushing excitedly from desk to desk. The heap on Lauren's desk grew. She'd like to open them but there was just too much going on and she had to make sure that everyone took all their stuff home. Robert had acquired an extra pair of wellies, which he'd have to carry home together with his model of a spaceship, complete with plasticine aliens. And how was Chang going to manage the paper chain?

The home bell rang.

'One row at a time, then.'

Laden with extra garments, carrier bags, satchels and assorted models, the queue got longer, the desks emptier.

'Happy Christmas all of you. I'll see you in January.'

'Happy Christmas, Miss Massey,' and they were gone.

Thank goodness Fiona was giving her a lift home, Lauren thought, as she packed her loot into carrier bags. Her grandmother liked poinsettias. Would it be very terrible to give her one of them? It would mean taking it home on the train. Certainly her landlady would be the lucky recipient of the other one.

Back in Lauren's flat, Fiona and Lauren sipped tea and

dug into the box of M & S chocolate biscuits. There would be wine later, when they'd be meeting other members of staff at the Fisherman's Arms.

Staff members and their partners would assemble before going their separate ways. Mrs. M would not be present but Hugo Preston would be there, possibly wearing his magnificent maroon velvet jacket. There was a Mrs. P but she never attended school functions. Someone had once bumped into Mr. and Mrs. P while on holiday in Bruges. All they could offer by way of a description of her was, 'Well, she's not at all what I expected,' which only deepened the mystery.

Lauren had piled her cards up on the coffee table, smallest on top.

'You haven't opened your cards,' Fiona said. 'Go on, it won't be the same if you do it tomorrow.'

They admired the variety: drawings of snowmen who looked as if they could do with a hearty meal, forests of Christmas trees, cards dripping surplus glitter ... but on balance this seemed to be the year of the overweight robin.

Lauren opened the last envelope, by far the biggest addressed, in beautiful italic writing, to 'Miss L. Massey.'

It was a drawing: a picture of her, Lauren, complete with red bobble hat, on stage, with her guitar, surrounded by Class M.

'Here, let's have a look.' Fiona took the card from Lauren's hand.

'Wow. It's you. Who's it from?'

Lauren didn't need to look. It could only be from one person.

Fiona read out, 'We wish you a very Merry Christmas and a Happy New Year and it's signed by Michael, Alan,

Adam and Amelia Gregory. Fiona looked at the picture again.

'Lauren, this is amazing. Here's this face, a little bigger than my thumbnail and it really is you. Mr. Gregory is a blurry genius.'

As was usual on Christmas Day, Lauren accompanied her parents to church. Her mother quite happily left the turkey roasting in the oven. 'The good Lord is a far better cook than I am,' she declared. Perfect Sunday roasts had been entrusted to the Lord's culinary skills for as long as Lauren could remember. The only time He got it badly wrong was on her mother's first attempt at cooking a goose. Sarita had placed the bird in a shallow tin, too shallow as it turned out. The family had arrived back from church to find goose fat pouring out of the oven door.

As usual, the church was packed. People nodded and waved at each other as they spotted an old friend or neighbour they'd seen only yesterday.

The brand new vicar, the Reverend Stokes, had brought with him a brand new Nativity scene. The old vicar had been such a softie that every offer to replace a broken figure had been graciously accepted. The result was a group ludicrously out of scale. The assembled sheep looked as if they had been victims of sinister experiments with vitamins: some the size of horses, others barely visible to the naked eye. A giant shepherd had towered over the Holy Family, like a heavy from central casting, acting as their not-to-be-messed-with bodyguard.

This new Nativity, tastefully carved from pale wood, was spare and cleverly lit, throwing dramatic silhouettes from different angles.

The choir had certainly improved. When they began singing, Lauren nudged her mother and gave her the thumbs up.

'Vicar's wife, Mrs. Stokes, takes the choir now,' her

mother whispered.

And there he was; the Reverend Stokes, standing at the pulpit beaming down at his flock. Lauren had heard a great deal about the new vicar from her mother. He was not what she expected. Lauren wondered what she had expected – her mother's reports on him positively glowed. Lauren surveyed the man in the pulpit.

No longer smiling, in his white robe he looked exactly like a rabbit; a contented rabbit that had just been stroked, ears back. A prominently protruding tooth gave the impression that he only had the one. Lauren reckoned there probably were other teeth somewhere, but they were overshadowed, insignificant. The large brown eyes and eyebrows were fairly standard issue, but his nose was, somehow, triangular; fleshy and triangular, broad at the base, parallel with his mouth, ending in a point between his eyes. And there was a hint of pink to this triangle; perhaps a ray of weak winter sun casting its glow on the parson's nose, through a stained glass window, turning it a soft rabbitty pink.

The choir finished singing and the Reverend Stokes began his sermon. He had the congregation wrapped around his little finger. They leaned forward eagerly listening to a story every one of them could have recited backwards.

Lauren found her mind wandering to wonder about vicars in general and this one in particular. Any vicar's status in this village was a given. Lauren's mother had been looking a trifle smug ever since Lauren arrived. It turned out that the fifth person for Christmas Dinner at her family's table would be none other than this Rev Stokes himself. This was something of a social coup for Sarita.

Upon hearing the news that Mrs. Stokes would be away in New Zealand to spend Christmas with newly arrived twin grandchildren, and therefore the vicar would be on his own on Christmas Day, a flurry of invitations ensued. Sarita's had been accepted. Her mother had won.

Lauren felt herself redden as she remembered the lie she'd told Mrs. M about her imaginary uncle, the vicar, who had allowed Santa into church. Perhaps she'd ask the Rev Stokes if he would allow … No, on second thoughts she wouldn't ask. She'd rather not know the answer. Correction; she did know the answer. But what if Mrs. Montgomery, forgetting the Ding Dong exchange for Santa Claus is Coming, in a fit of religious zeal decided to track down the profane clergyman in order to have him defrocked … what then? What if the church dignitaries came knocking at her father's door wanting to know the whereabouts of the blasphemous vicar who had let Satan, no Santa, into his church?

Lauren decided that her new year's resolution would have to include no more porkie pies, along with healthier eating...

Considering the number of women in the congregation this Christmas morning, Lauren reckoned the good Lord must be keeping an eye on a great many turkeys.

Having harkened to the herald angels and joined the throng of the joyful and triumphant, the service came to an end.

The queue to compliment the vicar on his sermon moved at an irritating dawdle. Everyone had something to say to him. Solid, otherwise sensible, tweedy countrywomen positively simpered when they reached the

Rev. Stokes.

As her family left, Sarita said, rather too loudly, 'We'll see you at one, Vicar.'

Back home Lauren knew the drill: turkey out in half an hour, then spuds and parsnips top shelf, carrots and sprouts on stand-by ready for last minute steaming. After the Rev arrived there would be plenty of time for a festive sherry or two and nibbles. They'd be having lunch at two and the Queen at three.

Surveying the kitchen table Lauren decided that her perfect Christmas dinner would consist entirely of nibbles. The ready-and-waiting carrots and sprouts looked accusingly healthy and horribly worthy.

Grandma arrived first. Entering the kitchen, she took a step back, studied Lauren from top to toe and declared, 'I do believe you've put on a pound or two. It's better … better than when I last saw you, but you could still do with a few more curves. Lovely to see you, darling. Anything I can do?'

Lauren's mother was still changing from her church best into cooking clothes. If she added enough bling no one would notice that the jumper was, of necessity, gravy-coloured.

Rabbit or not, the Rev Stokes was a charmer. Promptly at one he arrived bearing wine and fresh flowers, stood for a moment at the front door, took a deep breath and said, 'Ah … this smells wonderful, absolutely wonderful, Sarita.'

Lauren's grandmother patted the seat beside her on the sofa and said, 'Come and sit next to me, Vicar.'

Lauren wondered if she'd imagined it or was her grandmother actually fluttering her eyelashes at him? Either that or a bit of tinsel had found its way …

Nibbles consumed, accompanied by a sherry or two and village news, and the meal was ready.

The Rev made short, but sincere, work of saying grace, napkins were expectantly spread and plates heaped. Lauren reckoned the meal was near perfect, if you discounted the sprouts. She placed her one sprout next to an extra large dollop of cranberry sauce. At least the green ball looked pretty next to the jewel red.

Grandma seemed to Lauren a tad merrier and more than a tad louder than usual.

'Poems time,' Grandma announced, 'everyone must say a poem. You start, Lauren.'

Only pausing for a second Lauren launched in to 'Oh Who Would be a Puddin'?'

When she finished the Rev said, 'Good gracious, Lauren I haven't heard that in years. I must remember it for my grandchildren, when they're old enough, in a year or two.'

'Your turn, Vicar,' Grandma said, hiccoughing ever so slightly.

'Ah … all right then.

I went to the bishop's to tea,
and when all was as quiet as could be,
the rumbling abdominal was simply phenomenal,
and everyone thought it was me.'

The game was brought to an abrupt halt when Sarita absolutely forbade her husband to recite 'The Green Eye of the Little Yellow God.' He had been known to declaim the entire opus with elaborate hand gestures, endangering any ornaments within his orbit. Once he got going he was like a wind-up toy that didn't run down. Dad's father and grandfather had both been afflicted with the reciting bug, both favouring 'The Green Eye of the Little Yellow God'. It was Sarita's life mission to kill that particular family tradition stone dead.

Perched on the sofa, accepting a cup of coffee from Sarita the Rev looked more than ever like a rabbit, a rabbit that had just emerged into the sunshine and liked what he saw.

Helping her mother clear away, Lauren realised that her mother's invitation had been accepted because the Rev Stoke wanted a bit of serious man talk. He had probably had his fill of simpering village women. The Rev and her Dad were replaying, second by second, a recent rugby match – both of them animated and seemingly knowing the life history of every player.

But what was this? Grandma joining in with her comments on the match?

Grandma wandered into the kitchen.

'I didn't know you were interested in rugby, Grandma,' Lauren said. 'You seem to know a lot about it.'

'I don't, darling. I don't know anything about rugby.'

Grandma stopped, gazed into the middle distance and sighed. 'I watch it because of all those lovely thighs.'

Chapter 22

Cameron hung around, hovered, requiring frequent swatting away. Lauren felt like telling him to go and sit down and draw a picture. He reminded her of George, the miniature monk in her class, but George always got there in the end, George was going to be all right. Cameron, on the other hand …

It was taking a long time to register with Cameron that she, Lauren, would not be at the New Year's Eve bash at the tennis club. Her mum seemed to be feeling sorry for Cameron and muttered something about there having been an 'understanding' between them.

Pairing off for bike rides and the cinema, and the fact that Cameron's happened to be the spare knee when the gang crammed into taxis did not, in Lauren's book, amount to an understanding. He'd gone off to Australia, for heaven's sakes. There had been some letters of the 'what I did on my hols' variety, (very badly punctuated letters, Lauren recalled) but Cameron was … her grandfather would have called him gormless, no gorm at all, not a shred.

Trying very hard to stick to the truth Lauren hinted that there was someone else.' She couldn't be more precise, even to herself about the identity of 'else.' And it didn't matter one jot, in spite of her grandmother's insistence that Lauren would be happier with a 'lovely young man' in her life. Lauren decided that she was absolutely fine as she was.

Fiona had volunteered to come and fetch her and Lauren looked forward to introducing her to the family. Grandma had perked up considerably when Lauren mentioned that Fiona had four brothers.

'Any of them older than Fiona?' Grandma asked.

'Yes, Fee is the second of the five children.'

'What is he like, Fiona's older brother? I knew some lovely brothers. There was a family with five boys, every one of them ...' Grandma drifted off into a happy reverie.

Lauren thought about Miles; thoughts not unpleasant at all, but she was not about to fall into her grandmother's trap.

'Miles? He's nice enough I suppose. Works in sausages.'

'What do you mean works in sausages? With sausages?'

'No, Grandma, not with, not alongside. Miles is heavily immersed in sausages.'

Lauren was treated to one of her grandmother's long disapproving looks, followed by an almost inaudible 'tut.'

As expected, Fiona was a great hit with the family.

'I don't suppose Lauren told you,' Fiona said over lunch, 'that her class was the star turn at the Christmas concert. Seriously, it was brilliant. Lauren have you shown them the card Mr. Gregory drew?'

Lauren fetched the card. It was passed round the table evoking appreciative noises.

'Very clever,' her mother said, 'This really looks like you. And were the children really bundled up like that, with scarves?'

When the card reached her father, he looked at it for a long time.

'Can I keep this, love?' he asked.

'Course you can, Dad.'

Lauren felt herself blushing. She was absolutely sure

there was going to be a whole book of drawings of her by Michael Gregory, no point mentioning it. They'd find out soon enough.

Fiona explained that the New Year's Eve party they would be attending would be held in a large house. Fiona assured Lauren that she had been invited as Miles' plus one.

Aware that her grandmother was about to chip in Lauren asked, 'Is it going to be very posh, this do?'

'Posh as it gets,' Fiona replied, 'bring every bead and sequin you've got.'

Fiona's house looked more than ever like a child's drawing. Every window had been framed in fairy lights; the effect quite wonderfully naive. Inside, it resembled a railway station: constant comings and goings, boxes being left to be picked up, or exchanged, the house scoured for props for the pantomime – and there was a new hazard.

Joe, Fiona's youngest brother had a gleam in his eye. Every time a brother crossed his path Joe pounced and attempted to wrestle him to the ground. If no brother ventured within pouncing range, Joe grabbed Fiona.

'Stop it, Joe,' had become the family mantra.

The brothers each had their own way of dealing with the impending wrestle. Harry, being very light on his feet, managed a few side steps, a nifty soft shoe shuffle, then turning on his heel he'd pin Joe's arm behind his back.

William's, often successful tactic, was to insert one leg between Joe's legs, thus throwing him off balance.

Lauren was reminded of the wild-life programmes where young lions tested their strength tumbling round the edge of the jungle.

Miles's response to Joe only added to the jungle impression. Being taller and stronger than Joe, Miles simply grabbed the back of Joe's collar and held on tight.

Mrs. Bates seemed completely oblivious to the behaviour of her offspring; simply going round or stepping over the heap of writing bodies when necessary.

'I think you might have guessed, Lauren, that Joe has taken up wrestling.'

Joe and Harry were heading up to London to Trafalgar Square, and William to his girlfriend's. So only four of them would be going to the New Year's Eve party: Fiona, Lauren, Miles and Ben. Lauren had heard about Ben, Miles's best friend from school. Fiona hadn't said much about him, except that Ben was in the RAF and Fiona had once had a serious crush on him.

Fiona and Lauren made a great fuss of getting ready for the 'ball', experimenting with face packs that made Lauren feel as if her skin was being pulled, although she couldn't work out in which direction it was heading. Whichever it was she hoped it would find its way back. 'It's meant to be soothing,' Fiona said with great difficulty; the tight mask making it difficult for her to move her lips.

Perfume dabbed behind ears and on wrists, hair sprayed with some invisible magic potion that would keep every hair in place come hell or high water, they descended the stairs feeling like a pair of giggly teenagers from a Hollywood B picture.

Turning into an impressively scrunchy drive Lauren noted the mansion and someone directing cars to a field behind the house.

'Whose house?' Lauren whispered.

'Lord of the manor, sort of,' Fiona replied. 'He was a great friend of my dad's, so we get invited to these do's.'

Lauren realised this was the first time Fiona had mentioned her father but this was not the time to question her.

Walking into the bright house smelling of Christmas trees and food, (sausage rolls, Lauren wondered, hoped?), their coats vanished, drinks appeared and introductions were made.

It occurred to Lauren that this was probably the first proper grown-up party she'd ever been to. It was not like the tennis club hop where someone was bound to arrive dressed in bin bags or wearing the mayor's chain of office, which they had somehow 'borrowed'. Here, every group could be posing for a sober, society magazine. Lauren giggled.

For the first time Lauren got a good look at Ben. He was a fraction taller than Fiona, with curly brown hair and very dark brown eyes. No one would call him handsome, but he had a kind, friendly face, the sort you wouldn't hesitate to go up to and ask for help. Ben gazed at Fiona. Lauren reckoned the crush was the other way round this time.

Dancing with Miles, Lauren asked, 'How are the sausages?'

'History, I'm happy to say. Did Fee tell you they sent me to Germany to research sausages?'

Lauren nodded. There had been frequent messages from Miles.

'Do you know how many different kinds of sausages there are in Germany?'

'No,' Lauren said, 'but I have a feeling I soon will.'

'Ha', Miles laughed. 'Well if you do, you'll be the only person who does. Germany, being Germany insists that sausages are registered before you can sell them, but as every frau makes her own from her great-grandmother's secret recipe, which she is not going to reveal, sausages remain unregistered. Ghost sausages, if zey are not registered zey cannot exist. I was supposed to find a way of making our sausages more appealing, more like the German ones. Not much chance when they're called wurst. I am now advertising whisky and very pleasant it is, too.'

On being introduced to Lauren and Fiona a plump young man said, 'Two teachers you say, I'd better behave myself then.'

'Don't you just hate it when people do that?' Ben said. 'I get the stupidest cracks about being in the RAF.'

Lauren realised that she was very comfortable in Miles's company. He was about as unlike Cameron as it was possible to be. For a start he didn't follow her around looking like a lost puppy dog.

Waking late, on New Year's Day, in the Bateses' spare bedroom, Lauren realised they'd be heading back to work in a day or two. Christmas had been great, pretty nearly perfect, but she was quite ready to get back to her pack of little people in Class 3M.

All the Bateses, Lauren and Ben went to the local pantomime on the 2nd. Lauren decided that amateur pantomimes were a whole lot better than professional ones: a custard pie inexpertly thrown, the pantomime horse sitting down and splitting in two and the entire audience booing at the mention of a proposed new road.

Lauren thought how her class would love it. She could just imagine them joining in with 'Oh no he isn't!'. Then

Widow Twanky appeared; the generously-padded landlord of the local pub. With his dark-rimmed specs, magnificent bosom and oddly-shaped medieval headdress, he was the image of Mrs. M.

Chapter 23

Lauren opened the classroom door with a little flutter of excitement. It looked very empty. And sad. The cleaners had no doubt done their best, but little flakes of sparkle still clung to the weird, brown oily stuff that covered the classroom floor after every holiday.

A corner of the blue backing paper had come loose from its drawing pin, curling back on itself like wallpaper in a neglected house. The classroom lacked ... life, and there wouldn't be any of that until tomorrow. The children would be back on the 7th and there was a lot to do before then.

They came in, beaming, bursting to tell about Christmas.

'Happy New Year. We'll have News Time after I've taken the register.'

They answered to their names, loud and clear and everyone followed the 'Yes' with 'Miss Massey', until she got to Bradley.

Lauren stopped, looked up and frowned. She'd called out Bradley's name and he'd replied, 'Yes, Miss Missy.'

Cheeky beggar, Lauren thought and called out again, this time very loudly, 'Bradley!'

Visibly cowering, he replied, 'Yes, Miss Massey.'

There was a knock on the door and Rose Dawkins, the school secretary, came in followed by a plump boy of Afro-Caribbean origin.

'Excuse me, Miss Massey. Mrs. Montgomery says this boy is to be in your class. I'll bring you the forms when they're ready. His name is ... I think he'd better tell you his name himself.'

In haste, and just a little flustered, Rose Dawkins departed.

'Come in. What's your name?'

For a moment the child stood silently looking round the room. Then he beamed and said, 'My name is Thanta Clauth Joenth.

Lauren stared. Was it possible? Could this child be trying it on? In spite of the lisp there could be absolutely no doubt what he said his name was.

'No way!' Col said.

'Uh huh. That'th my name, Thanta Clauth Joenth.

'And what do you want us to call you?' Lauren asked.

'Thanta ith fine, mith.'

'All right, Santa. I think we've got a desk for you. There, beside Col.'

Col beamed.

'And where have you come from Santa?'

'From London, Mith.'

'My name is Miss Massey.'

'Thank you Mith.'

Lauren decided to let it go. In time he'd learn to call her Miss Massey, but, with that lisp, she could imagine the amount of spray this was going to generate.

The class, to a man, to a child, were staring at Santa with an attention Lauren rarely managed to achieve.

The boy didn't seem to be in any way uneasy. When she gave out books or asked the children to do something, Santa looked around to see what the other children were doing and did likewise.

Just before break Rose Dawkins came in again.

'Mrs. Montgomery says, would you go and see her at

break time. Here are the forms.'

Lauren glanced down at the pink form. There it was, clear as daylight, 'Santa Claus Jones. Date of birth 25th December.' Well of course, it would be. What had his parents been thinking of? They hadn't even given him a middle name.

Lining up to go out to play the children were jostling to try to be nearest to Santa. Lauren could see a battle royal brewing between Bradley and Col, elbowing each other out of the way, both wanting to be instant best friends with Santa.

'Before you go out to play,' Lauren said, 'I'd like you, Adam, to show Santa where the cloakroom and toilets are and will you take Santa to the canteen at lunchtime, please Adam.'

Adam beamed, 'Cool,' he said.

'Cool' was not a word Adam usually used. He was obviously delighted to be Santa's chosen escort.

A few minutes after playtime started Lauren glanced out of the window and saw Santa holding court, surrounded by children, with Adam standing guard beside him, relishing the role of chief courtier.

She made her way to Mrs. Montgomery's office.

'Come.'

Mrs. M's coiffure had slipped; one bump still in place the other listing precariously leftwards.

Lauren hadn't quite reached the seat opposite Mrs. Montgomery before she launched forth.

'The new child in your class, Miss Massey. I sense mockery.'

'Mockery?'

'Yes. I was not aware that in a Christian country

137

parents could name their child anything that took their fancy. Where will it end? I am sure the child must be registered somewhere with a more ... suitable ... indeed a more acceptable name. It will not do, Miss Massey.'

Mrs. M glared at Lauren. Lauren stared back. What was she supposed to do about it? Get the child rechristened?

'Perhaps, Mrs. Montgomery, you could have a word with Santa's parents.'

Mrs. Montgomery winced visibly. Lauren wasn't sure which word wounded Mrs. M most: 'Santa' or 'parents.'

The silence lingered.

'Very well, Miss Massey.' Mrs. Montgomery turned her attention to the papers on her desk.

Very well what? Lauren wondered, hoping Mrs. M wouldn't take her displeasure out on Santa.

Bouncing in after playtime Louisa reminded Lauren, 'We didn't do our telling about Christmas and George went to Lapland and his gran took him and his cousin and they saw Santa's helpers and reindeer and everything.'

'Suppose we let George tell us about it, all right, George?'

Lauren glanced at Santa to see if hearing his name in the Lapland context had any effect on him. Apparently not, he listened as eagerly as the others.

'Come on, George, come up here and tell us all about it. It sounds very exciting.'

George, still by far the smallest member of the class, got up and walked slowly to the front of the class. Standing beside Lauren, legs apart, he hung his head.

'Did you go by plane?' Ashok asked.

George nodded, then he said, 'It was cold and we went

on a sleigh and the men covered us up with real furs. It was dogs like wolfs pulling the sleigh. Huksies.'

There was an awed silence. No-one could follow that. Lauren decided to let the 'huksies' go. Never before had George been bathed in such unanimous admiration.

George suddenly beamed. That smile on his usually solemn countenance was as if the sun had come out … and a hitherto undetected dimple appeared on his left cheek. Then, just as suddenly, overcome by the attention, George dashed back to his seat.

After a brief pause Maria revealed that she and Suzanna had gone up to London to see the lights 'on top of a bus.'

Spencer had received a transformer.

Pritti said, 'We don't do presents at Christmas time, but my uncle gave Ashok and me each a Rubik's Cube and whoever gets it right first is going to get five pounds.'

This was followed by a recitation of 'I got …'

In an attempt to get nearer to the spirit of Christmas, Lauren said, 'Did anyone have a family Christmas dinner with grandparents or aunties and uncles?'

Sally's hand went up. 'Miss Massey, you know plaster?'

'Plaster, like you put on a cut finger?' Lauren wondered where this was leading.

'No, no that sloshy grey stuff like the builder's men put on our kitchen wall.'

'Yes, I know about that kind of plaster, what about it?'

'Why would they put it on people, Miss Massey?'

'I don't think they do.'

'Yes, they do,' Sally insisted, 'Mum said Auntie Vera was thoroughly plastered, so that means they did it well, doesn't it?

Lauren thought for a moment.

'Does your Auntie Vera wear a lot of makeup?'

'No, she's very pink already.'

Joanna said, 'My mum is an Avon lady, she's got heaps of makeup, all kinds and perfume and special bags to carry things in.'

Bless you, Joanna, Lauren thought, then she said, 'I'm glad you all had a lovely holiday. Graham, will you please give everyone one of these red circles.'

Lauren was about to find out what, if anything, class 3M remembered about basic fractions.

Chapter 24

Every morning in January Lauren wondered which members of class 3M would have succumbed to the prevalent coughs and colds. They'd start with red noses, yawns and arms on the desk cradling a wobbly head. Lauren now had a box of man-sized tissues permanently on her desk.

Very rarely, since the beginning of the spring term, had all 24 desks been occupied. Maria had already been away twice – leaving Suzanna bereft.

Lauren had been feeling unusually tired, and she was trying to ignore the sensation in her throat which had started out as a tickle and now, every time she swallowed, felt as if it was lined with a row of razor blades.

Attendance among class teachers at Springmeadow was little short of extraordinary. They were rarely away. Looking at a register an outsider might wonder how this group managed to keep in such good health. Were they fitness fanatics? Did they take vitamin supplements?

The simple answer was: Hugo Preston. The thought that her class would have to endure the ministrations of Hugo Preston was too much to contemplate, so teachers dosed themselves with tablets and linctus and, somehow, dragged themselves into school.

Lauren, voice rapidly disappearing, managed to keep going until one Friday, at lunchtime, Fiona said, 'Enough, girl.'

It was Fiona who braved Mrs. Montgomery and told her that Lauren Massey was ill and should be at home in bed before she got something really serious that would keep her away for several weeks.

Lauren took a taxi home, then slept from two in the afternoon until one in the morning.

Fiona arrived on Saturday with, soup, cold chicken, grapes, bananas and magazines. Lauren wondered how she could possibly have forgotten the pork pies and Prosecco.

'And don't you dare go in on Monday,' Fiona said. 'I'll tell them you won't be coming in. I don't trust you to do it.'

Lauren examined her hands, wondered if she was turning into a bear. She was definitely hibernating. Sleep never seemed to be more than a few minutes or inches away.

On the phone her mother sounded concerned.

'It's only a cold Mum, just about everyone in my class has either had it or has got it – and anyway, Fiona is looking after me.'

Monday dawned, and with it feelings of guilt and worry. She was feeling better. Lauren did a check: nose – streaming, throat – O.K., head – O.K. Two out of three was a pass mark.

Taking a cup of coffee back to bed, Lauren plumped up the cushions and climbed back in. The room looked different somehow. It was Monday morning and she shouldn't be here. The wallpaper seemed to be another shade of green; it was pea soupier, and wasn't the sun – there definitely was some sun, supposed to have reached the chair by now?

Lauren glanced at her watch: 9:15. Hugo Preston would have taken the register. What would the class be doing now? Fiona had bundled her off in such a hurry there had been no time to plan anything.

Trying to visualise her class, Lauren wondered why she'd suddenly conjured up a picture of a hippopotamus in an aviary. She wondered what HP would make of Santa and vice versa. Santa was definitely a character. He had presence. Things happened around him, the children deferred to him. Santa had already persuaded the class that they needed to save the baby seals who were being killed for no reason, they hadn't done anything bad. Santa and Adam had become inseparable. When they weren't kicking the sponge ball around the playground they could be seen, heads together, conferring about something serious.

Trying to reassure herself that there was nothing she could do about Hugo Preston now, Lauren vowed she'd go back tomorrow.

She was greeted at the staffroom door by Fiona.

'You shouldn't be here – you're a right nutcase. But listen, you're on playground duty, only you're not. I'm doing it, no argument. You can do mine one day. Anyway there's not a bat's chance in hell that anyone is going out on the playground today; icy patches have been reported. But you just come up here at break times, make yourself a warm drink and I'll do the patrolling. '

Springmeadow's arrangements for the break times when the children couldn't go on the playground were, to say the least, haphazard. Teachers on duty patrolled the classrooms, (downstairs and upstairs) with Hugo Preston doing likewise – only on these occasions he was invariably 'otherwise engaged.'

'Thanks Fee, and I really will do your playground duty one day. Honest … and thanks.'

When the children came in and saw Lauren at her desk, they smiled at each other.

Charmaine said, 'We've got to be good today, else Miss

Massey will get poorly again.'

Her pronouncement was greeted without comment.

It was hard to work out exactly what the class had done on Monday.

'Mr. Preston didn't like us singing our names when we answered the register,' Mark said.

'And we did silent reading,' Adam added, 'lots of it.'

Mark put his hand up. 'Miss Massey, you know your guitar? Would you bring it back, so we can have songs in the classroom? Like we did for Christmas?'

'That's a lovely idea, Mark. I'll tell you what. We can learn the songs I'll be teaching everyone to sing in assembly.'

Sally said, 'Miss Massey, if we can't go out at playtime this afternoon, could we do you a play? We've been practising.'

'No we haven't,' Bradley said.

'Yes we have, Bradley Hawkins and if you want to do a play this afternoon you'd better get practising.' Sally folded her arms and stuck out her chin. Lauren could just see what Sally would look like twenty years hence.

'That's a really lovely idea. Thank you, Sally. I would be delighted to come and see your play at this afternoon's break.'

Sally immediately began making gestures that looked like the signals tic-tac men make at races. No doubt she was giving instructions to her cast.

Two bells indicated indoor play again this morning. As Lauren was leaving the classroom Col said, 'Miss it's not fair, we can't go on the playground. It's not fair.'

'It's the weather Col. Who can we blame for that?'

Spencer, who was standing near by, pointed his

thumb heavenward and said, loudly in his deep, deep voice, 'Big G.'

Knowing Hugo Preston would make some crack about her class, Lauren half dreaded going into the staffroom.

He looked up as she came in, 'That ginger boy – one man wrecking gang, away, is he?'

'Ginger boy? I don't know who you mean.' This time Lauren really didn't.

'Fully paid up member of the awkward squad. Looks like a rat.'

Lauren knew exactly who he meant, and wished she didn't. The boy was not in her class but Lauren knew that every time she saw him she'd think of …

Mercifully Brenda Cunningham came over.

'I hope you're feeling better, Lauren. Are you sure you should be here?' She gave Lauren's arm a little pat. 'Could we have a word at lunchtime? Someone from the office has been in. She wants us to have a go at Music and Movement. It's a radio programme, it's … well in the dance and drama area. Mrs. Montgomery said if we must, it's your class and my class should do it. Have you brought a packed lunch? Good, I'll see you at lunchtime.'

After several days of unrelenting indoor playtimes, the air in the classroom was stale. Always damp and musty, on some mornings it reeked of de-icer, due, no doubt, to a child being helpful, getting the frost off a car and getting de-icer on the sleeves of a sweatshirt. The children were lethargic, it was a struggle keeping their attention on the task in hand. Lauren longed to open all the doors and windows in the school, and to hell with the consequences. She needed AIR!

The play Sally and co were putting on would, at least

be something different.

Two bells rang for the afternoon break: indoors, yet again.

Sally took over. 'Miss Massey, you have to come and sit here and shut your eyes while we get ready.'

'How about me sitting on your desk, facing the other way, but keeping my eyes open.'

Sally pondered for a moment. 'All right, Miss Massey, but promise you won't peep.'

Facing the back of the classroom, Lauren became aware of a group of boys who also seemed to be rehearsing.

Col said, 'You can't say that! It's me what 'as the money.'

This was followed by some whispered conferring.

Lauren heard the door open. She turned round. Hugo Preston stood in the doorway surveying the chaos. Lauren's chair was now covered with a badly dyed pink sheet with a hole in it, over which dangled several strands of tinsel. A group of girls wore assorted headgear from the dressing-up box and the sparkly scarves that had featured in their Christmas costumes.

Hugo Preston opened his mouth, then closed it again. He looked around the room, stared at Lauren, then retreated.

Sally announced, 'We're ready. You can turn round. Oh, you peeped, Miss Massey.'

'Mr. Preston came in,' Lauren said.

'We are going to do a play about the story Mr. Vicar told us about King Solomon.'

Lauren searched her mind, wondering if she was going to have to press the 'censored' button.

Sally continued. 'Mr. Vicar said two ladies came to

Solomon and said the same baby belonged to them. In our play there are four ladies, so more people can have parts. I am King Solomon.'

Sally sat on the chair and draped the tinsel around her.

Louisa, wearing a headscarf, faced the audience. 'George didn't want to be the baby, so we made one from a cardy.'

Louisa, Inga, Pritti and Kylie also wore hats or bits of cloth on their heads, but it was Kylie cradling the cardigan. She approached the throne.

'Oh wise and powerful King Solomon. These terrible women want to take my beautiful baby from me.'

Louisa piped up, 'It's not your baby. It doesn't even look like you. It's mine.'

Inga and Pritti said woodenly, in unison, 'No, no it's my baby.'

'You aren't looking after it properly,' Pritti said, 'give it to me at once.'

Sally said, very loudly, 'Silence. Stop your chattering ladies. Page, bring me my sword.'

Charmaine, standing beside Sally, produced a ruler from behind her back.

'The fairest thing to do,' Sally said, 'is to cut the baby in two and you can have half a baby each.'

Lauren sighed. As she feared, Class 3M's grasp of fractions was very shaky.

'No, no,' Louisa said, 'that will kill the baby.'

'We must draw lots,' Pritti said, 'See, I have papers. The one who draws the cross will get the baby. All agree.'

They all said 'agree', including the page and Solomon, who was still holding the ruler/sword at a menacing angle.

Lots were drawn. Kylie kept the baby. The girls

147

bowed.

Lauren led the applause.

'Can we do ours now, Miss Massey. It's not very long.'

Glowing, the girls removed the scenery and their headgear.

Adam came up to Lauren. 'Miss Massey, I think we should have a talent show, you know, the kind they have on television. I can do a magic trick and Santa can make fart noises with his armpits.'

The boys were ready.

'We're in a pub,' Col said, 'and we're gangsters workin' out 'ow to rob a bank an' get rich.'

'I'm the barman,' Jonathan said,' but I'm a baddy, as well.'

He turned to the actors. 'What would you like to drink, gentlemen?'

The door opened, and once again Hugo Preston surveyed the scene, just in time to hear Bradley, who was frantically smoking a pencil, say, 'Just give me a pint of brandy.'

Chapter 25

Every child who came through the door noticed the second adult chair beside Miss Massey's. The weather had improved a bit so, bundled up in coats and scarves, the children were able to run around outside at playtimes. They'd come in, pink and panting, and Lauren fancied that as they came they brought some fresh air in with them.

Lauren and Carol Webb were studying the class timetable over in the corner. Carol Webb, a tall thin woman with short grey hair, was making notes. With her dark brown eyes and swift movements, there was something birdlike about her. She said softly to Lauren, 'Would you like me to just watch or join in?'

'Join in, please.'

Now seated, the children waited patiently for an explanation. On the blackboard they could see stick figures making a sort of arrow shape. At the bottom, the pointed end, was a stick figure labelled, 'you.'

'We have a visitor,' Lauren said. 'Her name is Miss Webb. Would you like to say good afternoon to her.'

There followed six robotic syllables. Lauren could have conducted them with her ruler: three, low, drone-like notes, a high fourth one for 'noon' followed by two more drone notes.

Lauren hoped this dirge wouldn't count against her.

'We're going to look at your families and then talk about what life was like in your grandparents' time. This little figure is meant to be you, here are your mum and dad – so how many grandparents are there, Spencer?'

'Four,' Spencer rumbled, 'two grandmas and two grandpas.'

'Yes, and great-grandparents, Maria?'

'Eight, Miss Massey.'

Adam had been staring at the blackboard in something like disbelief. He put his hand up.

'Miss Massey, does that mean that I have, I mean there were 16 great-great-grandparents? Everyone has 16 great-great-grandparents?'

Bless you, Lauren thought.

'Yes, it does, Adam.'

Santa's hand went up. 'My granddad in Trinidad is called Thquirrel.'

Mark started giggling, setting the others off.

Miss Webb stood up, and with a piece of chalk wrote 'Cyril' on the blackboard.

'Could that be his name?' she asked. 'It sounds just like squirrel.'

Head on one side Santa considered the possibility.

Louisa put her hand up, 'George's grandma took him to Lapland.'

This information was for Miss Webb's benefit.

'You've given me an idea, Louisa. Shall we save what we know about our grandparents until next News Time? And I can tell you about my grandma, too.'

Seeing the look of disbelief on their faces she added, 'Yes, I do have a grandma. How are we going to find out what it was like in your grandparents' time.'

Several hands went up. Pritti offered, 'We can ask them. We can do interviews like they do on television.'

'Yeah!' came from Bradley, 'cool, like on telly.'

'That's what I'd like you to do. And if there are no grandparents living near you, you could interview a neighbour or friend of your parents' and if you can't find anyone to interview, Mrs. Graham, who is a grandma, and our caretaker, Mr. Beamish, have both said they'd be happy to be interviewed. Now how do we go about interviewing someone?'

'Be very polite', Suzanna said.

'Good. What sort of questions are you going to ask?'

There followed a succession of suggestions regarding toys, food, holidays, amount of pocket money received, means of transport … Lauren managed to deflect some of the dafter ones.

'Now, what about a practise. Would someone like to come and ask Miss Webb a question?'

Santa's hand went up.

'All right, Santa, perhaps you should have a pencil and notebook to take down her answer.'

Fortunately Santa was beginning to grow into his teeth; the lisp becoming less pronounced. He approached Miss Webb.

'Excuse me, Mith Webb, how old are you?'

Lauren barely managed to stifle a gasp but, without missing a beat, Carol Webb said, 'I'm as old as my tongue and a little older than my teeth.'

Santa stared.

'Think about it,' Carol Webb said. 'You're born with your tongue, but a baby's teeth don't come in for several months.'

Santa beamed. 'That's really funny. But …'

'Santa,' Lauren said, 'It's not considered polite to ask people how old they are. I'm not sure why that is...'

'My mum told me that,' Santa said, 'you don't athk them unless you can thee that they are very, very old. Then it's O.K.'

Louisa's hand was up. 'May I do a question, Miss Massey?'

'Come along then,' Lauren's heart was sinking. She wondered if it could get any worse.

'Miss Webb, if you didn't have telly when you were eight years old, what did you do when you got home from school?'

Carol Webb listed the games she'd played, giving detailed instructions and a demonstration of 'kick the can', finishing off with, 'You could play it on the playground here. I think you've got enough hiding places.'

The home-time bell sounded. Children gone, Lauren waited apprehensively for the verdict.

'Do you need to get away in a hurry or could we have a chat now?' Carol Webb asked.

'I'm not in a hurry,' Lauren said, fearing the worst.

Carol Webb leaned back in her chair, 'I really enjoyed that. And you know, that boy is absolutely right. It is acceptable to ask a very old person their age – or a child, but not the people in the middle. Why?' Looking over at Lauren she said, 'Don't look so worried, that was a great lesson. You're doing very well. Has Mrs. Montgomery discussed your teaching with you? Anything?'

Lauren shook her head.

'Mrs. Montgomery will tell you that she runs a tight ship, and so she does in some ways. There are other ways of steering a ship, especially where the waters are not eternally choppy. Mrs. Montgomery told me she thought you might be a "soft touch, unable to grasp the nettle, should it be necessary." Have you sent many children to her to be disciplined?'

'No, it hasn't been necessary. I threatened two boys

once, well, it wasn't even a threat, I just floated the possibility that ...'

'It seems to me, Miss Massey, that Class 3M is a nettle free zone. Is there anything worrying you?'

'Yes. I worry a bit about Chang. He's so quiet. He's never spoken in class, I mean, he never volunteers information or asks questions. His work is good ... everything, written English very good, and he can draw anything.'

'Does he interact with the other children?'

'Oh yes. He's got some kind of card exchange business going on with George and Robert. The girls talk to him, especially Pritti and Charmaine. Chang's parents, on Open Evening were ... lovely. They kept thanking me.'

'I think it's a cultural thing. I'd leave him alone, praise him quietly, perhaps ask him privately if all is well. Not everyone I know is a chatterbox. Do you intend to stay on at Springmeadow?'

'For another year, I think ...'

'Good plan. Another year here, then look around carefully. I probably won't see you again, there's no need. Good luck, and I only wish I could see what your interviewers come up with.'

Putting some exercise books into her rucksack Lauren wondered if 'I probably won't see you again,' meant that she had passed her probationary year. It couldn't mean that, the school year wasn't even half over. It probably meant that when a supervisor came, it wouldn't be Carol Webb.

Pity.

Chapter 26

Lauren stopped at her classroom doorway. There was a distinct whiff coming from ... She took a couple of sniffs; definitely coming from somewhere inside the classroom. Since the brilliant Dr. Della Ryan-Jones had solved the noisome Col problem, the classroom had been a pong-free zone. But this musty smell ... no, worse than musty, much worse – there were unmistakable overtones of decay.

Fiona appeared in the doorway, 'May I borrow your ... what's that horrible smell?'

She took a few steps into the classroom. 'Ye gods, dead mouse springs to mind. We had one once, under the cooker.'

Fiona began circling the room taking exploratory sniffs as she went. Lauren followed echoing Fiona's non-rhythmic sniffs.

Fiona stopped and pointed at a cardboard box on the radiator. 'Whatever or whoever it is, is in there.'

For a second or two they surveyed the stinking box.

'Ahh ...' Lauren said.

Holding her breath Fiona peered in. The box was full of polystyrene trays that had once contained raw meat. The blood that had once been red was now a sticky brown.

'Oh dear,' Fiona said, 'I suppose this is my fault.'

A few weeks ago Fiona had held up a child's picture of a house with a tree, swing and stick figure. The page was entirely red except for the white drawing.

'How did you do that?' Lauren had asked.

'Easy: polystyrene trays, the kind you buy meat and fish in, stuff like that. You wash and dry the tray. The underside is smooth. Child draws on it with pencil or biro.

You roll paint on it and print. Voila! Instant masterpiece. Send a letter home asking for the trays. There is polystyrene specifically for printing, but I can't see Mrs. M allowing Brenda to spend good money on anything like that.'

Lauren had sent the letter home. It had not occurred to her to ask for the trays to be washed. The reeking pile of trays before them still bore traces of mince, little crumbs of suet and fragments of bone. This lot had never come into contact with water.

'Tell you what,' Fiona said, 'until we can get rid of them, put the box under the stage. No one goes there. We can chuck them properly later.'

Holding her breath, Lauren picked up the box and headed for the hall. She wondered what the conversation would have been like if she'd asked Brenda Cunningham for shop-bought, lovely, clean, specifically-for-children-to print-with polystyrene.

Brenda Cunningham was in charge of The Arts at Springmeadow; the Arts, the whole jing bang lot of them. Not that there was any drama in the school, nor dance nor even a great deal of painting. Painting paper was doled out at the rate of one sheet per pupil per lesson. Any nod at sculpture was confined to now grey/beige plasticine, completely colour-free, except for the rare, sad swirl of orange echoing its former glory.

Mrs. M's job description for 'person in charge of The Arts', if there was such a thing, would have been brief and most likely entirely in capital letters. DO NOT WASTE MONEY ON FRIVOLITY. For one thing, a lot of art was messy and Mrs. M did not like mess. More seriously though, it might be hard to keep control, if the arts were allowed even a little licence.

Music didn't really count as one of The Arts. Music was desirable, as at Springmeadow it manifested itself mainly in hymns, which were by definition: godly.

There was a distinct hierarchy in Mrs. M's view of the subjects on the curriculum. At the top, no argument, came Religious Education. Mrs. M had assumed the onerous responsibility for that, herself. A long way behind R.E. came mathematics. Lauren assumed that mathematics had Mrs. M's blessing because numbers and plus signs were totally predictable – they weren't going to come up with anything alarming or unexpected. History and geography were thoroughly respectable because they could be held firmly within the confines of carefully chosen facts and maps. Science passed muster, provided it stuck to plants and nature trays. Biology caused extreme anxiety. You never knew what living creatures might get up to. Well you did, and that was the problem.

The Arts were definitely the lowest of the low: frivolous and unnecessary. Even English, when not sticking to spelling, grammar or comprehension, could get out of hand.

Brenda Cunningham, nominally in charge of The Arts at Springmeadow, was very nearly unemployed.

At the urging of 'the office', Music and Movement was to be a tentative nod in the general direction of The Arts.

With Class M seated in the hall, Lauren switched on the radio.

The tune, though not familiar, was like a dozen airs you might hear in a lift. Muzak, Lauren thought.

The voice from the radio said, 'Stand up children.

Stand up and stay where you are keeping perfectly still. You are a forest now, and each of you is a tree. When there is no wind, trees are perfectly still. Keeping quite still now, listen to the music.' The children stood up, some looking sheepish: a bit embarrassed. A few bars of soft, string music sounded from the radio. 'There is going to be some wind soon, but you can't move your feet, a tree's roots stay firmly in the ground, so now, sway, as a tree might sway, with this wind music.' A fractionally faster tune sang out from the radio. Some of the children had their arms up and swayed hesitantly, as requested. Santa, eyes closed, and completely unselfconscious, waved his arms from side to side. Lauren reckoned he'd done this kind of thing before. George's arms stayed glued to his sides. He gave the occasional nod. 'Now the wind is getting stronger.' The music was now louder and a bit faster. Bradley started blinking manically and opening and closing his hands.

'I'm a Christmas tree Miss, with lights and all.'

Lauren decided she'd have to ask Brenda if Music and Movement could be recorded, so that it didn't plough inexorably on. She definitely needed a pause button.

The weather was still cold, but snowdrops appeared on lawns, and the stiff green spikes, heading out of the ground or plant pots, would become daffodils or tulips within a few weeks.

The 'interviewing grandparents' lessons had gone down a storm. In addition to answering the children's questions, several grandparents had sent in notes and photographs. Alan Gregory sent in a beautifully handwritten page about his school days and a photocopy of one of his school reports saying, 'this boy needs to pay attention in lesson times.'

Lauren told the class about her grandmother's extraordinary childhood bathing costume, and about her grandfather, Laurence, helping out in a bakery when he was twelve.

Santa's grandma, living with the family, was a dressmaker. The stories about her childhood could have kept lessons going for a whole term. Lauren had thought how much she'd like to meet her. By coincidence, Santa arrived with a letter from his mother. Brief and to the point it said, 'Dear Miss Massey, I would very much like to meet you. Would it be convenient for me to come to the school one day at home time? I promise I wouldn't keep you long.'

Lauren was glad that half term was going to be uneventful. Her mum had booked her an appointment at the dentist and had planned a shopping trip to Oxford with gran. Mum hoped Lauren would join them. Apart from that Lauren intended to sleep and go for long walks in the country air.

One morning, in late February, Adam came in with a large brown envelope.

'Miss Massey, my dad said he'd like you to have a copy of his latest book.'

Lauren stared. Was this it, was this the one where she was being exposed as a greedy idiot?

Lauren managed to say, 'Thank you, Adam.'

The envelope lay on her desk all morning. She couldn't stop thinking about it. The likeness Michael Gregory had got of her, on his Christmas card, would leave no doubt in anyone's mind who the 'heroine' was.

At lunchtime, heart thumping, Lauren took out the book. The title was, 'Where's Scratch?' The cover showed a puppy bearing an expression guaranteed there would be no punishment, no matter what he had done.

Glancing through the pages there was no sign of anyone looking remotely like her. The puppy, Scratch, arrived as a birthday present. Another present, arriving in a huge box, was a comfy bed for Scratch. Leaving the puppy for a moment, the family go to the door to greet a guest. Back in the lounge – no sign of Scratch. The family search and begin to panic. Eventually puppy is found asleep inside the box which had contained his bed.

Lauren felt herself flooded with relief. This wasn't it. This wasn't her humiliation. The book, like Michael Gregory's other books, was brilliantly illustrated and, yes … funny. She'd been reprieved, but for how long?

Lauren sat down to write a letter thanking Michael Gregory. Her pen hovered when she wondered whether to ask him the plot of his next book, but decided against it.

Waiting for the bell to ring, Sally put her hand up. 'Miss Massey, could we do another play, about the olden days, our grandparents' time?'

Remembering Hugo Preston's two glimpses at the last theatricals Lauren hesitated. But only for a moment.

'Of course you may, Sally.'

Santa put his hand up. 'My mum ith coming to see you, but I'm going home with Adam. Mum said to tell you or you might think I'd forgotten she'th coming.'

'Thank you Santa.'

Lauren didn't have to wait long.

There could be no doubt that the smiling woman with her hand outstretched was Santa's mother. Smart and colourful, she somehow filled the room.

'Miss Massey, I've heard so much about you from Santa and Adam. You might want to know how Santa got his name. His birthday, of course. But with Jones it was going to have to be something a bit different, wasn't it? So my mother said to my husband, "go the whole hog and call him Santa Claus". She was joking, but the baby got himself registered that way. We could have ignored that and called him Billy at home, but Santa stuck like glue. Now, I don't want to keep you. I want to know how I can help.'

'Help?'

'Yes, at Santa's last school I used to go in and take little groups for cookery, and if there were outings I came as an extra supervisor. I work from home, so I can be flexible. Call on me when you need an extra pair of hands, Miss Massey. Does the school have a cooker outside the kitchens?'

'I don't know. I don't think so.'

'Would you like your class to have cookery sessions? I used to take four children at a time.'

'I'd love it, Mrs. Jones. The children would love it, but …'

Mrs. Jones laughed. 'I was pretty sure you would, but I thought I'd better check before I tackle Mrs. Montgomery. Thank you Miss Massey. I hope to be getting back to you soon so we can start with the cookery rotas.'

As she said goodbye Lauren noticed a gleam in Mrs. Jones's eye; a decidedly mischievous gleam.

Chapter 27

Half term at home had been exactly what Lauren needed;
peaceful and uneventful – except for that one night. She'd
woken at about three in the morning, suddenly
remembering the bloody polystyrene trays she'd put under
the stage.

Lauren visualised a plague of flies zooming out in the
middle of one of Mrs. M's assembly sermons. She'd be
dismissed immediately, never again able to get
employment. And there was no way she could get in touch
with anyone. Fiona was spending the week with Ben and
his parents.

Lauren wondered whether to phone the school and
fling herself on Mr. Beamish, the caretaker's, mercy. But
there was little or no chance he'd be in the secretary's office
or that he'd even answer the phone. It was already Friday,
so she'd be back at school at the same time as a letter could
arrive. Perhaps by now the whole school would be stinking
to high heaven and the hygiene people would have been
called in. They'd come in wearing their white coats, gas
masks and fumigating gear, and they'd spray the entire
school with a noxious chemical. The school would have to
be closed and the whole thing would get into the papers
and Lauren knew she would be unemployable for ever.

Getting into school early, Lauren raced for the school
hall and made her way under the stage. It smelt a bit dusty,
a little damp but nothing else. The box was gone.

A beaming Fiona was waiting in her classroom.

'Fee, those bloody, smelly meat trays ...'

'Oh, didn't I tell you? I chucked them that evening. Mr.

Beamish said it was O.K. to put them in that skip. How was your half term?'

Revelling in the feeling of relief now flooding through her, Lauren said, 'Lovely, peaceful, how was yours?'

'Absolute heaven. Can you keep a secret? Course you can, silly question. Ben thinks we should get married, then we could live in married quarters. It will depend on his postings of course, but ...'

'Whoa ... too fast. Are you telling me you're engaged?'

'Yes ...YES! Well I don't know if Ben's aware of it, but we've been engaged since I was about seven. Is that the time? More anon.'

It wasn't officially spring, but class 3M bounced in full of the joys.

Register taken, all present and correct and every child adding, 'Miss Massey', to 'yes'. Good: full house, so it could be full steam ahead with the lesson plans Mrs. M had approved with her perfunctory tick. Mrs. M had approved content, but Lauren had not been too specific when it came to methods.

Mental arithmetic and silent reading over Lauren asked, 'Does anyone know about the game of skittles?'

Several hands went up.

'Like bowling', Graham said, 'You sort of roll the balls and knock down the skittles.'

'Are we going to play ski'uls, then?' Bradley asked. Bradley seemed to think putting his hand up a waste of valuable energy.

'No. You're not. I am. You are going to be the skittles and I'm going to try to knock you over. You all sit on top of your desks. I'll give you a word to spell and if you get it wrong you have to sit down. Last man ... er ... child

standing, I mean sitting, wins. It's called "spelling skittles."
Right, on top of your desks everyone.'

It took George two attempts, but within seconds chairs
had been vacated, desk tops occupied. Clipboard in hand
Lauren walked up the aisles before pouncing on Chang.

'Spell "coat".'

Chang answered softly, but correctly.

'Good. George, spell "best"'. 'Best' was George's
favourite word. His brief compositions invariable included
the word.

Closing his eyes, concentrating hard, George said, 'B-
E-S-T.'

'Good.'

George beamed, revealing the rarely seen dimples.

Kirsty's word 'twin' had been carefully chosen. Like
Chang she answered correctly, but almost inaudibly.

Once round the class Lauren said, 'I'm not doing very
well am I? Half term has done you good. I haven't
managed to knock anyone down yet. Right, the next lot of
words are going to be really difficult.

'Ignacio, spell "rabbit."'

Without hesitation Ignacio said, 'R-A-B-I-T'. Someone
coughed.

'No Miss twobees, twobees, twobees, please Miss
twobees.'

Robert was the first to go, felled by 'cloud'.
Surprisingly, 'money' was Col's undoing.

Santa put a 'g' after the 'n' in 'donkey.' Just for a second
Lauren mused that as mistakes go, this was a good one.

'George, spell banana.' The word had appeared in a
recent composition.

'B-A-N-A.'

Silence.

'More George, 'Charmaine said, 'the banana is longer than that.'

'B-A-N-A'.

'Keep going,' Charmaine said, in what she imagined was a whisper.

'N-A.'

'Yessss', from several children.

With a handful of children still atop their desks and the others watching intently, the door opened and Hugo Preston appeared. He looked around, opened his mouth, closed it again and retreated. Lauren decided that he looked like a very large fish, grounded and gasping. It needed to be thrown back into the sea, immediately.

Soon only three children remained; Suzanna, Pritti and Adam.

'Laughter' turned out to be Suzanna's undoing. Pritti and Adam seemed unstoppable; tackling 'macaroni', 'earache', 'obedient', and 'daffodil' without hesitation.

The playtime bell sounded.

'Well done. It's a tie, a draw. Adam and Pritti are the winners. Why don't the rest of you look for some really hard words to see if our two champions can spell them.'

Expecting a tirade from Hugo Preston, all Lauren got on entering the staff room was a dirty look. She reckoned HP was working up to saying something really scathing, when he had a big enough audience.

Fiona's 'more anon' was more of the same. Ben was now very much aware that he was engaged to Fiona and as delighted as she was. There were messages to Lauren from Miles, who was now in Scotland doing something about whisky.

164

'Something's up with Mrs. M,' Fiona said. 'Something's bugging her. I asked her if my class could plant some vegetables in the far corner of the field and instead of her usual "we'll see" she snapped, "that would not be practical." And have you noticed the position of the bosom? Permanently on high alert.'

As Lauren did her best to avoid Mrs. M whenever possible, she hadn't noticed any change. But assemblies were becoming haranguing sessions. Fiona was right. Something discombobulated Mrs. M.

The windowsills of class 3M were now lined with jam jars. Chang had provided the notice. 'Class 3M Bean Race. Start date 15th of March 1976.'

With every child now in possession of a labelled jam jar, lined with old-fashioned blotting paper, with a bean wedged between the glass and the blotting paper and a carefully measured half an inch of water at the bottom the of the jar – the race could begin. With the jars lined up at the starting gate, (the window sills,) friends' jars together, of course, in unison the children said, 'Ready, steady, grow.'

Charts had been made and beans drawn. Now the class waited expectantly for changes to occur. First it was just the wrinkling of the skin. Then, causing great excitement, a little white, not green, as the children had expected, root appeared.

It looked as if Inga's bean was pulling into the lead, but, sounding old and wise, Adam said, 'Actually, it's still early days.'

One morning the water in Bradley's jar looked decidedly murky. It had turned brown.

'What's happened to this, then?' Lauren asked.

'Well, my dad said if I wanna win the bean race, bean needs a bit of fer'ilizer, so I put in some Growmore.'

'That's cheating, Bradley Hawkins,' Sally said.

'It's never. My dad says it's usin' your noddle. That's what it is.'

'All right,' Lauren said, 'let's see whether it makes any difference.'

One afternoon, when a pile of letters for the children to take home appeared on her desk, Lauren discovered what had been upsetting Mrs. M.

'Dear Parents,

I regret to have to tell you that parents have not been complying with my request to park further away from the school gates when bringing or fetching their child to and from school. In addition, the school's neighbours have been complaining that their drives are frequently blocked and parents' cars have been driving over verges, permanently ruining the grass.

Several items of clothing now in the Lost Property box are unnamed. Please ensure that all items of clothing bear your child's name at all times.

It has come to my attention that some children are not wearing the recommended footwear for their P.E. lessons. It is essential that standard issue plimsolls be worn. Both shoes should bear your child's name, written in indelible black ink on the inside of the shoe. It is acceptable for an additional piece of elastic to be worn to keep the shoe in place but this elastic must be black.

At no time may jewellery be worn. Hair slides should be sensible and serviceable and preferably brown. Hair slides bearing glitter or rhinestones are merely an unnecessary distraction, not conducive to good work habits. I must also add a word of caution here with regard to pencil cases. These too, are becoming unnecessarily frivolous.

I must also ask parents to refrain from telephoning the school unless the matter is absolutely necessary. Our hard-working school secretary, Mrs. Dawkins, has recently been telephoned, on more than one occasion, by parents enquiring about the dates of school terms and half terms. Every child was given a comprehensive list of dates at the beginning of the school year. May I suggest that, upon receiving this information you place it in a safe place where you can refer to it as needed.'

Reading through the letter Lauren reckoned that up till now it was all pretty standard stuff. What followed was not.

'A group of parents has approached me, asking if they might hold a Fete this summer to raise funds for some new equipment the school could make use of. An overhead projector and a free-standing cooker to be used for educational purposes have been suggested.

These parents are willing to form a committee to organise the Fete. I have agreed to allowing this, provided enough parents show an interest. Should this be the case, Fete committee meetings will not be held on the school premises. They will be held in the homes of the parents concerned.

Should you be interested please do not contact the school; write to:

Mrs. D. Jones, 14, Birch Drive or Mr. A. Gregory, 52,

The Meadows.

Yours sincerely, N. Montgomery'

Ouch, Lauren thought, both addresses for children in her class. That was not going to get her any Brownie points with Mrs. M.

Clearly, Mrs. Jones's offer to come in and cook with groups of children had been quickly dismissed by Mrs. Montgomery, due to the lack of a cooker. Equally clearly, Mrs. Jones was not put off that easily.

Lauren smiled. How she would love to have overheard that conversation.

Chapter 28

Longer days, spring flowers and the dawn chorus now near deafening, there was a general feeling of busyness in the air – things were moving.

The prospect of a school fete in the summer had the staffroom buzzing. Opinion was divided.

Hugo Preston predicted unmitigated disaster. Allowing parents to form a committee for whatever reason was tantamount to inviting them to come in and take over the running of the school.

'Thin end ...' he muttered darkly, 'thin end.'

Others, Fiona and Brenda Cunningham in particular, were enthusiastic.

'Lovely idea,' Brenda said, 'I'll get my family knitting miniature teddy bears.'

'However did she do it?' Fiona asked, 'Your Mrs. Jones, I mean. She's only been here five minutes, she braves Mrs. M and gets her to agree to holding a fete. It's pretty obvious Mrs. M doesn't think there'll be much interest. I think there might.'

Inga's bean continued to flourish, growing steadily. Lauren decided to declare the race over when, growing lopsidedly, some of the beans began to keel over. Inga was declared the winner. Bradley's bean had proved to be no advert for Growmore. It did only averagely well, but looked miserable the entire time being the only bean growing in murky, brown water.

Chang's drawings of the growing process could have graced a Botanical Encyclopedia.

One of the school's governors, a Mr. Farley, was causing a bit of a stir by sponsoring a 'Decorate an egg' competition. An ordinary hen's egg, either blown or hard boiled, had to be decorated; the decoration had to be 'all the child's own work.'

Class M received the news with mild bewilderment.

'What kind of paint stays on eggs?' Adam asked.

'I expect you'll have to experiment,' Lauren replied, having no idea.

'You can stick stuff on an egg,' Sally said, 'my mum put a moustache on one and my Dad wouldn't eat it.'

'Well, I hope you're all going to enter the competition.'

Considering that he'd had several days to work on his comment, Hugo Preston's reaction to seeing her class sitting on top of their desks, could only be described as feeble.

'Have you got rid of the mouse, then, Miss Massey?'

Without replying Lauren waited for further explanation.

'When I went into your classroom it looked as if the children were getting their feet away from the floor. I assumed they were fleeing from a mouse – that or a flood.'

Lauren reckoned that her encounter in the park, with Goldie, had been long enough ago for the children to write about their pets. If they didn't have a pet they could write about an animal they'd like to own. They'd need to say where it would live and find out what it ate and if it needed exercise, how much.

Lauren intended to milk the topic for all it was worth.

'Could we have a class pet, Miss Massey?' Louisa began, 'My cousin's class has a gerbil called Bilbo and the children take it in turns to take it home and it jumps ever so high once it escaped even and the caretaker found it behind the pipes.'

'Yes, a class pet. A dog would be good,' Robert said, 'a labrador.'

'A cat's better,' Maria said. 'Cats are more peaceful.'

'If we did have a pet', Lauren said, 'it might have to be a goldfish.'

'Spiders aren't much trouble,' Spencer rumbled.

Having spent a great deal of time deciding what anyone needed to know in order to keep a pet well and happy and to keep mum and dad happy, 'and the neighbours,' Adam added, the children set to work.

There were some surprises.

George turned out to be the proud owner of a corn snake. It only ate one 'mowse' a week and mostly slept. 'It doesn't need walks.'

Pritti would dearly love a pet monkey, but decided it could be too mischievous so her wish-pet was a white cat.

Maria had a rabbit whose feet and teeth needed constant and expensive attention. Her dad was not over-impressed by this.

Kirsty had once had a 'budgerigard' but it was now in heaven. What she would really like was a wee pony.

The bar chart showed: Dogs 6, Cats 5, goldfish 2, guinea pigs 2 (but both owned by Joanna), rabbits 1 and corn snake 1.

George, by running his orange-paint-laden brush all over the paper, had a dramatic portrait of Cob, his apparently mile long, snake.

Joanna's pictures of her guinea pigs were just blobs, with barely discernible eyes. Lauren studied them carefully. Actually, she thought, they were quite accurate; guinea pigs really were just living fur balls with feet.

Leaving Adam's work until last, knowing he would be

writing about Goldie, Lauren paused and studied one paragraph.

'Goldie steals socks. She doesn't steal anything else. But we can't ever leave a sock where Goldie can reach it. My grandfather doesn't know how she knows the difference between a sock and a big hankie. But she does.'

So when Michael Gregory said, 'She's never done anything like that before,' after Goldie had pinched her lunch, he wasn't really telling fibs.

Still, he probably would put the whole episode in a book, wouldn't he? There weren't that many plots involving dogs.

One morning Santa arrived with a letter.

'Dear Miss Massey,

The pets project has really got Santa going. He's not sure whether he's going to own a pet shop or work in a zoo.

The reason I'm writing to you is that my neighbour asked if your class would like two guinea pigs, both female. My neighbour's daughter is leaving home soon and they will be travelling, so the guinea pigs are looking for a new home. There is a sturdy cage and a good supply of straw and food. We have owned guinea pigs ourselves so would look after them during the holidays. We are near enough the school to come in and tend to them during weekends, or bring them home if that is preferable. Should there be no fund in the school under which 'guinea pig food' might come, we would be happy to provide the necessary food and straw.

Let me know if you would like them.

Yours sincerely, Donna Jones.'

Lauren glanced around the classroom. There was certainly room for a guinea pig cage, on the spare desks or on top of the book cupboard. Yes, that corner would be better, more stable, no draught.

Suddenly, it became imperative that Class 3M should have two guinea pigs. Mrs. Jones had faced Mrs. Montgomery and, almost single-handedly, amazingly, had gained permission for a school fete.

Lauren, inspired by Mrs. Jones, would brave Mrs. Montgomery with regard to the guinea pigs. She would rehearse her speech carefully. There was no need, in this instance, to invoke an imaginary vicar, but she might need a nod to the good Lord, by way of recommendation.

Chapter 29

Lauren decided to go and speak to Mrs. M sooner rather than later. Her dwindling courage would desert her completely if she left the interview too long. It would have to be tomorrow because, today, Lauren was on playground duty, and Mrs. M did not like to be disturbed during her lunch break.

Walking around the playground Lauren realised that the sun was gaining strength, she also realised that she'd been muttering, rehearsing the speech – the plea – she would be making to Mrs. M.

Sally had already come up to Lauren, looking crestfallen.

'You know we're going to do a play about grandma's and granddad's time?'

'Yes, Sally.'

'Well, it was ready but it's going to be not quite soon because Pritti thinks we should write it down and learn the words properly.'

Sally drifted off. Arabella could be seen heading purposefully towards Lauren.

'Miss Massey, Louisa is telling lies about what her mum and dad did for her to get borned. My mum and dad wouldn't do that. Gran told my little sister there's a special room at the back in Mothercare where mums and dads go for the special chocolate the mum has to eat, only sometimes they give her the wrong chocolate and the baby comes out the wrong colour.'

Fortunately there was only enough time for Lauren to say, 'I see' before Kirsty, who had been searching for her, pulled Arabella away to join in a complicated skipping game at the far end of the playground.

After three deep breaths and firm knock, Lauren heard the 'Come' she'd anticipated and dreaded. Shoulders back, head high, Lauren entered and waited to be invited to sit. The invitation didn't come. Mrs. M. assumed, hoped, that the meeting would be brief, very brief.

'Mrs. Montgomery, I believe you are aware that Class 3M has been doing a project on animals, on their pets. This has proved to be very educational in many areas of the curriculum. I have shown the children maps and …'

'Yes, Yes …' Mrs. Montgomery said, tapping her biro on her desk, 'Yes?'

Lauren realised that the carefully rehearsed speech would have to be ditched, pronto.

'Mrs. Montgomery. My class would dearly like to have a class pet. A parent, (she had the sense not to say which parent), has offered my class some guinea pigs. Two guinea pigs.'

'TWO!' The word shot out like a bullet. The implications of a pair, a pair of anything, reached Mrs. M in a nanosecond. Her entire being was affronted, she quivered, even her hair registered indignation.

'Two?' she repeated, face like thunder.

'Two female guinea pigs, Mrs. Montgomery. A cage, food and straw will be provided by the donor, who will also look after the guinea pigs during the holidays. I really think it would be in the children's interest for them to be responsible for the survival and well-being of some of God's creatures.'

Mrs. M still looked stunned but … was there the merest softening of the dead straight line that was Mrs. M's mouth? Did the shoulders relax infinitesimally?

The door opened and the school secretary appeared holding a sheet of paper.

'Two females, you say?' Mrs. Montgomery was already concentrating on Rose Dawkins.

'Oh, very well, Miss Massey, but I will hold you personally responsible should anything … is that the list, Rose?'

Lauren slid out of the room unnoticed; Mrs. M and Rose Dawkins already deeply involved in 'the list.'

What Lauren needed right now was a strong cup of coffee. Prosecco would have been better; coffee had to do.

What had she done? Suppose the guinea pigs died and were found, one morning, stiff and cold, little pink guinea pig feet pointing heavenward? The children would never forgive her and they'd probably be traumatised for life, developing twitches and neuroses, and would need expensive psychiatric help for years to come.

Right, Lauren decided, on the way home she'd find every book available on the care and maintenance of guinea pigs. She'd write to Mrs. Jones but only tell the class on the day the animals would be arriving. Santa and Adam would be in on the secret. The caretaker would also be told, just to keep him on side.

Fiona was nearly speechless at the news.

'Did Mrs. M actually say "yes?" I didn't think the word was in her vocabulary. She must see you as a one woman wrecking ball. My class are going to be so jealous. Do guinea pigs smell?'

Oh, Lord, I hope not, Lauren thought.

Information in the local library was sparse and patronising. Most of the books, intended for small children, had about four words per page. Lauren needed something heavier, meatier, more scientific. It took a while to find their Latin name: Cavia porcellus. Seeing that, Lauren felt calmer; but not for long. The list of things that could go wrong was endless: 'they have sensitive digestions, are prone to mange, eye infections and can succumb to bumblefoot.'

Lauren made copious notes: green vegetables but never lettuce which could cause diarrhoea. (For years she had been convinced it was spelt 'dire rear'.)

Something else about guinea pigs was a little odd. Lauren had scrutinized dozens of photos. They had feet, but didn't seem to have legs. Lauren searched but there was no sign of them. Guinea pigs had eyes, teeth, fur, feet and multitudes of possible problems, but no legs.

It took a while for Lauren to get to sleep, worrying … bumblefoot sounded clumsy and painful. She fell asleep visualising a legless guinea pig with a miniature crutch stumping about the cage.

Mrs. Jones had been thanked and arrangements made for the guinea pigs to arrive one lunchtime. Lauren reckoned that would cause the minimum, disruption. Going to meet them, Lauren hadn't reckoned with the sensation that Mr. and Mrs. Jones, crossing the playground, carrying a large cage, would cause. Helped by Santa and Adam, Lauren cleared a way, as hoards of children descended, like iron filings to a magnet.

'What is it?' 'What is it?' 'What's inside?'

Somehow the procession reached the classroom.

Cage in position, Mr. Jones put out his hand. 'I'm really glad to meet you Miss Massey. Donna and I persuaded Adam and Santa to write a booklet on the care of guinea pigs and they've done a great job.'

Adam and Santa beamed. The booklet was produced.

Mrs. Jones said, 'These are very young guinea pigs. My neighbours would never have bought them if they'd known their daughter would be moving away. They don't even have names yet.'

'Thank you so much,' Lauren said, 'please give me the name of your neighbours so the class can write and thank them.'

As the rest of the class filed in, Lauren looked over at Santa. Having now met both of his parents, she could understand why Santa was so much at ease with the world.

The cage stood higher than Lauren imagined, comprising of two stories with a ramp to join them. Under the ramp, an enclosed box with an opening, provided the guinea pigs with a bolt hole.

'It's no good crowding round the cages. The guinea pigs have gone into their private space for a bit of peace and quiet. So sit down and we'll decide how to organise looking after them.'

Lauren knew there was no point trying to keep to the timetable on this momentous afternoon.

Santa and Adam, assisted by Joanna, who had guinea pigs of her own, gave the class a lecture. Joanna's contribution included an introduction to germs. 'Always wash your hands after you've handled them.'

Adam said, 'And they don't like too much noise, either.'

Brilliant, Lauren thought, another possible way to quieten the class.

The booklet would be kept beside the cage, alongside the rota. A large notice was made, to be hung on the classroom door for use when it was exercise time. It read, 'Please Keep out, guinea pigs running loose,'.

Excitement was waning just a little, probably due to sheer exhaustion, when an unfamiliar squeak was heard, followed by some little scuffling noises.

And there – noses twitching, scuttling fussily round the cage were the two guinea pigs: two perambulating balls of fluff, one beige, one black and white.

For a moment the children just stared.

'Keep in your seats, children, we don't want to frighten them.'

'What are their names?' Joanna asked.

'Ah,' Lauren answered, 'we can decide on that.'

'One of them is the colour of sticky toffee pudding,' Adam said.

'Could we call it Princess?' Louisa asked.

'Nah', from Bradley.

Weeding out 'Snuffles,' 'Tiger', 'Twitchy' and 'Piggy' from a short list, a vote was taken and the animals became 'Toffee' and 'Chips.' 'Chips' only just beat 'Panda' as the name for the black and white one.

Some of the children wanted to stay in during afternoon playtime to keep watch over their new classmates. Assuring them that the animals would be absolutely fine on their own for a quarter of an hour, Lauren headed for the staffroom.

Adam called after her, 'Miss Massey. I nearly forgot to ask you. My Dad is coming to fetch us this afternoon, and he wants to ask you something. Will it be all right for him to come ... I mean today, after school? Is it all right?'

Lauren's heart sank. This was it. She was going to be told about the book or ... or shown the draft ...

She managed to say, 'That's fine, Adam.'

Once again, in the staffroom, opinion was divided. Some teachers declared that they, too, would be having a class pet. Hugo Preston's muttering changed from 'Thin end of the wedge,' to 'Making a rod for your own back, young Lauren, mark my words.'

The guinea pigs continued to get a great deal of attention for the rest of the afternoon. Lauren fervently hoped the novelty would wear off.

When she had dismissed the class, Lauren realised that Toffee and Chips would be entirely alone from the time she left until tomorrow morning. Would they really all be right? They looked so small.

'Miss Massey? Ah, there they are.'

It was Michael Gregory. Holding Amelia by the hand, he came over to study the cage. Adam stood beside him beaming.

'These guinea pigs have caused no end of excitement. Adam and Santa have been consulting encyclopaedias for information for the booklet.'

'Their booklet is really very good,' Lauren said. 'I had to go to the library to learn about guinea pigs, too.'

Lauren wondered where all this was leading.

Michael Gregory turned to Lauren and said, 'Milly, Amelia, wants to learn to play the piano. Will you teach her?'

'Please,' Amelia said softly.

Chapter 30

The caretaker came up trumps. 'There's no need to take the little fellas away at weekends, unless the kiddies want to that is. I can give them a handful of greens – see there's plenty of water.'

Lauren thanked Mr. Beamish profusely and didn't point out that the little fellas were, in fact, little lassies. His offer would serve as insurance, should no one be able to take them at the weekend. It wouldn't solve the instruction, heavily underlined, in Santa and Adam's book, that said 'Toffee and Chips must get runabout exercise every day.'

The book had been rewritten, and now included the guinea pigs' names and an admonition in capital letters to, 'USE BOTH HANDS when you pick them up.' There had been a moment of high drama when Graham nearly dropped Chips.

On the first Friday afternoon it was Donna Jones and Alan Gregory who came to fetch the guinea pigs. Mrs. Jones didn't ask how things were going, she told Lauren, 'You're doing a great job. You know something? By now I think Adam and Santa could get a PhD on guinea pigs.' She laughed, 'And why not?'

Most weekends Fiona and Lauren spent a day or an afternoon together, going to the cinema, and now that the weather was improving, to parks and sometimes up to London. Plans were being made for the Easter holidays.

Lauren would be spending five days with her parents.

Thanks to some complicated and ingenious manoeuvring, both Ben and Miles would be staying with Fiona for two nights of the Easter week. Theatre tickets had been booked, meals planned.

Lauren reckoned that her friend had many fine qualities; subtlety was not one of them.

'Fiona, tell me the truth. Are you engaged in a tad of matchmaking ... me and Miles?'

'Matchmaking? You've got to be joking. Miles has been trying to wangle a visit with me, to see you again, ever since Christmas.'

Lauren studied Fiona's face; a picture of innocence.

'I hope you've done all your teaching by now,' Fiona said. 'The summer term is hopeless. Children go away, there's the class outing, Sports Day and this year there's the Fete. I know that's going to be on a Saturday, but there's bound to be a bit of disruption on the run up to it.'

'What do you mean, disruption?' Lauren asked.

'We've no idea what it will entail. It's all gone very quiet out there,' Fiona said, 'all I know, all anyone knows, is that it is going to happen. Perhaps it'll be a handiwork stall and a cake stall, with perhaps someone serving warm lemonade.'

The guinea pigs seemed to be thriving. If their health was measured by the rate of knots with which they raced around the cage and up the ramp, Toffee and Chips would be classed as Olympic athletes of the guinea pig world. Lauren was still trying to work out how they managed this when they were seriously deficient in the leg department. There was a hint of legs round the back, nothing discernible at the front and they didn't seem to have any bones.

Ignacio had got himself firmly in the dog house with the rest of the class.

One morning he announced, 'My mum, she said in Peru everyone keeps guinea pigs. They run around a floor in the kitchen, ten, twenty … more, all happy, happy, then one, he gets picked up,' here he mimed picking up a guinea pig, 'is dropped in the pot and is eaten.'

The speech was met with stunned silence.

'You are a horrible boy, Ignacio,' Sally said, 'and it's all lies.'

'I don't think Ignacio should be allowed to play with Toffee and Chips because if they were listening, they would be very frightened and, anyway they would hate Ignacio, Toffee and Chips hate Ignacio very much, they do, they do, they hate him.' Louisa, pink with indignation, eventually ran out of breath.

Lauren was faced with a dilemma: Ignacio had told nothing but the gospel truth.

Lauren had written to her parents, in her weekly letter, that she may have a piano pupil, a five year old girl. She would be going to the child's house during the Easter holidays for the first lesson and after that, if all went well, there would be a weekly lesson after school.

Fiona laughed when she heard the news. 'Lauren, you're just being disruptive, on purpose. You bring ungodly songs in at Christmas, introduce rodents into the classroom, one of your parents is organising a fete and now … horror of horrors … you are venturing into enemy territory. You are going into the house of a, (Fiona's voice fell to a whisper,) … a … parent. Is there no end to your mischief?'

The response to the school governor, Mr. Farley's, offer to sponsor a 'decorate an egg' competition had been lame, flabby … almost non-existent. Teachers were encouraged to encourage.

'Perhaps we should display the prizes,' Brenda Cunningham suggested.

Two large chocolate eggs in elaborate, shiny boxes, labelled 1st and 2nd and a box of chocolate bunnies with a 3 on it, were displayed in the cabinet in the lobby. The cabinet had previously held a collection of, totally ignored, shields.

The effect was electric. The children, mercenary to the core, became heavily involved.

'Mine's going to be a rabbit,' Maria said, 'with ears and a fluffy tail.' Ashok declared his egg-car would have real wheels and Mark was constructing a wall for his Humpty Dumpty.

'Guess what?' Fiona said one lunchtime, 'Charlie Farley, the governor chappie, asked if two teachers would help him judge the Easter eggs. Mrs. M has volunteered Brenda and me. So the eggs will come in on the Monday. Monday lunchtime Mr. F, Brenda and yours truly will patrol the corridors where the eggs will be displayed on windowsills, clipboard at the ready, and do the judging. Now, that really is going to look good on my CV. Aren't you the least bit jealous, Lauren?'

'Not even a smidgeon.'

Egg day arrived. The children were shown on which windowsill each class's eggs were to be displayed. Carefully placing them, the children prised themselves away from their eggs with the greatest reluctance.

'Suppose someone touches my egg.' 'What if someone steals it?'

Eventually, abandoning their masterworks, the children went to their classrooms.

184

Joanna handed Lauren a letter.

'Dear Miss Massey,

I know Santa was going to take the guinea pigs home for the Easter holidays, but I wonder if he would mind Joanna having them, just this once. We were planning to take our family to Bournemouth, but my mother has been taken ill, so we've had to cancel the holiday. Joanna is very upset, at her gran's illness, and missing the holiday. Looking after the class guinea pigs would take her mind off it.

I hope you understand,

(Signed) A. Taylor'

At break time Lauren wrote to Mrs. Jones. She already knew what the answer would be.

Lauren spotted Fiona and Brenda accompanying Mr. Farley round the corridors. Mr. Farley, a kindly man, who advanced with tentative shuffles, would not have looked out of place in Victorian costume; his grey moustache, abundant and a little untidy. He blinked, frequently and benevolently from behind his thick glasses.

At afternoon break Fiona was on the point of exploding.

'"All the children's own work" is what it said on the letter; the children's work my eye. There's a Cinderella coach that would give Fabergé a run for his money, a peacock with a feathered tail, several perfect chickens, one even laying perfect eggs. It should have just been a parents' competition and be done with it. Judging was really tricky. We couldn't exactly ignore the amazing creations, but Mr. Farley was adamant that an egg, clearly a child's own

185

work, should also be rewarded.'

Ignacio was once again an accepted member of the class. He arrived one morning with a large, strong cardboard box labelled, 'Please do not throw away.'

'Is for when we clean the cage,' he said, 'Toffee and Chips come in here to play.'

Of course Mrs. Jones understood, so Joanna would be taking the guinea pigs home over the Easter holiday.

Excitement, the hope of chocolate to come, intruded on the children's concentration during the assembly and sermon by Mrs. Montgomery. Mercifully, the Rev. Palmer was otherwise engaged and unable to come and explain to the children the true meaning of Easter.

Everything Mrs. M said was lost on the children. They were waiting for the judges' decision. With the prizes, on a table beside him, eventually Mr. Farley got up to speak.

'I'm very happy to be here with you. There are great many beautifully decorated eggs. Perhaps some of you got a little help from your parents or brothers and sisters.'

He paused, possibly searching for a sign of guilt here in there; no reaction. The looks on the children's faces registered, 'Just get on with it, will you!'

'The third prize goes to this igloo. It was such a clever idea. Will Anthony Rogers come and get his prize.'

A beaming Anthony, a boy of about nine, gratefully received the box of chocolate rabbits. Lauren could see that the igloo was placed on an ice floe on which stood a perfect, white plasticine, polar bear.

'Second prize goes to this wonderful, Mad Hatter.' The large top hat, still sporting its price tag, sat at a rakish angle; the expression on the egg suitably mad.

'Will Belinda Butcher come and collect her prize.'

Six year old Belinda shyly accepted the smaller Easter egg.

'The judges thought long and hard about who should get the first prize. This might not be the most beautiful egg, nor the cleverest idea.'

Mr. Farley held up a pathetic specimen. Three mismatched strands of brown wool stuck clumsily on top. An attempt at a paper nose had missed its target and, too high and slightly to the left, it nearly obliterated one of the eyes.

'We decided to award this egg first prize because it is clearly a child's own work.'

Before Mr. Farley could read out the name of the winner, Santa stood up.

'But my daddy did it,' he said.

Chapter 31

Lauren's 'to do' list for the Easter holiday was getting complicated:

    1)   Find poem about guinea pigs (seems to be a dearth. Plenty about mice.) Has to be solid sort of poem, like the g p's, nothing airy fairy

    2)   Find book about underground trains for George

    3)   Plan class trip to Kew Gardens. How many extra adults needed? Mrs. Jones. Who else? What do I do if H Preston offers to come? Does School Sec book coach etc.?

    4)   Plan piano lesson for Amelia

    5)   Flat lease up end July. Stay? Find new one? List pros and cons

                pro: landlady almost invisible

    6)   Sports day. Are we supposed to train children? How? Weight lifting? Ask Fee.

    7)   Mend skirt? Safety pin do?

    8)   End of year reports? Ask Fee.

Being on holiday and not going home immediately felt odd to Lauren; spookily grown up. There was plenty to do. Summer term lesson plans would be finished before going home.

'The Outing' had come and gone and had been everything she'd hoped for. Miles was even better looking than she'd remembered. Lauren vowed she'd make sure he never got anywhere within range of her grandmother, or grandma would be licking her lips and matchmaking with the zeal of a medieval astrologer. Lauren smiled to herself and awarded Miles a solid nine – and she'd be seeing him again.

Ben and Fiona alternated between looking like a pair of love-sick puppies and sounding like an old married couple; sure signs of a solid relationship.

And now, on this sunny morning, she was on her way to the home of Amelia, Adam, Alan and Michael Gregory.

The Gregory house, bigger than she expected, stood well back from the road. Its symmetry spoilt by an addition to the left hand side. Lauren guessed that would be Michael Gregory's studio. The cement path, bisecting the lawn, was fringed with daffodils. Wasn't there a poem or something about a flowery path, Lauren mused. No, it wasn't daffodils, it was primroses, and if she remembered correctly, going down that path led to certain disaster. Already wondering if she'd done the right thing, agreeing to teach Amelia, Lauren had butterflies in her tummy, exactly like she used to get before games at school. Lauren wished she hadn't remembered about the ominous path, only she hadn't remembered it, not properly, just knew it <u>was not a good sign</u>. At the top of the path the daffodils ended, replaced by ... a cluster of butter-yellow primroses.

The front door opened before she reached the doorbell. Michael Gregory stood there, a smiling Amelia by his side.

People looked different out of context, only this <u>was</u> Michael Gregory's context. He'd looked more formal in the classroom, older. Now, dressed in jeans and faded red sweat shirt, the look was beyond casual; accentuated by the smudge of black ink on his cheek.

'Come in, come in, Miss Massey, we'll have some coffee first if that suits you.'

O Lordy, Lauren thought, I suppose I'll have to be

Miss Massey here, but already feeling horribly grown up, i.e. older, the spinster piano teacher image felt positively … fuddy duddy.

The front door opened onto a flagstone-floored hall, with stairs going up on the right-hand side. Stair number four was occupied by the thieving Goldie.
She lifted her head, took one look, lost interest and went back to sleep.

'That's her look-out post,' Michael G said. 'May I take your coat?'

Lauren followed him and Amelia into a sun-filled lounge. Most of the furniture, a biscuity-cream, was like a chorus supporting the soloist; one sofa upholstered in a patchwork of wildly clashing colours. Framed illustrations from M Gregory's books hung on the wall. Through the glass doors leading to a patio, Lauren could see Alan Gregory at the end of the garden instructing Adam and Santa on the complexities of cricket.

Michael G came in with the coffee and a plate of shortbread.

'Adam and Santa know you're coming. I've said they can come and say hello after Milly's lesson. I hope that by agreeing to come here today, we're not keeping you from your home in the Cotswolds.'

How the hell did he know that, Lauren wondered.

'Not at all,' she said, realising she was sounding prissy. 'I'm going home at the weekend.'

'Please have some shortbread, Miss Massey. My dad made it. He'd be most offended if you don't.'

'If it's anything like the mince pies he made …'

Amelia was, reasonably politely, showing signs of impatience.

'Miss Massey,' she said in a small voice, 'the piano is in the dining room.'

Spending time making sure Amelia was seated at the best possible height, the lesson began.

With the half hour nearly up, Lauren said, 'Now Milly, (the request to be called Milly came three minutes into the lesson,) now Milly, I want you to play a duet with me. You play just this note, like this: one, two, three, stop, one, two, three, stop. Do you think you can do that?'

Milly nodded and tried it out.

Lauren accompanied Milly's note. 'Lovely, keep going.'

When they'd finished, a round of applause erupted from the doorway. The two older Gregorys, Santa and Adam stood there registering amazement and delight.

'Was Milly doing that?' Adam asked.

'She was.'

'Well done, Milly,' Santa added.

A beaming Milly gave Lauren a swift hug before disappearing with the boys. While Lauren was gathering up her belongings, Michel Gregory said, 'Can you spare a minute? I'd like to ask you something?'

Well if it's permission to put me in one of your books the answer is absolutely not, no way, Jose, Lauren thought. She said, 'Of course.'

Following the two men back into the lounge, Lauren smiled at Alan G, 'Your shortbread is absolutely perfect.'

'You've said the right thing, my dear, I've already packed some up for you to take home.'

Michael G leant forward, hands between his knees.

'We don't want to put you in a difficult position, Miss Massey, but Alan, Donna, that's Santa's mum, and I,

191

wonder how much you and the rest of the staff know about the Fete.'

'Absolutely nothing,' Lauren said, 'all we know is that it is going to happen. My friend pictures a cake stall and someone dispensing lemonade.'

The two men exchanged glances. Alan Gregory laughed, 'Come and have a look at this.'

Lauren followed them into the kitchen and joined them in facing a large notice board bearing a label: 'The Fete.'

Neatly pinned onto it were a series of typed lists of names and a plan of the school playground.

The lists were headed: 'Committee', 'Treasurer and assistants,' 'Class liaison', 'Help on the day', 'Printer', 'Call upon for transport,' 'Flyer Deliverers', 'Electricians,' Music', 'Stall organisers', 'Clearer uppers', 'Liaison with local shops and press', 'Garages available, collection, storage etc.'

Lauren felt her jaw drop as she studied the map. The school playground was dotted about with rectangles and circles bearing labels: 'tombola', 'bric-a-brac', 'crafts', 'books and cards', 'tin can alley', 'cake stall', 'tea tent', 'burgers and bangers', 'instant portraits', 'makeup adults', 'makeup children.' At the bottom of the board was a list of times.

Lauren found herself sitting at the kitchen table with Michael and Alan Gregory. The three children could be heard playing outside.

Reeling from what she'd just seen, Lauren said, 'I'd no idea ...'

'Donna is the driving force,' Michael G said. 'She really ought to be running the country.'

'What we want to know is,' Alan Gregory said, 'do you think the teachers will want to be involved?'

'Some will,' Lauren said, 'some definitely will.'

'Nobody wants to put any pressure on them,' Michael G said, 'and we wouldn't want anyone to get into Mrs. Montgomery's bad books.'

The silence that followed lasted a bit too long.

'We don't want the teachers to feel left out,' Alan G said, 'we'd just like them to know that they are included if they want to be, and can be as involved as they'd like to be.'

'What do you want me to do?' Lauren asked.

'Nothing that would upset Mrs. Montgomery,' Michael G said. 'Perhaps just find out which members of staff intend to come to the Fete, and if they'd like to be involved in any way.'

Thoughts of Mrs. M's displeasure loomed large in Lauren's mind. The sound of the 'TWO' that exploded from Mrs. M after Lauren's request to enrol the guinea pigs, still hurt her ears.

'I can do that, of course I can,' Lauren said, not feeling as certain as she hoped she sounded.

Date for Milly's next lesson fixed, Lauren set off wondering whether it would be better to tell Mrs. M what she was going to do before she mentioned the Fete to the rest of the staff. Or, should she say nothing to Mrs. M? No, that wasn't going to work. When he got wind of it, Hugo Preston would inform. He would snitch on her. And he would love it.

Walking back to the High Street Lauren realised how little she knew of the school's catchment area. (Catchment: funny word that, reminding her of butterfly nets and battlements.) She recognised the names of some of the streets from the class address book. Spencer lived on this road and ... was it Joanna? Were their parents involved with the Fete? Judging by the length of the lists she'd seen, just about everybody was involved.

Somewhere nearby a dog expressed its indignation – loudly and insistently. The constant hum of traffic from the nearby High Street was punctuated by the occasional backfiring of a car. The plane high overhead, leaving a scribble in the sky, sounded like a lazy bee. Funny how on warm days planes sounded like lazy bees and in winter they just sounded like planes.

Lauren recalled the noticeboard in the Gregory's kitchen; comprehensive lists of helpers, sideshows, tea tent ... Mrs. M considered this, out here, as enemy territory. If she ever gave it any thought, she must assume that little pockets of foot-soldiers were known to each other. But she could have no idea what was brewing now. The foot-soldiers were coming together; the entire catchment area encircling the school joining up, joining forces. The school, bang in the middle of roads and roads of parents, was about to be invaded.

And what was her own role, Lauren wondered. Mrs. M would surely guess that she, Lauren, had crossed into enemy territory. And she had been tasked with asking the staff if they wanted to collaborate. Had she, ever so subtly, been asked to persuade them to collaborate? That would make her more than just a messenger ... was she a traitor? A spy? For which side?

Whatever her role was, just at that moment, it felt very solitary, and quite ridiculously scary.

Chapter 32

'I'll do it.'

Lauren slid into the seat opposite Fiona at the Apollo cafe; a fish and chips lunch together before they went their separate ways for the remainder of the Easter holiday.

'What is it you will do?' Lauren asked.

'Be ringed. I'll be ringed but I refuse to be pinnied.' Fiona looked indignant.

'Fee, could we start at the beginning of this conversation, please?'

'I always vowed I would never wear a ring like some ruddy pigeon, a ring that showed I belong to someone, like a brand they put on cows. I've told Ben I don't want an engagement ring, waste of money, and they're only meant to ward off prospective suitors. I'll tell Ben I <u>will</u> wear a wedding ring.'

'So you will be ringed, but what is it you said you <u>won't</u> be?'

'Pinnied. I hereby swear I will never, ever, wear an apron, like frilly perfectly-made-up housewife rushing round to be sure the house is spotless and smelling of apple pie for homecoming hubby. Grrr.'

'What brought this on Fee? You sound as if you're about to go into battle.'

'Advertisements. Look at this.' Fiona produced a magazine open at the page where a simpering woman in a gingham apron gazed adoringly at a man, while serving him an elaborate meal.

'Anyway, if she was playing the part properly she would have removed the ruddy apron. How did the piano lesson go?'

'That was absolutely fine and ... I have news from the front.'

Lauren told Fiona about the lists and map she'd seen in the Gregory's kitchen.

'I tell you Fee, it's a squillion miles from a few cakes and a lemonade stall. It's going to be huge, like those fairs they have on Hampstead Heath on bank holidays.'

'Fantastic,' Fiona said, 'what fun, shall we, you and I, volunteer for the White Elephant stall, or bric-a-brac is it ... shall we?'

'We can do that. But the problem is Mrs. M has no idea of the size, the sheer numbers ... and they want me to ask if any members of staff want to be involved.'

'Simple enough,' Fiona said, wistfully studying her last chip.

'Not really, Fee. Why would I be asking everyone? Mrs M will know I have been speaking to ... parents, or even worse, they have been speaking to me.'

'Ah. I see the problem. What are you going to do?'

'Not sure.'

Once back home with mum and dad, there was an invitation to tea with grandma. 'I want you to myself, dear,' she said.

Lauren left her jeans and tee shirt slung over the chair and reached for a cherry red skirt and shirt with red buttons.

Grandma didn't do casual. Even if the postman was the only person she'd be facing that day, grandma would present herself with nose properly powdered, earrings neatly anchored into plump pink lobes and perfume dabbed behind said lobes.

Lauren reckoned that grandma was permanently prepared for a chance encounter, perhaps someone asking for directions or delivering leaflets. This someone would be of the gentlemanly persuasion, getting on in years a little, but who still had a spring in his step and a twinkle in his eyes. Grandma was not giving up and she would be ready. Grandma was PREPARED.

She greeted Lauren with genuine delight.

'That's more like it, dear.' This was a reference to gran's unspoken dislike of jeans. 'You scrub up beautifully.'

There followed some obviously rehearsed enquiries about school, before grandma introduced the purpose of the invitation; an interrogation into Lauren's love life.

'You're not one of those ...?' gran had finally asked looking seriously worried.

'No gran, I'm not one of those.'

'You are interested in men, aren't you, dear?'

'Yes gran, but not now and not very. Just at the moment, not very.' This was not entirely true but not a subject for discussion.

'I really don't understand you young things. You're trying to fight nature, my dear. It won't work, you know.'

'Grandma, at least let me qualify as a teacher before I go on the prowl.'

'On the prowl?'

'Husband hunting.'

'Lauren, sometimes you really can be quite ... really quite awful.'

There had only been one occasion when Lauren got her dad to herself; a walk through the countryside to inspect the new reservoir. As they walked, Lauren noticed that the hard edges of the paths were now blurred by green shoots. The stark, dark silhouettes of Winter branches had disappeared into a soft green fuzz.

Lauren told her dad about the Fete and her dilemma.

Her dad said, 'Ahh.'

'What sort of "Ahh", dad?'

'A sort of "I see" Ahh.'

'The thing is I seem to have the knack of upsetting Mrs. M.'

'On purpose?'

'Once, yes. I admit it. Once on purpose, but since then I've tried to keep my head below the parapet but things keep happening, either she sees something she doesn't approve of when she walks into my classroom, misunderstands or a parent asks her about something … I'm sure she sees me as a bad influence.'

Her father laughed, 'As villains go … I'm afraid you're not very convincing, Lauren. Everything else O.K.?'

Lauren nodded.

'You'll know what to do, love.'

Of course she knew what to do; if she didn't get the interview with Mrs. M out of the way as quickly as possible, she wouldn't be sleeping and it would get in the way of absolutely everything else.

The rest of the holiday whizzed by; helping her mother choose an outfit for a 'do' at dad's work, a trip to the garden centre where an extra pair of hands was needed, and a visit to the dentist.

The first day of the summer term dawned bright and beautiful. The school, accompanied by Lauren on the piano, dutifully sang at assembly, about all things bright and beautiful. There would be more about creatures, great and small, later.

Class M seemed taller, more solid, delighted to see each other and the return of the guinea pigs, which was perfectly timed. They arrived just as Lauren finished taking the register.

Robert put his hand up. 'Miss Massey, I think Toffee and Chips should be on the register, too.'

'Toffee?' Lauren called.

'Here, Miss Massey,' Robert said in a high squeak.

'Chips?' Lauren called.

'Here, Miss Massey', Mark said, in an even higher squeak, then erupted into giggles, setting off the rest of the class.

At playtime Lauren headed for the secretary's room.

'Rose, could you tell me when it would be convenient to er … speak to Mrs. Montgomery?'

Rose Dawkins looked up. 'If you're thinking of leaving, Lauren, I'm afraid it's too late … you have to give …'

'No. I'm not thinking of leaving.'

Rose Dawkins waited for an explanation. Lauren said nothing.

Ostentatiously, Rose reached for a large diary and studied it.

'Unless something else comes up, I suggest afternoon playtime. I'll send a message if it's not convenient.'

Right up until afternoon playtime Lauren half hoped that a message would arrive telling her it would not be possible for her to see Mrs. M.

Lauren knocked at Mrs. Montgomery's door. On entering she noticed that Mrs. M's bosom lay at maximum height. The expression on her face could only be described as curious; curious with overtones of impatience. The 'thinks bubble' above her head would read, 'What does she want now?'

Bearing in mind the frailty of Mrs. M's attention span, Lauren plunged straight in.

'It's about the Fete, Mrs. Montgomery.'

A loud 'tut' escaped from Mrs. M's lips, her shoulders drooped and she leant back in her chair.

'I was afraid of this Miss Massey. I was afraid of this … that this frivolous idea of a school Fete was going to impinge on the smooth running of the school, impinge on the children's education. It's all so unnecessary … *de trop* … we've managed perfectly well for years, without the intrusion of parents. Why people try to take over matters that have nothing to do with them, I really don't understand.'

Mrs. Montgomery paused and sighed, 'Well, Miss Massey, what about the Fete?'

'One of the parents has asked me to find out if any members of staff would like to be involved.'

'Asked YOU?' It was nearly as loud as that 'TWO', but not quite.

Mrs. Montgomery took a deep breath. 'In that case I recommend that you inform that parent that the staff do not wish to be involved. I only gave my permission, against my better judgement, on the clear understanding that nothing regarding this proposed Fete would impinge on the school – no communication, no goods, no interruption, nothing to be stored on the premises. If the parents really want this to happen, and I can't think why they should, they will be allowed to come onto the premises on the day of the Fete and there are to be no traces of it on the following Monday. Thank you Miss Massey.'

Lauren stood her ground.

'Mrs. Montgomery, some members of staff have already shown an interest. I believe several of us will be attending the Fete.'

Lauren gave herself an invisible pat on the back for the 'us'.

Mrs. Montgomery glared at Lauren, her pink face turning puce, then crimson.

'And this is your doing, Miss Massey?'

'My doing? What do you mean? What is my doing?'

'This ... this staff involvement this ...'

Clenching her fists Lauren managed to say, 'Mrs. Montgomery, I was merely asked to find out if anyone wanted to join in. The parents don't want the teachers to feel left out.'

Mrs. Montgomery had run out of steam. Somewhat feebly, she echoed, 'left out? left out?'

Without waiting to be dismissed again, Lauren headed for the door expecting another outburst. It didn't come.

Having got that out of the way Lauren expected to feel relief. She didn't. Her heart pounded and the blush that had started a few minutes ago, felt as if it had reached her fingertips. And absolutely nothing had been resolved. If anything, she felt worse.

Back in the classroom, after several deep breaths, Lauren glanced down at the lesson plan. Was she over-milking the pets project? Probably, but the children were enjoying it and 'all creatures great and small' certainly included Toffee and Chips and Cob, George's snake.

'Everyone has a card on their desk with a poem about an animal. We're going to use these for handwriting practice. After today, you can choose the ones you like and make a little book of animal poems.'

'Is my one really a poem?' Col asked, 'Is it?'

'Yes. Would you like to read it to the class?'

Somewhat haltingly, Col declaimed, 'Who's that ticklin' my back?' said the wall? 'It's me,' said the small caterpillar, 'I'm learnin' to crawl.'

'Neat,' Bradley said.

'Short,' Col said.

Santa and Adam, clearly delighted with the poem on Adam's desk, nudged each other and pointed. Adam put his hand up.

'Mine's about a hippopotamus.'

'There are some more verses of that poem, if you'd like them, Adam,' Lauren said. She'd left them out, thinking the vocabulary too advanced even for Adam. Perhaps not.

'Mine is lovely,' Pritti said, 'It's about cats. Cats sleep anywhere ...'

George put his hand up. The entire class froze to attention. This was a first.

'Mine's about a snake,' George said miserably, 'But Cob doesn't bite, he doesn't.'

Lauren sighed. She'd spent hours searching for just the right poem, now she'd offended Cob. And George might never forgive her.

Chapter 33

Lauren noticed Inga's hairdo as soon as the class trooped in that morning. She couldn't take her eyes off it. Bunches, the hairdo was called: bunches. Most bunches lay to the side, or back of the head. But Inga's hair, parted down the middle from forehead to the back of her neck had been gathered up each side and clasped in unrelenting rubber bands, completely covered her ears. The resulting effect was two collections of hair; one pointing due east, the other due west. There was not enough hair for a graceful falling of tresses. Two aggressive little brooms stuck out, one each side of Inga's head.

One word sprang to Lauren's mind, why?

Make your maths lessons relevant. With that mantra firmly in mind, Lauren addressed the class.

'There are 24 of you in the class. You're going to find that 24 is a very useful number. I've put 24 counters on your desks. Working together, I want you to find out how many ways we can put the class into teams, fair teams, with equal numbers.'

'If it's football teams, I don' want no girls in my team,' Col said.

'No girls,' Bradley said.

'It doesn't matter what the teams are for,' Lauren said, 'I just want you to work out how many different ways we can divide you up.'

'You said fair teams, Miss Massey. It's not fair if you make me have girls on my football team,' Col said, 'they're useless.'

'Not as useless as you,' Sally said, 'you are as much use

as a chocolate tea pot.'

'What's one of them?' Bradley asked, perking up at the word chocolate.

'That's enough of that. There are 24 of you. Could we make two football teams, with an extra, someone spare to be … on the bench, perhaps?' Lauren asked.

'No, we couldn' do that. Girls can't play football,' Col said.

'All right,' Lauren sighed, 'two teams for a spelling competition, how many on each side?'

Robert said, 'Adam's team would win. Pritti would have to be on the other team so it would be fair, and Suzanna's a good speller, so, for it to be fair …'

'We're not going to have a spelling competition, I only said, if we had a spelling competition, how many would be on each side, same number on each side.'

Several hands shot up. 'How many, Ashok?'

'Twelve.'

'Good, everyone agree with that?'

Somewhere from deep in her memory a solitary fact drifted to the surface; polo teams consist of four members.

'How many polo teams could our class make? There are four people on each team?'

'Woss polo?' This from Bradley.

'Those sweeties with a hole in it, dumb dumb,' Sally said.

'You play it on horses,' Adam offered.

'Bet I could ride juss like a cowboy,' Bradley said.

'I got on a horse once, in the New Forest, it's a special kind of pony ever so little but dad says they are really strong and they're sort of wild only they do get looked after …' Louisa said.

'Where would we put the 'orses?' Col asked.

'We're pretending, Col. How many pretend polo teams could our class make?'

'Could we play 'orses, gallop an' trot, could we, Miss Massey?' Col's head nodded in a horse-like fashion.

Pritti's hand went up, 'We could have six polo teams, Miss Massey.'

'Good, Pritti.'

Relieved, Lauren gave thanks for at least one sensible child.

'My dad says they play polo in India, Miss Massey. The Indians are very good at it, and they're very good at cricket, too. We could have a cricket team. Girls do play cricket.'

Lauren groaned inwardly.

'Right, so far we've worked out that we can have two teams of 12 and six teams with four people in each team. I think there are some teams with eight people in them. How many of those – how many teams of eight could we have?'

'What are we goin' to play?' Col asked.

'It doesn't matter,' Lauren snapped, 'how many lots of eight?'

'You said it 'ad to be fair,' Col said.

Robert put his hand up, 'Three teams of eight, Miss Massey, but it wouldn't work very well because, if you had two teams playing against each other, one team would have to wait.'

Lauren ignored this.

'Right, now we're getting somewhere.' On the board Lauren wrote: '2 teams of 12 children 6 teams of 4 children, and 3 teams of 8 children.' Eventually the four teams of six and eight teams of three were added.

'Three's not a good number for a team,' Sally said. 'People would quarrel.'

Getting better at ignoring unhelpful comments, Lauren said, 'Now, if we had a three-legged race how many lots of two would be entering the race?'

Before any mathematics was applied to this question, the children began negotiating noisily for partners for the three legged race.

Lauren made a mental note to rethink 'relevance' in maths lessons.

At playtime Inga crept up to Lauren.

'My hair hurts, Miss Massy. This one.' She patted her left ear.

Shall I take the rubber band out?

Big-eyed, Inga nodded.

Careful not to tug, Lauren tackled the rubber band. The rubber band resisted, hung on.

'Will it be all right if I cut it?'

'Oh no, Miss Massey, I want proper plaits, really long ones.'

'I mean, the rubber band. I can cut that without cutting your hair.'

'O.K. My mum has lots.'

Inserting one side of the scissors under a piece of rubber, the released hair sprang away.

'Thank you Miss Massey.'

'Here, let me do the other one.'

'The other one doesn't hurt,' and Inga, with a no-longer-symmetrical hair style, bounced off.

Since that last interview, Lauren had done her best to keep out of Mrs. M's way. But it was impossible to hide. Every afternoon between three and four Mrs. M barricaded herself in her room, out of range of stray parents. This guaranteed that during that hour Mrs. M could not possibly be anywhere else. At any other time, in spite of her bulk, Mrs. M. appeared, materialised, in unexpected places and whenever she came across Lauren, her face registered alarm, followed by close scrutiny, as if she could hardly believe what she saw.

On one occasion Mrs. M emerged from a broom cupboard. There was no obvious explanation for what she had been doing in there. Lauren wondered if, tucked somewhere among the cleaning fluids, there might lurk the odd bottle of vodka or gin. Might that explain the permanent pinkness of complexion?

As for possible staff interest in the Fete, Lauren decided to tackle the easy ones first. Brenda Cunningham was delighted and would most definitely be involved.

'You've told Mrs. M?'

'She's no idea what the parents are planning. All she knows is that I'm asking if members of staff are interested in joining in.'

'And she's not best pleased?'

'You could say that,' Lauren replied.

Brenda gave Lauren a little pat on her shoulder. 'Leave Hugo P to me. We won't get an answer, but at least he'll know … what he needs to know.'

With varying degrees of enthusiasm every member of staff except one would attend and several were willing to join in the fray. Amanda Scott regretted that she would be unable to come as the Fete clashed with her brother-in-law's wedding.

Friday afternoons, after school, had been set aside for Milly's piano lessons. On the first Friday of the term she appeared at the classroom door 'To take Miss Massey home.' After the lesson there had been tea and a slice of coffee cake, baked by the senior Mr. Gregory, with Santa, Adam and Michael G milling round the kitchen. The sole topic of conversation: guinea pigs.

Lauren realised that in addition to finks, kelses, nuffs and their mates, all too often guinea pigs squeaked their way into her dreams.

The following Friday, after Milly's lesson, Lauren handed Alan Gregory a list of teachers who would be coming to the Fete, with stars besides those who'd like to be involved.

'Michael is in London, with his publisher,' Alan Gregory said. 'I'd be delighted if you'd have a cup of tea with me. Are you feeling brave, Miss Massey? No, that's a silly question. You are brave. I must say I was a bit concerned about asking you to do this.' He waved the paper with the list of teachers on it. 'Knowing Mrs. Montgomery's er ... mixed feelings about the Fete ...'

'It's fine Mr. Gregory. I think they ... we ... appreciate being included.' Lauren winced, cringing inwardly. That sounded like a bit of clunky dialogue from a badly rehearsed play.

'The reason I'm asking if you're feeling brave is that I've just baked some banana bread. The trouble is, I've no idea what it should look like, or taste like. Do you know anything about banana bread?'

Lauren shook her head.

'What do you think?'

Lauren inspected a darkish loaf. 'Well if it's banana bread, as in ginger bread, that looks ... absolutely fine.'

'Will you do the first tasting with me?'

Lauren smiled, 'It's Friday and I'm feeling reckless.'

She watched Alan Gregory, as carefully as if he was filleting a fish, cut two slices from the loaf.

Lauren sniffed it, then took a bite. 'Mmm. I really like it.'

'This is a dummy run. If it works – you're not just being polite, are you? If it works, I'll take a loaf to Donna. It's her birthday at the weekend.'

Donna … Santa's mum; the Joneses and the Gregorys seemed to spend a lot of time together.

'By the way, Mr. Gregory, Milly is doing so well I'd like her to have another music book. Would you like me to buy it or shall I tell you what we need?'

'You've got enough to do, Miss Massey, just tell me what's needed and where I can get it.'

On her way home Lauren thought about the Gregorys. Michael G seemed … what? All Lauren could think about was that one day she was going to feature in one of his books, looking stupid. But Alan Gregory was different. He was just a really lovely man.

Lauren giggled. If grandma ever set eyes on him, he wouldn't stand a chance.

Chapter 34

One of the traditions at Springmeadow, laid down with the ferocity of the laws of the Medes and the Persians, decreed that class outings took place in May. Also decreed, was the place where they took place. Last year class 3M had gone to the Natural History Museum. And, according to Fiona, who heard it from Amanda, this outing had not been an unqualified success. Rumour had it that as Kirsty approached the brontosaurus, Bradley said he saw it move, sending Kirsty rushing from the scene sobbing and hiccoughing. One adult had to spend the rest of the day in the museum restaurant, soothing her.

And the command for Class 3M this year ordered: Kew Gardens, on the 18th to be precise, and every detail of the forthcoming event already set in stone. The letter to the parents bore Mrs. M's unmistakable style, peppered with 'it is essential that', 'under no circumstances' and a 'will not be tolerated' tossed into the mix for good measure.

There was also a list of instructions to accompanying teachers and parents, and a worksheet for each child to fill in. Rose Dawkins had booked Kew Gardens (all of it? Lauren wondered) and the coach.

The most entrenched, though unwritten, law was; 'thou shalt not deviate one jot from these instructions.'

All Lauren had to do was find three adults willing to accompany the class.

Santa went home with a letter.

'Dear Mrs. Jones,

You very kindly said I could call on you when I needed a parent's help. We'll soon be sending a letter out telling parents that Class 3M will be visiting Kew Gardens on May 18th. Would you be able to come with us? I shall be asking two other parents so there will be four adults and twenty-four children.

      Yours sincerely,

        Lauren Massey'

The reply arrived the following day.

'Dear Miss Massey,

      I'd be delighted to accompany Class 3M to Kew Gardens on May 18th. If you haven't already asked any other parents, I think Christine Harding could come and Alan Gregory. Although I hate to admit it, it can be handy to have a man with us. Would you like me to ask them?

      Forgive me for asking, but will this be your first class outing?

      Yours sincerely,

        Donna Jones'

'Dear Mrs. Jones,

      Thank you for agreeing to come, and yes, please do ask Mrs. Harding and Mr. Gregory.

      This will be my first class outing. I have been issued with instructions, but it all looks very theoretical. I should be grateful for any practical suggestions.

      Yours sincerely,

        Lauren Massey'

'Dear Miss Massey,

      I suggest you remind the children to bring rainwear

and if possible, drinks in boxes with straws. May I also suggest that on the 17th you divide the children into 4 teams so that each adult will be in charge of six children. It would be a good idea to place potential 'wanderers' in different teams.

Might we have a competition amongst the teams? Best behaved team to get some extra playtime back at school?

I've been on several class outings, and in my experience worksheets are of little educational value. The children look at the work sheet, copy answers from each other and never notice anything.

Perhaps you could ask the children to look for something nobody else will notice, to tell the class about later. By all means let's take drawing materials.

I'm looking forward to the outing. Please let me know if there is anything else I can do.

Sincerely,

Donna'

Lauren put the letter down. She'd seen a copy of the work sheet. Twenty-four copies would materialise on her desk on the morning of the 18th. The work sheet, though adequate, was uninspiring and far too long.

The most annoying thing about this whole enterprise was that it had been sprung on her, sprung – like her having to accompany the Nativity play.

During a coffee break Lauren asked Fiona. 'Why didn't anybody tell me about the Kew Gardens visit?'

Fiona stared. 'Sorry. I assumed you knew. It's a fact of nature. You don't talk about the sun coming up, because it does, no room for discussion. I'm sorry Lauren. I'll have a serious think and see if I can find anything else absolutely everyone knows but nobody's told you.'

'Please do that, Fee. And, those work sheets. Does anyone look at them when the children have filled them in?'

'I don't think so. No. Why?'

'I just wondered.'

When she'd first joined Springmeadow there had been instructions, the curriculum, the shalt and shalt not lists, but nowhere was there any mention of Kew Gardens nor a concentration on plants.

Starting with, 'Remember when we grew the beans?' 3M was bombarded with information – everything and anything to do with plants.

Four teams of six should be easy enough, but none of the boys should be in their parent or grandparent's team; so Adam and Santa couldn't be with Mrs. Jones or Mr. Gregory, Robert couldn't be with Mrs. Harding, Lauren would keep Kirsty and Arabella with her, and she'd better keep and eye on Bradley, and Col and Bradley should be in different teams. But whose?

After several false starts Lauren put the children's names on slips of paper. Juggling the slips around for several minutes Lauren came up with the list. She made three copies so everyone would know where everyone was.

MISS MASSEY	MRS. JONES
Kirsty Fraser	Louisa Hughes
Arabella Miller	Kylie Fletcher
Bradley Hawkins	Spencer Baxter
Robert Harding	Mark Murray
Charmaine Abbott	Graham Collins
Joanna Taylor	Colin Riley

MR. GREGORY	MRS. HARDING
George Webb	Pritti Patel
Chang Liu	Ashok Patel
Ignacio Hernandez	Inga Karlsson
Jonathan Wheeler	Sally Newman
Maria Stewart	Adam Gregory
Suzanna Kowalski	Santa Jones

On the afternoon of 17th of May Lauren told 3M that they would be put into four teams for the trip to Kew Gardens tomorrow.

'There will be a competition for the best-behaved team. That means the team that doesn't complain, that is always polite, kindest to everyone else, least trouble and most cheerful will win. And the team that wins will be allowed onto the playground ten minutes before everyone else.'

Lauren hadn't worked out how this wonder was going to be achieved, given that both winners – on the playground, and losers, moping in the classroom would have to be supervised.

'The competition starts now. That means that anyone complaining about the team they are in will lose points for their team. Does everyone understand?'

Silence.

'Right. Robert's Mum, Mrs. Harding, Santa's Mum, Mrs. Jones and Mr. Gregory, Adam's grandfather, are coming with us.'

'I want to be …' Col started.

'Do you want to lose points for your team, Col?'

Lauren read out the teams to some delighted squirming, some pointing and a few signs that the information had found its mark.

'Right. Whose team are you in Jonathan?'

'Mr. Gregory's, Miss Massey?'

'Col, whose team are you in?'

'Team Jones, Miss.'

'Does everyone know which team they're in?'

Silence.

The 'best behaved' competition, with a ten-minutes-extra-playtime bribe, was having an immediate effect and Lauren had almost frightened herself with her fierceness.

Col put his hand up, a rare occurrence.

'Toffee and Chips can go on the back seat,' he said.

'No. Toffee and Chips will not be coming with us. Miss Bates and two children from her class will feed the guinea pigs and give them their 'runabout time'.

One or two 'buts' erupted, only to be swiftly swallowed.

'So what do you do first thing tomorrow morning?'

A sea of hands waved at Lauren. No one spoke.

'Spencer?'

In a voice that seemed to rumble from somewhere way down in his boots, Spencer said, 'We come in here, with our stuff.'

On the night of 17th of May Lauren hardly slept at all. Tomorrow she would be responsible, outside the confines of school, for twenty-four little people. Her imagination went into overdrive. Suppose one of them got badly hurt? Ate a poisonous berry? Got themselves kidnapped by someone lurking behind one of those giant fir trees, the ones whose bouncy branches reached right down to the ground? Suppose someone got lost and was never seen again? Lauren tried telling herself that school trips took place all the time, were well organised; tried and tested. All true ... but she hadn't been in charge of any of those. Telling herself three other adults would be there didn't help. She was in charge. This one was her responsibility.

THE DAY dawned, with an overcast sky; the grey blanket of cloud covering the Earth matched Lauren's mood. With a dry mouth and something going on in her tummy (nothing as delicate as butterflies), judging by the erratic swooping, it could only be bats; Lauren hoped no one could tell how she was feeling.

Class 3M trooped in with their 'stuff'. The 'stuff', receptacles for packed lunches, consisted of an array of carrier bags advertising local supermarkets, shocking pink plastic cases with my little pony on them, and Bradley's hefty rucksack. Once they were seated, the children, in their anoraks and clutching their stuff, began behaving decidedly oddly. Every time Lauren caught someone's eye, that someone bared their teeth. What on earth was wrong with them? They looked like a litter of angry puppies.

Halfway through taking the register Rose Dawkins walked in, juggling two carrier bags and a sheaf of papers.

'The work sheets, Miss Massey, and clipboards. I hope you have a lovely day.'

The carrier bags landed on Lauren's desk with a clunk. As Rose Dawkins retreated, Mrs. Jones, Mrs. Harding and Alan Gregory came in. Both the women had cameras hanging round their necks.

Lauren introduced them.

'Hands up Mrs. Harding's group.' Amazingly, everyone still knew which group they were in. From time to time someone bared their teeth at Lauren. It suddenly dawned on her that they were demonstrating being cheerful – just as she had instructed them to be. Lauren hoped they'd soon forget about that or the whole lot of them would look completely gormless. Rose Dawkins reappeared.

'The coach is here Miss Massey.'

Class 3M performed a collective wriggle of delight.

Alan Gregory held up a holdall. 'Miss Massey I've brought a supply of drawing paper and a collection of pencils. I see we have clipboards?'

Lauren nodded. Donna Jones picked up one of the clipboard bags and handed the other one to Mrs. Harding. Donna Jones looked at the worksheets on Lauren's desk then at Lauren. Was that the merest hint of a wink in Lauren's direction?

Lauren opened the desk drawer and pushed the worksheets in. The nod of approval from Mrs. Jones couldn't be mistaken for anything else.

'Mr. Gregory's group line up ...'

And they were in the coach with the four adults at the front.

Seated beside Mrs. Harding, with Donna Jones across

the aisle, Lauren wondered how she was supposed to talk to a parent. Would she have to talk about Robert all the way to Kew? Lauren remembered Mrs. Harding from Open Evening. Robert had inherited her ears. His, with a short hair cut, were in full view ready for the next high wind to carry him off. Hers, though visible, mingling with thick wavy hair, had to be searched for. Lauren remembered that the woman had been kind, asking her how she was settling in and whether her accommodation was comfortable.

The driver revved up the engine and the coach moved away from the school. Lauren found herself willing for four o'clock to come, with everyone home safe and sound; trip over. She turned round to look at the children and gasped. Where, less than a minute ago a child had occupied a seat, that seat was empty.

Donna Jones looked round then spoke to Dom, the driver.

Over the loudspeaker, Dom said, 'Children, you must keep two to a seat. If there are three of you, you'll be getting me and your teacher into trouble.' As if by magic, Sally appeared from across the aisle, slid into her seat and bared her teeth at Lauren.

'How did you know?' Lauren asked Donna Jones.

'They always do it. It's understandable, they rattle around in these seats. Tell me are we booked in for a lesson?'

'No, Mrs. Montgomery didn't think it necessary. We've got the 12:30 slot for packed lunches, someone will meet us when we arrive.'

'That's good. Christine and I have been on several school trips. We'll make sure your first is a really good one.'

Donna Jones's smile both warmed and reassured.

Talking, or rather, listening to Mrs. Harding, Robert's name didn't come up once. Lauren heard about the Fete and the 'magnificent' response from the parents and how the Joneses and the Gregorys were the 'brains and heart of the whole thing.'

As the coach scrunched into the 'Parking For Coaches' bay, Donna Jones turned to Lauren.

'Well, it didn't happen. I fully expected at least one child to come and complain about something. This is a first.'

A young woman, holding a sheaf of brochures, bounded into the coach. Looking around, her eyes rested on Lauren.

'Good morning Miss Massey. Here are your leaflets with information and map. I believe you're following route two (news to Lauren). It's marked in blue. You can keep together but, as there are a lot of school parties here today, you might be asked to split into two groups when you visit the Temperate House. Please don't hesitate to ask one of us if you need any more information.'

The woman glanced over her shoulder as another coach drew up.

'I hope you have a lovely day,' and she was gone.

The anxiety that took hold of Lauren at the word 'map' (Lauren found maps and mazes interchangeable), disappeared at the news that the groups could stay together.

And they were on their way. Alan Gregory and his flock at the head; Kirsty and Arabella staying close to Lauren. Bradley's rucksack had been replaced by a string bag, straining over several small parcels, two hard boiled eggs and a banana.

Following the designated route and stopping at the designated spots, Lauren relaxed a little; not completely, there were too many people around.

'Woss 'at?' Bradley indicated the pagoda with his chin. 'Looks like a yooj pile of sangwiches.'

'It's a pagoda. A Chinese building,' Lauren pointed at the picture in the leaflet.

'Did Chang live in one of those?' Bradley asked.

'Nah,' Robert said, 'this one was built about a million years ago.'

Lauren glanced at the leaflet. 'The pagoda … completed in 1762.' Clearly her efforts at teaching mathematics were not … taking.

Keeping in sight of each other or agreeing where to meet, the four groups separated.

A sudden shout of 'Stop that, stop that at once.'

Lauren froze, looked around and relaxed. Not one of her flock; the girl being berated wore blue; 3M wore green.

Green. Lauren looked around her and up at the branches. They were surrounded by dozens, maybe hundreds of colours, and every one of them called green.

Kirsty pulled Arabella away to make a close examination of ladybirds on a leaf.

Bradley began a running commentary, which Lauren feared might go on for the rest of the day. She couldn't decide which was worse; this stream of consciousness or not knowing what he was up to.

'My gran's got some of them on her lotment. Lotments all very well but people nick things. They do. Gran says she's goin' to grow only ne'uls. Stinging ones. See how the pinching people like that. Woss that bird there, that one?

No Miss. Pigeons is brown. Cor that must be the biggest tree in the world.'

'Perhaps not that one,' Lauren said, 'but one like it. Can you see what it's called, Robert?'

'It's a giant redwood,' Kirsty said. Did her voice quaver a bit at 'giant'?

At the Temperate House they were asked to go in twelve at a time; Lauren's and Alan Gregory's groups were first. Alan Gregory pointed out leaves like spirals, a plant sprouting a shoot bearing a miniature versions of itself and one like a giant pineapple. He encouraged the children to draw them. Lauren's group joined in. In Victorian times Kirsty could have made a living painting miniatures; her drawings resembled postage stamps.

Outside again, Alan Gregory said, ' Would you take four of my flock with you, Miss Massey? If you just follow this path you'll get to the Orchid House. Chang wants to finish his drawing of the Temperate House. We won't be long. Is that all right, with you?'

'Of course,' so Lauren's group now included Ignacio, Jonathan, Maria and Suzanna. No need to map read, (thank you Alan Gregory), Lauren knew where she was heading. She turned round to see Chang busily drawing and George, sitting on the bench, legs dangling way above the ground, laughing, and chatting away to Alan Gregory. She felt something like … was it jealousy? He'd never chatted like that to her.

Suzanna couldn't get enough of the orchids. She darted from one to the other, 'Maria, look at this one, it's like a bee, and this one, like a spider. Maria you draw that one and I'll draw this one. Roots are usually in the ground, aren't they Miss Massey?'

Bradley managed, 'Orchids is expensive. This lot muss be worf a lot, Miss.'

Alan Gregory caught up with them. He seemed to be doling out an endless supply of drawing paper. From time to time Lauren noticed one of the women taking photographs. She'd been expecting to line up for a group one. It didn't happen.

Seated at tables for lunch, Donna Jones produced 28 gingerbread men. 'We did the buttons,' Adam said, pointing at the Smarties.

'Can you peel my eggs, Miss?' One in each hand, Bradley presented Lauren with the eggs. The twist of salt was the size of a ping pong ball.

'I'll show you how to do one and you can do the other one.'

Lauren rolled the egg around on the table top, exerting slight pressure. When the egg shell looked like crazy paving, Lauren peeled it.

'That's neat, Miss.'

Watched by the rest of the class Bradley imitated her..

'Can I do one?' This was Col.

But there were no more eggs. Mesmerising the audience, Bradley peeled his egg like a magician performing a near-impossible trick.

A break, sitting on the grass, had been part of the plan.

'Why don't you draw each other?' Alan Gregory suggested.

There was a great deal of giggling and 'keep still', 'don't look down,' 'but I have to, I'm drawing Miss Massey.' Lauren heard cameras clicking.

By some marvel, bringing a wave of relief to Lauren, 24 children and four adults boarded the bus at a quarter past three, with nothing worse than a blister; Kirsty's, and a lost string bag; Bradley's.

Just before the coach took off Sally, hands clasped behind her back, approached Lauren.

'Miss Massey,' Sally swayed from side to side, 'Miss Massey, would we lose points if we asked which group won?'

Lauren, almost asked, won what? Such had been her preoccupation to get them all back safely, she'd completely forgotten about the 'best behaved' competition.

'No Sally, no one will lose points. I'll let you know as soon as we get back to school.'

The consultation with the group leaders took a matter of seconds.

Tired, elated, relieved, grateful to the other grownups, Lauren sat back while Mrs. Harding and Donna Jones discussed some finer details concerning the Fete.

A knot of parents waited at the school gates.

Lauren stood up. Twenty-four faces looked up. Lauren had never had such absolute, unanimous attention before.

'The winner of the best behaved group is ... all of you.'

A cry of 'Yessss' filled the coach, fists punched the air.

The receiving parents probably got the impression that this school trip had been the best ever. Lauren knew that the group euphoria could be explained by only one thing; every member of class 3M knew that tomorrow morning they would be out on the playground ten minutes before anyone else.

Chapter 36

Back at her flat Lauren fell asleep without undressing. She hadn't realised how exhausting relief could be.

Taking stock the following morning, Lauren planned her day. Major achievement: everyone back safe and sound. Now what? How was the follow up going to work? And there was the question of the worksheets which she'd somehow have to get rid of.

What if Mrs. M or Hugo Preston asked to see them? 'I left them behind, by mistake,' wouldn't wash. Rose Dawkins delivered them only minutes before take off. The wording on them sounded more like Mr. P than Mrs. M, a lot of 'how manys?' and 'where would you finds?', so if anyone asked for them it would be him. She'd keep her fingers tightly crossed and hope and pray that Big G had forgiven her for inventing a blasphemous vicar.

Lauren wrote herself a large note: 'take class onto playground at 10:20.' That, too, would have to be explained. Should she tell 3M not to explode onto the playground like a marauding hoard. (Adam might understand that.) If she told them to sneak out, that might only make matters worse with Mr. P. Though Mrs. M was clearly M-press indoors, Hugo P was undisputed Lord of the Playground.

In the classroom, still fizzing with excitement, having not seen them for a whole day, the children greeted the guinea pigs like long lost relatives.

'Miss, are we really gettin' extra playtime?' Col asked.
'You are.'
'I told Billy in Miss Scott's class an' he called me a liar.'
'Did he? Well he's going to find out that you were

telling the truth. Before we do anything else I want you to write and thank the three grownups who came with us. I'd like two people from my group to write to one of the leaders of the other groups.'

Taking a chance Lauren asked, 'So how many letters will Mrs. Jones, Mrs. Harding and Mr. Gregory get?'

Several hands went up.

'Jonathan?'

'Eight Miss Massey, but don't you get a letter?'

After some careful selecting of writing implements, all Lauren could see was the top of 24 heads; the hands hard at work with the occasional pencil getting a chew in the search for inspiration. George's tongue, on view well to the left of his mouth, indicated serious concentration.

While the children wrote, Lauren glanced at the clipboards she'd collected on the coach yesterday. They would be given back to the children after break. Charmaine's ferns reminded Lauren of the pattern on her silk scarf. Santa's drawings: chunky, square and solid like him, bore his unmistakeable style. They couldn't have been drawn by anyone else. Lauren remembered Santa's first day. Fortunately he'd grown into his teeth now, and the lisp had all but disappeared. Suzanna's orchids, with their trailing roots, scrambled over several pages.

Lauren had already looked at Chang's drawings. Alan Gregory said they were remarkable, 'They remind me of Michael at his age. He once got into trouble at school, because a teacher wouldn't believe a drawing was all his own work.

Lauren noticed the classroom clock getting a great deal of attention. The clock read 10:18.

'All right, leave your work where it is, we'll carry on

after … early playtime. I want you to go out very quietly and don't make too much noise when you get onto the playground.'

Lauren followed them out and stood in a corner watching. As usual the girls formed little knots to decide what they were going to play, who was going to be allowed to play it and whose turn it was to be leader. These discussions usually took up the whole of break time. The boys hit the ground running. In no particular direction.

Fiona happened to be on playground duty. 'What are your lot doing out here?'

'Aah. It's a prize, ten minutes extra playtime for being little angels yesterday.'

'Really?'

'Yes, little lambs they were.'

'Make up your mind, Lauren, angels or lambs?'

'Angelic lambs and don't tell anyone, Fee, I didn't take the worksheets.'

'What? Is there no end to your … your rebellion?'

Lauren smiled, 'See you at lunchtime, Fee.'

At lunchtime, as Lauren entered the staffroom Hugo Preston looked up, frowning. 'I had to check my watch. I believe it was your class Miss Massey, who were on the playground well before 10:30, well before the bell. It is the bell that indicates playtime. I thought at first the children might have been undertaking a scientific observation, but soon realised by their behaviour that this was not the case. Was there a reason for this … premature playtime?'

'Yes, Mr. Preston. It was a reward for exemplary behaviour in Kew Gardens yesterday.' Lauren wondered where that exemplary had come from.

Hugo Preston glared.

'This is not ... this is not Springmeadow policy. I strongly advise you not to do it again, Miss Massey.'

Lauren crossed her fingers tightly behind her back hoping he was angry enough to forget all about worksheets.

Letters finished and collected Sally put up her hand, 'Can we do telling now, Miss Massey?'

'Remember I asked you to try and notice something nobody else might have noticed?'

Louisa said she noticed lots of different tree barks and it was funny because bark was written the same way as you spell it when a dog barks only sometimes words sound the same and you spell them different and one tree had a bark that was like lots of threads.

Kirsty said a man told her ladybirds were really beetles, wee beetles.

Adam and Santa saw a dragonfly, blue as if it had a light on inside it and it gave them the idea to write a book about flying dragons; small ones.

Bradley learnt how to peel a hard boiled egg.

Charmaine said water lily leaves were much bigger than her ruler, this way, lying down, like.

Pritti said she could spell rhododendron and she liked the pink ones best.

Jonathan said dogs weren't allowed in Kew Gardens but he saw one.

Ash asked a gardener if he did the gardening all by himself and the man said no he didn't and anyway there were nearly a thousand people working at Kew. (Ash loved big numbers, and if they weren't big enough he could always ... enlarge them a bit. Lauren wondered if this number was true.)

Ignacio said, 'Bananas grow wrong way round, going up and they the wrong colour. Should be yellow, Miss.'

For a moment Lauren wondered if it had been a mistake to leave the worksheets behind. Was it possible to tell what the children had learnt? If anything?

Had everyone reported on the day?

'George, did you notice anything?'

'Mr. Gregory said Kew Gardens people collect plants from everywhere in the world and they look after them. He said Kew Gardens is like a Noah's Ark for plants.'

Chapter 37

On Monday morning Robert arrived with four packets of photographs; every child pictured at least once. Lauren found herself in several, most of which were taken when she wasn't looking. Some of the photographs could, perhaps should, be entered for a competition: Suzanna and Maria gazing up in awe at an orchid, Charmaine bending over a pond, Col, examining a twig held up by Graham, and Bradley, almost cross-eyed with concentration; peeling a hard-boiled egg. Lauren's favourite showed the children sitting on the grass; some drawing and others looking intently at another child.

'Can we see them, Miss Massey?' Sally asked.

'I'll lay them out on the spare desks at dinner time and you can look at them, one row at a time.'

Lauren had decided to make a really big scrapbook. She'd mount the children's work, the writing and drawings, and dot the photographs around in appropriate places.

When it came to writing Col asked, 'Can I do a poem?'

A casual observer might be touched by Col's fixation on poetry, or rather on his determination to write a poem every time Lauren mentioned writing. Lauren knew Col now legitimised his four line offerings, written in huge letters with gaping spaces between each word, by calling the result a poem. Giving Col that short verse to read had been a big mistake.

The class decided; Chang's drawing of the Temperate House should go on the scrapbook's cover.

'Should our book have a title? 3M's Visit to Kew?' Lauren asked.

Spencer put his hand up, 'I think it should have the title that George said, what Mr. Gregory said about a Noah's Ark for plants.'

That suggestion met with unanimous approval.

On playground duty again, as a favour to Brenda Cunningham, Lauren had barely reached the playground before a posse of boys accosted her.

'Why did your class get extra playtime Miss?' 'Why Miss?' 'It's not fayah.'

Realising that replying, 'They were very, very good' would not satisfy the questioners, Lauren said, 'It was a mistake.' This, according to Hugo Preston, was true.

The three miniature ruffians stared. One narrowed his eyes menacingly, signifying ... disbelief? 'But ...'

Lauren stood her ground, sipping her coffee, and waited for them to lose interest.

On a corner of the playground Sally, carefully watched by a line of girls, could be heard teaching them 'Save All Your Kisses For Me.' The accompanying dance, stepping from side to side and doing hand movements which looked as if they were winding wool, also involved the waggling of non-existent hips.

Col, Bradley and Mark came over to speak to her.

'Sally says she's going to be a pop star,' Mark said.

Doing a little sideways dance, (dribbling a ball, perhaps?) Bradley said, 'Me, I'm gonna be a footballer, Miss.'

'Are you?'

'Me an' all,' Col said, 'I'm gonna be Chelsea. Up the bloo-oohs.'

Adam and Santa joined the group.

'What about you, Adam, what are you going to be?'

Lauren asked.

'I'm not absolutely sure yet. My grandpa says I like food so much I should be a chef.'

'That's a cook, like, innit?' Col asked. 'My uncle's one of those in McDonalds.'

'I like chips,' Bradley said.

'Chicken nuggets and chips is best,' Col said.

At some invisible signal, Bradley, Col and Mark marched off chanting, 'chips, chips ...'

'Santa, what about you, what are you going to be?'

'An inventor, Mith Massey. My neighbour has a cat with three legs and I'm working on a crutch thing with a roller thkate, and a sort of saddle to hold it on. George likes tunnels, he says he wants to drive an underground train.'

After a brief pause Adam asked, 'Miss Massey, if there's room in the scrapbook, when everything else is in, if there's room, would you put in the story of the very small flying dragons that Santa and I are writing?'

'I'll make sure there is room.'

With half term barely a week away, Lauren looked forward to days full of sunshine, getting up late, a long weekend at home, then back to the flat to prepare for the last half term of the school year when just about everything would be happening. Big decisions had already been made: she'd stay in her flat for another year. Luckily Fiona wouldn't be leaving Springmeadow for the time being, either. 'We've no idea where Ben might be based, it could be anywhere in the world, but that won't be for another year or so.'

The conversation took place while they filleted newspapers.

Fiona had alerted Lauren to the 'fruity' pictures on

page three of some of the papers the children brought in for covering their desks while they painted. Lauren never dreamt that being a teacher would involve censoring newspapers, yet here they were, the two of them, carefully removing screeds of bare-bosomed beauties and tucking the offending pages into carrier bags to be disposed of well away from the school premises. The Kew Gardens worksheets had met a similar fate.

Catching sight of the obituary page, Lauren found herself wondering, not for the first time, why only good people died. There wasn't much incentive to behave yourself, be kind and support charities. Good people died, the evidence was here, in the obituaries. All the, seemingly immortal, baddies were still out there, living it up, having a whale of a time.

While in Rose Dawkins' office to borrow the school's one and only long arm stapler, Rose asked, 'Lauren, has Mrs. Montgomery spoken to you lately?'

Lauren wondered for a moment how long away a meeting had to be to qualify for 'lately.'

'No. Why, am I in trouble?'

Rose laughed. 'I expect Mrs. Montgomery is waiting for a suitable moment to tell you. As for being in trouble … no quite the contrary, my dear. Mrs. Jones phoned and asked me to tell Mrs. Montgomery that on your visit to Kew Gardens, class 3M were a credit to the school.'

'The parents who came with us were … absolutely brilliant.'

Rose smiled. 'You have to allow yourself some credit, Lauren.'

Bless you Donna Jones, Lauren thought; how many parents would have bothered to phone the school with a message like that?

The getting-ready-for half term scramble seemed to be completely different in summer. With little outer wear cluttering the place, the classroom itself seemed larger ... airier, even the 'stuff' took up less space.

Alerted by Fiona, Lauren made sure she'd grabbed, and put in a place of safety, everyone's best work for the final Open Evening. 'There won't be much more of that when we get back,' Fiona warned, 'and if it gets really hot you'll have difficulty getting the seat of your lot's pants applied to the seat of their chairs.'

The guinea pigs would be spending half term with Santa. The book on 'Caring for Guinea Pigs', now a vast tome, included such essential information as: 'Chips likes broccoli very much. She is greedy.' 'Toffee squeaks loudest.' 'Sometimes the guinea pigs bump into each other but they don't get angry. We think they are just playing.'

On the last morning before the half term break, Lauren found a message on her desk. 'Work this one out: TGIFAIHTT. Fee.'

'I couldn't resist it. Miles does those all the time. Did you get it? Thank goodness it's Friday and it's half term, too. Miles asked if you were coming to ours at half term. When I told him you weren't it seems he isn't either. Funny that.'

Santa and Adam stayed behind in the classroom after the final bell. Santa waiting for his parents to come for the guinea pigs and Adam waiting to go home with Milly and Lauren.

Santa beamed when his parents arrived.

Donna Jones said, 'I really enjoyed our trip to Kew. We're taking Adam, Milly and Santa to Kew again next

233

Wednesday. Will we be able to see this wonderful scrapbook I'm hearing so much about?'

'Of course.' Lauren hoped it would be the centrepiece for Open Evening.

Mr. Jones said, 'Well, we'd better be getting this pair of fur balls home.'

Mr. and Mrs. Jones, with Santa behind them, clutching a bag of straw, then manoeuvred the cage round the classroom door.

After the Friday piano lesson Lauren always stayed for a cup of tea with Alan Gregory. Lately Michael Gregory had been joining them. Lauren's impression of him was changing. He seemed almost shy. But she couldn't get rid of the thought of the wretched book that was probably, even now, coming into being on that huge drawing board of his.

Chapter 38

Grandma, with a completely new face, now sucked in her cheeks and turned slightly sideways before looking at herself in the mirror; a frequent happening. This new habit meant she had no idea what she really looked like full on, with her face in neutral.

Lauren gave the softer hair-do a plus mark, a tick, but the thicker foundation didn't move at the same speed as gran's face when she smiled, and the violet eye-shadow and eyeliner made her eyes seem smaller, beadier. Lauren wondered what had prompted this makeover.

'Lauren, darling, you look so much more approachable, softer, than last time I saw you. You've lost some of that spiky, suffragette, woman's lib look. And guess what! I've booked you a makeup session – an early birthday present. I've booked a session with Andrea, she likes to be called Andray-yah. I went to her myself, dear, a dummy run for you Lauren, just to see if she was suitable. She says I have amazing skin for my age.'

Then why did she completely obliterate it behind a good inch of 'wondrous dawn' foundation, or whatever that particular goo is called, Lauren wondered.

'I know you're going back on Wednesday, so the session is booked for Tuesday morning. I'm coming with you. I'll get my hair done while Andrea works her magic on you.'

Mum, too had something to say about Lauren's appearance.

'You look healthier Lauren, and at least you haven't lost any more weight.'

'Mum, every winter you said I looked peaky and

you'd dose me up with some ghastly tonic and every summer, by some miracle, I'd recover from my peakiness.'

Giving her mother a hug and a peck on the cheek, Lauren said, 'This is my summer look, Mum.'

Two, almost silent, walks with her father calmed and reassured Lauren. If not absolutely everything was right with the world, just now, just here, nearly everything was, walking along the banks of the Windrush, just perceptibly gurgling, little lights dancing round the water ... Lauren stopped, eyes closed and facing the sun, savoured the moment.

Her father watched her, then tucking her arm through his, set off again.

'Still find the head and deputy terrifying, love?'

'Not really. I'm beginning to realise ...'

'Good. I knew you would. Stop a minute, see that wren over there ... look it's heading for that clump of ferns.'

Lauren wondered how, by saying very little, her father could convey so much. On one occasion, when Lauren and a group of her friends had been hauled in front of the headmaster for being unkind to another girl, Lauren had come home indignantly protesting her innocence and the injustice of the headmaster. Without commenting, very quietly her father had asked Lauren exactly what happened and exactly what had been said, leaving Lauren burning with shame.

On Tuesday morning, with Gran looking on, half supervising, half cheer leading, Lauren felt like a poodle in a grooming parlour. Grandma had booked the works, involving steam cleaning (wasn't that what happened to carpets?), exfoliation (surely the fate of trees in autumn), eyebrow defining (painful) and endless putting on and wiping off of assorted potions. And a manicure.

Nails involved penetrating, pungent smells. Lauren wondered if she might get 'high' on them and begin behaving oddly. What if the effect never wore off? Perhaps that was what had happened to grandma.

Sitting with her hands on miniature cushions while her nails received attention, Lauren caught sight of a creature (she assumed a woman), hair in a towel turban, face a thick white mask, with weird, round panda-like eyes peering out of it. It was her own reflection; no escaping from the numerous mirrors tilted at every possible angle.

Lauren mused, if this is what it took to get the show on the road, there would be no show. Her own 'beauty routine' involved half a dozen pots and bottles, soap, brush and comb and some lippie for special occasions.

Hair happened last. Andray-yah scooped Lauren's hair up in her hands and held it at the back of Lauren's head.

'Have you thought of wearing your hair up, like this? We could perm it, then take the sides round like this, you'd only need to put a clasp in the back for this or use a long grip or Spanish comb.'

Having lost count of the 'thises', Lauren decided it would be too much of a faff. But with her hair up she did look completely different: different, more serious, more competent. Was scraping back hair enough to make a body look more competent?

Declining the perm, several things then happened to Lauren's hair: it got washed, conditioned, wrapped round large rollers, blow dried and sprayed – which left it looking exactly the way it had before Andray-yah's ministrations.

Grandma was ecstatic.

'Lauren, you look wonderful. Absolutely adorable and just in case you missed them, I've written down the names of the creams she used, and do keep to the routine Andrea recommended, darling. I'll make a copy of the products for Sarita, so you can get some for your birthday.'

Grandma was all but clapping, so pleased was she by the results, for which she obviously took complete credit.

Lauren kept wanting to open her mouth as wide as she could, just to make sure it still worked properly. Her face felt odd: trapped. Every time she caught sight of herself, all she saw was her too bright mouth; the fire-engine-red had a spotlight on it.

Nothing could be altered until Mum had surveyed Gran's achievement.

As if pulling a rabbit out of a hat, Gran presented Lauren to her mother with a 'Ta rah!'

Sarita put her head on one side, thought for minute, then said, 'I like your hair. I'm not too sure about the lipstick, it's too … too dramatic.'

'I'm sure you mean eye-catching,' Gran said, 'I see our Lauren as quite the *femme fatale*.'

That evening, when asked his opinion, her father winked, gave Lauren a kiss on the forehead and patted her arm.

Before retiring Lauren needed no encouraged to 'cleanse thoroughly' as Andray-yah had so vehemently urged.

Back at her flat Lauren studied her school diary. Apart from Friday afternoons, Milly's piano lessons, and her playground duties, June looked relatively peaceful. July would open with a bang: Sports Day. Reports had to be with Mrs. M by the 2nd, so they could be vetted, prior to said reports going home on the 12th to give parents' time to study them before Open Evening on the 15th.

So when did reports get themselves written? More questions to add to the 'Ask Fee' list.

Lesson plans completed, the flat felt stuffy. Lauren headed for the local park to sit in the sunshine with a book. She might meet a member of 3M. Lauren hadn't been to the park since last September; it seemed years ago, that meeting with Michael Gregory and the thieving Goldie. Lauren wondered if she really was going to be in one of his books. Surely, after all this time, Michael G would have said something. He saw her often enough.

The sunshine soaked into her. Lauren felt deliciously drowsy. Tomorrow she'd be meeting Fiona for lunch at the Apollo. Just now Mrs. M. and Mr. P didn't matter. She didn't even have to visualise them in the bath to allay her fear of them. What brought that on? Lauren struggled to get rid of an image of Mr. P at one end of a steaming bath with Mrs. M at the other end, glaring at each other, about to do battle with loofahs.

'Ah, reports; get them from Rose as soon as you get back, fill in the names etc., then do a few each week. You've only got four weeks.'

Fiona and Lauren sat in the window of the Apollo, eating salad; a nod to summer.

'Mr. P will issue instructions about Sports Day, then change them and blame everyone else for the chaos, for chaos it will surely be. You will be allowed two sessions on the playground to practice, but the sessions are overseen by

Mr. P who is more worried about everyone getting the right-coloured band than anything else – oh, that and "fair play." "Fair play" embraces the bands, worn across the body, sitting up straight and keeping quiet. You wouldn't believe how complicated an exercise it is to get children to put a loop of ribbon over their heads and through one arm. Mr. P wanted them all going the same way, for tidiness. He nearly had a breakdown before he realised it wasn't going to happen. The worst bit is on THE day, with every child, however small, taking his or her chair out onto the playground. Chairs for parents are placed behind the small chairs, only the big chairs get there first, taken by anyone who can be pressed into service, so everyone gets thoroughly bad tempered and everyone goes round muttering, "Why do I have to do everything?" Mr. P clearly sees the parents as an unnecessary, untidy extra. He almost chokes when he announces the parents' race.'

'Do the children enjoy it?'

Fiona thought for a moment. 'Not really, no. Well, would you? It's usually jolly hot, they're told to wear hats, which they hate, and most of the time they're just sitting, waiting for something to happen. The "something", the actual race, is over in a matter of minutes. Most of the time is spent getting the right contestants, wearing the right band lined up, behind the starting line for the next race. And the end product, what all the effort has been for, the glittering prize, is a certificate, signed by Mrs. M.'

'Hmm,' Lauren said, 'so it's an ordeal to be survived?'

'Exactly. And then there's the Fete, and you, Lauren, know a great deal more about that, than I do.

Chapter 39

The warm weather brought with it a ... loosening. The children came into the classroom almost languidly, spent more time daydreaming and sometimes even walked onto the playground instead of exploding onto it. Sally and Charmaine took to absent-mindedly twirling their hair round their fingers and Ignacio spent a great deal of breath blowing his fringe out of his eyes.

One thing, still as tight as ever was 'The Daily Shout.' This was the name Fiona gave to Mrs. M's notices, which appeared every morning in the staffroom. Far from loosening Mrs. M's mood, the heat made her fractious. 'The Daily Shout' became more irritable; favourite old phrases rubbed against newly-minted expressions of dissatisfaction. 'Cannot be tolerated,' 'I must insist upon,' and 'under no circumstances' were joined by 'constant vigilance' and 'prodigious amounts'. The latter referring to the stationery Mrs. M declared had been wasted during the school year.

The 'Shout's' closing salvo invariably included variations on, 'You must understand that while each class teacher has only one class's reports to attend to, it is my duty to deal with those of the entire school. I must ensure that every report complies with the ethos and standards of Springmeadow.' And, of course, those 'ethos-complying' reports must, absolutely must, be with Mrs. M by July 2nd.

At Fiona's suggestion, Lauren gave each child a small piece of card and asked them to write a sentence for their own report, starting with their name. One or two were fairly predictable.

'Bradley is brilliant.' Brilliant spelt correctly;

amazingly.

'Pritti is a good speller. She really likes school.'

'Sally is a good singer.'

'Adam's dad says he's a bit of a monkey because he does as little work as possible. I don't think he was really cross when he said that.'

'Ignacio English getting beta.'

'Ash is rubbish at maths.' This wasn't true. Ash compared himself to Pritti. No one should ever compare their school work to Pritti's.

Lauren flipped through them wondering whether to slip these reports into the envelopes with the official ones. Mrs. M. would never know.

She got to the last two.

'Santa has settled very well at Springmeadow. He likes his friends and his teacher.'

But it was the last card that made Lauren catch her breath.

'George can read really well now.' And it was true. He could. He really could.

On warm days the existence of the guinea pigs could not be forgotten for a single second. The guinea pigs themselves didn't smell, but the cabbage, cauliflower and broccoli in the basket beside them, did. Class 3M had the whiff of the end-of-the-day at an indoor market about it.

One fine morning a wasp joined the class. The caretaker, wielding the long pole, had opened the top half of the classroom windows and a meandering wasp found its way in.

Santa leapt to his feet, stood in front of the guinea pig's cage and said, 'We mustn't let them get thtung.' The guinea pigs were out of sight, having a snooze.

Kylie put her head on her desk protecting it as best she could with her arms. The other children, grimacing, swayed away and 'ooo-ed' as the wasp approached. Rarely had Lauren commanded as much attention as that two centimetre long insect. Lauren flapped at it with a large textbook, trying to persuade it towards the windows. The none-too-bright wasp clearly didn't know what was good for it, and continued to buzz and swoop erratically in every direction except up.

'Charmaine, open the door, please.'

Lauren reckoned the wasp was never again going to fly as high as the open window. By sheer luck it found the large hole where the door had been. Lauren slammed the door shut with a loud bang.

'Neat, Miss!' Bradley exclaimed.

The door opened. Mr. Preston, a new, deeper shade of puce, stood there heaving with indignation.

'I'm so sorry Mr. Preston, I didn't see you there. We were just trying to get rid of … trying to persuade a wasp …'

On cue the wasp, narrowly skirting Mr. Preston's left ear, made its second entrance, even more dramatically than the first.

'You let it back in, Mr. Preston,' Bradley accused.

'Yeh, you did,' Col echoed, 'you let it back in.'

Lauren wondered whether to comment. Bradley hadn't been rude, he'd simply stated a fact.

Twenty-four faces glared accusingly at Hugo Preston.

The following scene could have been the re-enactment of a classic Western: black-hatted baddie, confronting newly-brave, innocent villagers. Lauren half expected Hugo Preston to reach for his gun.

The stand-off lasted several seconds. Then Hugo Preston, doing his best to bluster, backed away.

The wasp, having found a window pane, silently and fruitlessly climbed up and slid down the glass.

'Let's forget about the wasp, shall we?' Lauren said, 'I think it's going to be too busy trying to get out to bother us.'

Sports Day practices were every bit as pointless as Fiona had warned. Lauren realised that constant, general berating had little or no effect on class 3M. Mr. P's default position, haranguing, created a general sense of unease but most of the children wore a 'nothing-to-do-with-me-guv' expression. Even being told they were a 'right shower' and 'the worst class it has ever been my misfortune to encounter', completely washed over them. Lauren knew this last comment was aimed at her. She joined the class and ignored it.

The real problem was that, thanks to confusing instructions, Lauren had very little idea what they were supposed to do. She understood that every child could enter a maximum of three races. Was it mandatory? No provision had been made for any child wanting nothing to do with the whole shambolic affair.

After a lot of coaxing and comments from the class, 'Robert and Ash are really good runners,' and 'Maria won the egg and spoon race last year,' every child had been persuaded to enter two races. Picking up beanbags proved to be the least popular event, and it was hard to imagine George in a three-legged race with very tall Chang. Such was the lack of enthusiasm for the coming event, Lauren made a notice, displayed on the classroom wall, so the children would remember what they'd agreed to enter.

Back at her flat Lauren contemplated the blank report forms, (Springmeadow didn't believe in reports passing on from year to year.) She wondered whether to do the easiest ones first. None of them were going to be difficult; she'd do rough drafts – perhaps more than one draft. Would it be an idea to do the reports for the children who were good at everything, first? And how did you say that in a more nuanced way, anyway?

Could she honestly say the children, most of them, had improved? Kirsty's spelling had moved up at least one notch. Most people would now get the gist of her stories. Graham no longer went pale when maths was mentioned and Charmaine's writing flowed easily across the page.

Lauren started on the marking. The task: to finish a story. 'The giant decided to go on a picnic. He packed himself a basket of food, put on his great big boots, reached for his fishing rod and set off. The giant didn't notice that Joe, a boy who had been hiding in the giant's castle, had jumped into the basket and was now hiding under a bunch of bananas. Giants don't take only one banana on a picnic, they take a whole bunch and …' The children had to pick up the story from there.

Lauren had kept an eye on Kylie while she read the story. Listening wide-eyed, Kylie now seemed able to take giants in her stride.

This time Col couldn't get away with a 'poem'. As usual, Lauren put the exercise books she knew she'd enjoy reading at the bottom of the pile.

Some of the children simply listed the contents of the basket and forgot all about Joe; Ash being sure the giant had 17 chickens and 97 cakes along with 45 cans of beer, to say nothing of the mountain of crisps.

Picking up Bradley's exercise book Lauren put down her pen in disgust.

Bradley had written, 'Even tho the giant had lots and lots of things to eat in his baskit he wanted somefink kelse.'

Lauren groaned and said aloud, 'Back to square one. What have I been doing all year?'

Chapter 40

Adam put his hand up. 'Miss Massey, what do those words mean?'

'I'm hoping someone will tell me.'

Lauren had written, 'fink', 'kelse' and 'nuff' on the blackboard.

The children stared, Bradley looking as puzzled as everyone else.

'We give up, Miss Massey. What do they mean?' Adam asked again.

'I haven't the faintest idea, but some people in this class write about them, like this ...' Lauren wrote on the board, 'The giant wanted some fink kelse to eat. Then he had a nuff.'

Bradley's writing hadn't included a nuff, but Lauren was not about to leave it out.

Adam stared, then he started giggling. Gradually some children got it, Suzanna explained, everyone got it, everyone giggled.

'Who did it, Miss?' Col asked.

'Never mind who wrote it, I just hope I never see a fink, a kelse or a nuff ever again.'

Adam, reaching for his exercise book, wrote something down then asked, 'Do you think they are creatures, Miss Massey?'

'Yes, furry ones.'

'An full o' fleas,' Col added. Bradley maintained his expression of total innocence.

That afternoon a drama unfolded at Springmeadow, involving a police car in the school car park. It slid in silently with no 'nee naw' but that did not detract from the drama.

Mrs. Graham's class had been to visit the Natural History Museum and returned, exactly as expected, at 3:15. Mrs. Graham left Springmeadow with twenty-five children and returned with twenty-six. A lassie from another school, taking a shine to a girl in Mrs. Graham's class, decided to join them. When the children boarded the bus and the roll was called, every child in Mrs. Graham's class replied 'here'. The spare child wasn't noticed, thanks to the children's fondness for sitting three to a seat.

Mrs. Graham only became aware of the spare, when she spotted an unfamiliar girl, wearing red gingham, standing expectantly beside the coach, waiting for something to happen. The child, mouse-brown hair scraped back in a wispy pony tail, had small gold studs in her ears. She clung to an obviously empty carrier bag.

The first thing that happened; gesturing in the direction of the blissfully unconcerned child, Mrs. Graham burst into to tears. The girl in her class, to whom spare child had attached herself, had long since departed.

Coming upon the scene, just as she was leaving for home, Rose Dawkins took charge. She phoned the Natural History Museum to ask for the names of all the schools visiting that day, and did they by any chance know which school wore red gingham?

Lauren found herself pressed into service to see if any information could be extracted from the foundling.

Her name: Belinda Baker and she would be seven in August. Her address 19 Cedar Road and her school was just across the road, from her house, then you went round the side of the park but mustn't go in the first entrance, that was naughty.

Rose also phoned the police, no doubt fearful that Mrs. Graham would be arrested for kidnapping.

There was no sign of Mrs. M. nor Mr. P.

With Mrs. Graham still in tears, Brenda Cunningham, Rose Dawkins and the two policeman doing their best to find out where the child belonged, Lauren suggested taking Belinda to see the guinea pigs.

'Good idea,' a policeman said.

As a distraction the guinea pigs obliged; snuffling busily around their cage.

'I've got a hamster,' Belinda offered. 'My teacher said I should call him Hamlet, my daddy said who is he when he's at home so he's called Omelette, he stuffs his cheeks with food like this.' Belinda demonstrated blowing out her cheeks several times.

Rose came in. 'We've found out where Belinda lives. The police are going to take her home, they asked if you'd mind accompanying her.'

'No, that's fine.'

With two policemen in front, and Belinda beside Lauren at the back, Belinda gave them chapter and verse on the bad behaviour at the museum, of one Christopher. Christopher smacked the museum man who told him not to touch. And he sweared at him. Christopher sweared. Will Christopher go to prison?'

With two officers of the law mere inches away, Lauren didn't think it her place to reply.

An answer didn't appear to be necessary. By the time they reached Cedar Road they knew every one of Christopher's misdemeanours, which started on his first day at school when he bit the teacher.

A policeman knocked on the door of number 19. A

small boy answered the door.

'Mu-um, there's a policeman here.'

Lauren got out of the car with Belinda. A woman wearing huge hoop earrings and several necklaces appeared. She glared at Belinda, then at Lauren.

'Where have you been, Binda? Trust you to get yourself lost. Get inside, go on, get inside.'

Somehow, Belinda, wafted behind her mother and disappeared.

The woman glared at Lauren, 'And as for you! Call yourself a teacher? Taking a child doesn't belong to you! It's a disgrace, a disgrace. I'm going to report this.'

With that she shut the door, firmly.

'A thank you would have been nice,' Lauren said to the policemen.

'Don't take it personally, Miss Massey,'

'Lauren, please.'

'I'm Don and this is Charlie.' They walked back to the car. 'Don't take it personally Lauren, they get worried, they lash out. We're used to it. Shall we take you back to the school, or home?'

'Home, please.'

Charlie drove. Don, in the seat beside him turned to give Lauren his full attention.

'We get the blame for just about everything, but that's O.K. and I wish I had a pound for every time I've been told we're not like the old Bobbies. Is this your first time in a police car?'

Lauren smiled, 'Yes, it is.'

'Well at least you're not asking to drive it. I've lost count of the number of men we've given lifts home to, who ask if they can drive the car. I think they see themselves with the siren screaming, chasing a villain, jumping the lights ... '

They reached her flat.

'Thank you Lauren. I don't suppose it would be right to say I hope to see you again.'

The following morning Lauren found herself something of a heroine in the staffroom. No word of the previous day's events appeared on 'The Daily Shout', but Mrs. Graham couldn't stop thanking Lauren. 'I used to have nightmares about losing a child on an outing,' she said. 'It never occurred to me I could acquire one. Thank you for going with Belinda. I don't think I could have faced her mother. Was she very upset? I expect she was distraught? I would have been.'

'Her mother was fine,' Lauren said, 'glad to have Belinda back safe and sound.'

The following week the spare child incident faded into insignificance.

At a morning break Suzanna knocked on the staffroom door, 'Please Miss Massey, please come to the classroom.'

There had to be a very good reason for knocking on the staffroom door. And everyone in the staffroom would have heard Suzanna.

Suzanna and Maria were taking their turn giving the guinea pigs their run-about time.

'What's the matter? Maria hasn't had an accident, has she?'

'No, Miss Massey. You have to see.'

'The 'Please Keep out. Guinea pigs running loose' sign hung on the door.

Suzanna knocked and shouted, 'It's me.'

Maria opened the door just enough to let Lauren and Suzanna in.

'What's the matter?' Lauren asked.

'Look,' Maria pointed at the cage.

Toffee and Chips were on the floor, but there were still some guinea pigs in the cage; three very small ones.

Chapter 41

The three of them stared.

'But ... but, Toffee and Chips are both females,' Lauren said, 'ladies ... women.'

'Yes,' Suzanna whispered, 'and they've had some baby guinea pigs.'

'Well, one of them has.'

'What shall we do?' Maria asked.

'Put Toffee and Chips back.'

'But what's going to happen to the tiny ones?' Suzanna asked, 'Will they be all right?'

'They'll be fine for the time being,' Lauren said. 'I'm sure a mummy guinea pig knows how to look after baby guinea pigs better than we do.'

Reaching into the cage, Lauren gently lifted one of the babies and cupped it in her hand. Its toffee coloured head, with large ears sticking up, was encircled by a wide white belt. From the waist down, had there been a waist, the fur was jet black. It seemed weightless; a bubble of air covered in fur. Lauren remembered recoiling at the sight of newborn mice; naked, hairless with their pink skin so transparent, you could see their veins. But these little fellows – were they fellows? Females? These were perfect, miniature replicas of their parents. Parents? Mrs. Jones had assured Lauren that these were both females. How could this happen?

When the rest of the class returned, with two of the newcomers still on view, the news spread instantaneously. Within seconds everyone knew, everyone crowded around the cage, jostling for a better view, and every child was ecstatic.

'They are <u>so</u> cute, so cute,' Sally said.

'Ever so wee,' from Kylie.

'When did they get born?' Graham asked.

Mystified; Lauren tried to hide it. The children had no problem accepting that here were two mummies and one of them had given birth. With difficulty, Lauren persuaded the children back into their seats.

Just as Lauren regained the children's attention, the door opened and Hugo Preston walked in.

'I've come to see what occurred during break time.'

'Our guinea pigs had kittens,' Mark offered, 'like puppies.'

'Babies,' Pritti offered.

'Three,' Suzanna added.

'Indeed.' Hugo Preston studied Lauren with disapproval.

'Yeh,' Bradley said, 'do you want to buy one?'

'I do not.' Mr. P walked over to the cage and peered at the evidence; one, tiny almost entirely black creature, stopping and starting, trying to find its way around the cage.

Mr. P didn't waste any time. Just before the lunchtime bell, Rose Dawkins came into the classroom and said Mrs. Montgomery wanted to see Lauren, straight away.

'In her lunch break?' Lauren asked.

'In her lunch break.'

It had been suggested that Mrs. M might be disturbed during her lunch break when the school was on fire, only if it became clear that the entire building would go up in smoke.

'Come!'

There was no invitation to sit. Lauren faced the

254

onslaught standing, noticing that the bosom stood alarmingly high.

'Against my better judgement I agreed to allow your class to keep two guinea pigs. You assured me, Miss Massey, that these were <u>two</u> <u>female</u> guinea pigs. What you told me was clearly not the truth. I cannot imagine what you were thinking of, keeping a pair of guinea pigs in your classroom. A pair! This … this unfortunate event will, no doubt, have a detrimental effect on the children. I foresee complaints from parents. And who can blame them? You have placed me in an impossible position, Miss Massey. The parents will be justified in their complaints and, ultimately the responsibility was mine, allowing you to keep them in your classroom. I bitterly regret my decision, Miss Massey, bitterly, bitterly.' Pausing for breath, Mrs. Montgomery glared at Lauren.

'Mrs. Montgomery. Mrs. Jones assured me that both the guinea pigs were female. I still believe they are …'

'Miss Massey. If that is the fact, how do you explain the … the appearance of three baby guinea pigs? Mrs. Jones you say? Huh.'

'I'm sure there is an explanation Mrs. Montgomery, I …'

Rose Dawkins appeared. 'That phone call you were expecting, Mrs. Montgomery.'

Lauren wondered whether it was sheer coincidence that Rose Dawkins rescued her, yet again. Still glaring, Mrs. Montgomery picked up the phone. Lauren fled to the staffroom. She'd expected the interview to end with the guinea pigs' banishment. That could still happen.

Everyone in Springmeadow, including the caretaker, who'd gone to check for himself, knew about 3M's happy event; now the sole topic of conversation.

'Mrs. M's already had a go at you?' Fiona asked.

'Yes, she is not, as the saying goes "best pleased". But I can't understand it, Fee. Mrs. Jones is sure Toffee and Chips are females and they haven't been anywhere near other guinea pigs, they've been going home with Santa and ... hang on a minute. Fee, you don't happen to know the gestation period for guinea pigs, do you?'

'No. Elephants yes, guinea pigs no ... why?'

'I've just remembered. Toffee and Chips went home with Joanna Taylor over the Easter holiday and ... Joanna has got guinea pigs.'

'Ahhh ...' Fiona said.

'Ahh, indeed.'

Lauren found Joanna on the playground, waiting her turn to join a skipping game.

'Joanna, when you took Toffee and Chips home at Easter, did they have their run-around time with your guinea pigs?'

'Yes, Miss Massey, but they kept hiding under the cooker and wouldn't come out. Daddy had to squirt them with that spray thing Mummy uses for ironing, to make them come out.'

It dawned on Lauren that if Toffee and Chips had both hidden under the cooker, there might be yet another happy event. Seeing the tiniest guinea pig do its best to burrow under Chips, Lauren reckoned Chips was their mother.

Lauren sent Santa home with a letter.

'Dear Mrs. Jones,

By now I'm sure you'll know all about the additions to the guinea pigs. I've found the answer. You may remember that Joanna Taylor took Toffee and Chips home for the Easter holidays. Joanna has two guinea pigs and she tells me all four of them spent much of the time under a cooker, refusing to come out.

Mrs. Montgomery is angry about the babies. She says I can't have been telling the truth when I said we had two females. I'm afraid she's going to banish Toffee and Chips from the classroom. If she does, would you look after them for us?

What do you suggest we do about the babies? Have you any idea when they can leave their mothers? Do they need any extra care?

I'm sorry to bother you with all this.

Yours sincerely,

Lauren Massey'

The following morning Santa placed a letter on Lauren's desk with a flourish.

'Dear Miss Massey,

I'm sorry you got into trouble with Mrs. Montgomery. May I suggest that you tell her exactly what you told me, about the guinea pigs spending Easter in a household with other guinea pigs.

Of course we'll have the guinea pigs, should that be necessary, but I hope it won't be. I know the children love having Toffee and Chips in the classroom.

I'll get some advice from the local pet shop owner about the care of newborn guinea pigs. For the time being, I'm sure they'll be fine. Perhaps the children shouldn't handle the babies just yet.

Please let me know if you need any help.

Sincerely,

Donna'

Lauren felt a pang of guilt. She'd picked up one of the babies.

Lauren hoped she could get in first; explain the births to Mrs. Montgomery before being summoned to hear that the guinea pigs were being expelled.

At morning break Lauren approached Rose.

'Do you think I could see Mrs. Montgomery during the afternoon break?'

Rose Dawkins looked incredulous. She reached for the diary.

'Yes, that should be all right.'

Lauren wondered if Rose's expression could be described as disbelief, or was it pity?

Back in the classroom, the story of the giant and the as-yet-unnoticed Joe, proved so popular with 3M, further instalments were underway, passing the time between lunch and afternoon break.

'Come.'

'Mrs. Montgomery. I have the explanation. Our two guinea pigs went home for the Easter holiday with Joanna Taylor. Joanna Taylor has two pet guinea pigs.'

'Well?'

Ye gods, Lauren thought, do I have to spell it out? Apparently so.

'Part of a guinea pig's routine, is exercise outside the cage.'

'Well?'

'Joanna allowed all four guinea pigs to … exercise at the same time and Joanna tells me they all disappeared for

258

a considerable time under the Taylor's cooker.'

'The cooker?'

'Yes, Mrs. Montgomery, and they refused to come out.'

Dawn broke slowly over Mrs. Montgomery's face but dawn did not bring with it joy and birdsong; thunder threatened.

'This, this is … still most unfortunate, most unfortunate. You knew the child had guinea pigs, yet you allowed …'

The feeble argument caused Mrs. Montgomery to bluster, thrashing around in search of a better one.

'The babies will be removed as soon as it is safe for them to do so, Mrs. Montgomery. Toffee and Chips are both females, as Mrs. Jones assured me they were.'

'Toffee … and Chips?'

'Yes, Mrs. Montgomery, those are the names of our guinea pigs and I must say the children have proved diligent and responsible looking after them.' How Lauren wished she could have added, so put that in your pipe and smoke it.

Chapter 42

Pet shop owners, vets and encyclopaedias, consulted for information on the care of newborn guinea pigs proved to be in total agreement: all the recommendations tallied. To Lauren's immense relief, among the screeds of 'dos' and 'don'ts', it was declared that new born guinea pigs could be handled without causing them harm.

Santa brought in another letter.

'Dear Miss Massey,

Bert Jackson, the pet shop owner, says the guinea pigs should stay with their mother for at least three weeks. I suggest that when we fetch Toffee and Chips on Friday we keep them here with us for that period. We can then bring them back to spend the last few weeks of term with you. If it's for the good of the babies I'm sure the children will understand.

Bert says you can sex the guinea pigs at birth. He said it's necessary to do this early because they can reproduce while still very young.

Let me know if you agree to our keeping Toffee and Chips for three weeks.

Sincerely,

Donna'

'Reproduce while they are still very young?' That's all I need; Mrs. M walking into the classroom, the floor heaving, ankle deep in tiny guinea pigs.

Clearly making a huge sacrifice, the children agreed, for the sake of the babies, that the guinea pigs should stay with the Joneses.

Lauren's birthday fell on a Saturday. Mum and Dad phoned, not too early, and Fiona took Lauren out to dinner. Along with the ones from friends from home and college, there were cards from Brenda Cunningham, Rose Dawkins and Amanda Scott. Lauren's presents included a silk scarf sporting a sinuous red dragon (did the dragon signify anything?) from Miles, two books from Fee, blouse and skirt from Mum and Dad and a pot of particularly viscous goo from Grandma. Lauren couldn't remember what she was supposed to do with this special goo – lather it on somewhere, but where? When? Night? Day? After bath? Andray-ah's instructions had been very specific about time and exact location on the body onto which every cream should be lathered.

Reports took up much of Lauren's thinking time. Her own had too often included, 'could do better,' 'must pay attention,' 'more care should be taken,' all of which, like background music, meant absolutely nothing. She'd already decided never to use any of those phrases, nor would she resort to 'satisfactory,' which too often meant, 'who the heck is this? I really can't place this child.'

Sports Day loomed. Although the weather seemed to get hotter every day, Lauren felt obliged to fan the flame of enthusiasm for Sports Day. The children's interests lay elsewhere. School work took on a different tempo, andante in the morning, slowing down even more as the day wore on. Serious work happened immediately after assembly; story time at the end of the day got longer, with the children often resting their heads on their desks while Lauren read.

She felt as if they were marking time until the three highlighted days on the calendar: Sports Day, the Fete, and

261

the end of term. Certainly time did funny things; the days dragged but the weeks flew, reports would have to be with Mrs. M. next week.

Milly's Friday piano lessons had become one of the highlights of Lauren's week. Bright and biddable, not even objecting to scales, Milly made excellent progress. Her particular delight; playing duets with Lauren.

Michael Gregory always appeared after the lesson to join Lauren and his father for tea and cake; cake freshly baked by Alan Gregory.

'Would you like Milly to take her Grade 1 piano exam?' Lauren asked.

'What do you think? My instinct is to avoid unnecessary exams. Shall we ask Milly?'

'Good idea.'

'What does it mean? Will my lessons be different, Miss Massey?'

'No. The only thing that would happen is that I'd take you somewhere and one, perhaps two people, would listen to you playing, and then give you marks. If you played well, and I'm sure you would, you'd get a certificate.'

Milly thought for a moment. 'Would they be nice people?'

'I think so, yes, they are usually nice people.'

'I like my piano lessons the way they are now, Miss Massey.'

'So do I Milly.'

'I think we have our answer, Miss Massey.'

Lauren was getting to know this family so well, the 'Miss Massey' was beginning to grate. But would it be appropriate for her to be called 'Lauren' here, with Adam – and very often Santa, too, and the boys then having to call her 'Miss Massey' at school? It would be fine with her, but what if the 'Miss' slipped and Adam called her 'Lauren' at school, with Mrs. M within earshot?

Michael Gregory cleared his throat.

'Miss Massey, I want to ask you something. You've given me an idea for a book, but I must ask your permission before writing it, and I'll quite understand if you'd rather I didn't.'

'Oh, you want to write a book about Goldie stealing my lunch and strewing it all over the park?'

Lauren blurted it out, more harshly than she'd intended.

Michael Gregory recoiled. He looked aghast. 'NO!', he almost shouted.

'No. How could you possibly think that? I was mortified when that happened. I'd have given anything to turn the clock back. You didn't seriously consider that I … that I'd … and all this time you've imagined … Oh no.'

'Yes, I did. Adam told me you based your books on things that really happened and I thought …'

'No Miss Massey, I never had the slightest intention. This is awful. Do forgive me …'

For what? Lauren wondered, feeling like a prize idiot.

'No,' Michael Gregory said, 'no, this is something that happened in your classroom. Adam couldn't stop laughing about it. I think it would work well. I've made some sketches. Can you spare a minute to come to my studio and have a look?'

Chapter 43

Sports Day dawned fine and sunny. The morning had a
robotic feel about it; something to be got through,
mechanically. The bell, after lunch break, bidding children
back into their classrooms, tolled fifteen minutes early to
ensure that everything and everyone materialised in good
time and in exactly the right place.

Napoleon Preston, wearing a Panama hat which might
have fitted him once, and rust-coloured polo neck shirt,
strutted around exuding irritability. Lauren wondered if
he'd consider it a defeat, should he ever have to
acknowledge that someone had got something right. With a
whistle dangling round his neck, Mr. P carried a large
handbell in one hand and a clipboard in the other. Two
biros stood to attention in his shirt pocket. The handbell
accompanied his movements with tinny sounds, at
unexpected moments.

Class 3M now wore plimsolls, hats and coloured
bands across their bodies. Springmeadow had a tradition of
dividing children across the age range into Houses. These
dormant Houses only came to life on Sports Day. 'Why
can't we swap, Miss Massey? Kirsty likes the blue one and I
really don't mind a green one.' Bluebell house wore blue;
Shamrock, green; Primrose, yellow; and Rose, red.

Hats had been insisted upon, 'preferably one that
protects the neck.' While Class 3M waited to receive their
summons, Lauren appraised the headgear: spotty beach-
type bonnets, straw hats (one bearing artificial cherries), a
cloth cap belonging to a much larger person, white cloth
ones, like those worn by bowlers, and Bradley's baseball
cap, which he'd attempted to wear back to front.

The summons came.

With Pritti at the head of the queue and Adam and Santa bringing up the rear, they set off for the playground carrying their chairs. George struggled a bit, but Lauren could see Chang keeping an eye on him. George would manage.

Mr. P indicated that Class 3M should place their chairs behind the line, in a straight line, 'I said a STRAIGHT line', one arm's distance, 'go on measure it, boy' from the chair at the end of the other class.

Mr. P was already having hissy fits and the races hadn't even started, the chairs weren't even in place.

Parents began drifting in, sitting behind their children where they could. Mr. P went over and asked if they'd please fill up the chairs in order. Most would, not all, one or two affected convenient deafness and stayed put behind their child.

Well behind the finishing line, at a right angle to the lines of chairs, a table had been placed, with two chairs behind it. An object, looking like a blue witch's hat stood on the table.

Watching the chairs arriving, Lauren wished she could draw. There was something odd and ungainly, angular, about the way the children held their chairs, almost as if the chairs impeded their forward movement.

Lauren glanced at her watch; a few minutes to two and surely, all present and correct.

For several minutes nothing happened. The heat, bouncing off the cement playground, seemed to throb. A plane could be heard and distant traffic. The children shuffled their feet. The woman seated behind Lauren wore far too much perfume. Someone should tell her.

Surreptitiously, Hugo P looked at his watch and did his best to smile.

Mrs. M appeared, with Rose Dawkins following a few paces behind. Every head turned in their direction. Mrs. M wore a dress of unrelenting beige, beige stockings and beige sandals. The wide brim of her straw hat undulated so that only half her face was visible. Mrs. M looked like a very large mushroom.

Rose Dawkins carrying a bag, no doubt containing the certificates, wore a hat with turned-back brim, revealing the whole of her face. Over her pale blue dress, she wore a loose-fitting chiffon jacket. Lauren gave Rose top marks for a Sports Day outfit.

Mrs. M and Rose took their seats behind the table. Mr. P picked up the witch's hat, which turned out to be an old-fashioned megaphone.

The megaphone worked. Only too well. Adopting his hearty mode, Mr. P welcomed the parents, burbled something about a time-honoured tradition, attempted a joke about the hare and the tortoise, and announced the first event.

Arm up, having waited for complete silence, Hugo Preston blew the whistle to start the race. Two dinner ladies held the finishing tape. Ordinary-straightforward running, House relay, three-legged and egg-and-spoon races were run. Even hard boiled eggs couldn't survive the amount of bouncing asked of them; dustpan and brush materialised and eggs were replaced. Knees and elbows were grazed, small children bumped into each other, there were tears, disinfectants, plasters and soothing. The 'collect the beanbags' took a great deal of preparation every time, Mr. P never being completely satisfied with the placing of the beanbags. The prefects on one occasion, misunderstanding his instructions, picked up the beanbags which had been carefully placed only seconds earlier. Beanbags featured heavily, handed from one runner to the next for the relay. Not every class's number could be divided neatly into four like 3M's. So when it came to 'running for your House,' a child wearing the correct coloured band was swiftly recruited from another class to make up the numbers. There was no question that when Fiona's class ran their 'House race', Ash won it for the Bluebells.

The procedure at the end of each race seemed a tad cumbersome to Lauren. Brenda Cunningham, eye firmly on the finishing tape, sole adjudicator of winner, second and third, asked the victors their names as they breached the tape. Reaching for one of the postcard-sized slips of paper in a box on the table, Brenda Cunningham repeated the name as she wrote it down. Rose Dawkins did her best to keep up, writing the child's name on the certificate in front of her which already bore Mrs. Montgomery's signature.

Having given their names to Brenda Cunningham, the children lined up in reverse order, beside Mrs. Montgomery. Brenda handed her piece of paper to Hugo Preston who bellowed out the name. Rose handed the certificate to Mrs. Montgomery, who baring her teeth slightly, handed it to the lucky winner. Lauren could only assume that the system was working. No child checked that the certificate in their hand actually bore their name.

Parents did their best to keep the perfunctory applause going.

Surprisingly Kylie and Louisa won 3M's 'class three-legged race,' getting into a steady rhythm from the start. Ash and Pritti came a close second. George and Chang brought up the rear, encouraged by cries of 'Go on George,' from the audience. Sally easily won the skipping race; the rope seemingly irrelevant as she ran.

Watching Amelia line up beside Mrs. Montgomery to receive her certificate for coming second in the egg-and-spoon race, Lauren noticed her give someone a little wave; just a small movement of her hand at shoulder height.

Lauren turned to see Michael Gregory, Donna Jones and Christine Harding waving back, echoing her gesture.

'And now, the race we have all been waiting for … the parents' race.'

A small cheer arose from the lines of children.

Imitating a fairground barker, Hugo Preston bellowed, 'Come along, don't be shy, it's the annual Springmeadow parents' race.'

Not 'parents' race' Lauren thought; mums' race. Michael Gregory was one of a small sprinkling of fathers. Donna Jones, Christine Harding and Maria's mum, Mrs. Stewart, all, Lauren noticed wearing sensible shoes, lined up with perhaps a dozen others at the starting line.

Hugo Preston blew his whistle. The mums set off, most of them running as if catching a bus at the end of a day's shopping. Christine Harding was doing something else; running like an athlete she won by several yards. Class 3M were ecstatic; they cheered, some children stood up and punched the air. This was one of their mums, they all knew her, she'd been with them to Kew Gardens and she'd won! Megaphone held to his chest, Hugo Preston looked disapproving. Mrs. Montgomery turned and glared. Mrs. Harding, facing Class 3M, smiled and applauded them.

3M subsided into their seats. No certificate, just the

honour of being announced, via the megaphone, that 'The winner of the parents' race is Mrs. Harding.' Only a camera would have been able to sort out second, third and every other place. Seeing Christine Harding so far ahead, the mums who followed collapsed into chaos, several giving up well short of the finishing line.

Rose Dawkins had been doing sums, her biro jumping down the page as she added.

'Ladies, if you'd take your seats again, I will announce which House has gained the most points.' Hugo Preston consulted Rose.

'Bluebell House has the most points, closely followed by Shamrock. Well done Bluebells.'

Perfunctory applause.

'Now, ladies and gentlemen, if you would remain seated, we'll ask the children to take their chairs back to their classrooms. The children will come and find you. Would you please remain seated, ladies and gentlemen.'

This last sentence spoken loudly: parents, were standing, greeting each other.

Hugo Preston waited. The parents sat.

A stream of small people bearing chairs wound its way round the playground and into the school building.

Back in the classroom the members of 3M flopped into their chairs. Some of them studied their certificates then showed them to their friends. The certificates bore the school crest, name of race, name of child, place, date and Mrs. M's signature.

'You behaved really well and all of you tried hard. Well done. Those of you whose mum or dad is waiting for you on the playground line up. Right, good afternoon children, you may go. The rest of you line up. Good afternoon.'

Lauren sat at her desk and, removing her straw hat, which made her head itch, ran her hand through her hair. Like everyone else she'd been sweating profusely. She needed a cool shower, now.

Sports day was over and Rose Dawkins had 3M's reports, which would be on Mrs. M's desk first thing tomorrow morning. Two things could now be written off with gigantic ticks: jobs done.

Fiona came in and, fanning herself with her hat, perched on the lid of Charmaine's desk.

'Hot or what? Something really odd is going on out there on the playground. I went out just now to retrieve Justin's hat, and all the parents were chatting away. Normally, after Sports Day they just drift off home with their offspring. This lot all seem to know each other. How come?'

Chapter 44

July, and only three weeks until the end of term. Lauren wondered if all Springmeadow's auspicious occasions had to happen on a Thursday: Sports Day, Thursday, Final Open Evening, Thursday ... end of term ...

The day after Sports Day the children looked slightly pinker than usual, thanks to their spell in the sun. Robert turned a deeper shade when Bradley told him his mum was, 'Dead cool.'

'She's a really serious runner,' Adam said, 'she does training, proper training.'

'Like footballers?' Col asked, 'Does she, Robbo? Does yer mum do proper training?'

Still glowing Robert said, 'Yes, she does.'

There followed an awestruck silence as the information sank in. The reflected glory was almost too much for Robert, who hung his head and opened his mouth as wide as it would go to stop himself smiling too much.

News time, usually on Mondays, had been switched to Friday due to a Sports Day rehearsal. Since the guinea pigs had gone home with him, Santa had top billing. Having informed the class that the babies were two girls and one boy, Santa said, 'it's the little one, the one that's all black that's the boy and he's bossy. He pushes the girl ones away. You'll see, they'll be coming back soon.'

Maria said her auntie had brought her a Spanish doll back from her holiday in Spain, 'like a Barbie with black hair and little saucer things in her hands.'

Ignacio's hand shot up. 'Is not saucers, is castanets, they go like this.'

Hands above his head, Ignacio opening and closing his hands, demonstrated the clicking of castanets. 'They do it when they dance.'

For some reason half the class joined in, clicking their invisible castanets; the demonstration in full flow when Hugo Preston came into the classroom.

With Mrs. Montgomery in deepest purdah, perusing every report, and Rose Dawkins fending off any attempt at disturbing her, Hugo Preston's authority swelled into absolute control. This period, and Sports Day when he'd conducted the whole performance as a one-man-band, justified his existence. Hugo Preston attempted a strut (not easy, given his bulk), took assemblies and ensured that his views were known on every subject including the correct way to stack books. Everyone must be aware, at all times, who was in charge. This reign lasted twelve days. Just as well, Lauren thought, no human could have kept up that level of interference for any longer. For the first time she understood what the phrase, 'micromanagement' meant.

Noticing the absence of the guinea pigs Mr. P said, 'Gone have they? About time, too.' Turning his attention to the children, he said, 'Two of the bands you were wearing yesterday are missing. They have not been returned. Will you now, each of you, open your desk and see if there is a green or yellow band in your desk, go on, do it now.'

Twenty-four desk lids stood to attention, the children disappearing behind them. Mark's vain attempt not to giggle set Graham off.

'This is not funny,' Hugo P thundered, 'someone, perhaps one of you, has misappropriated school property.'

Happier shielding behind their desk lids, the children stayed there, heads down.

'Well? Have you found the bands?'

Some completely out of sync, feeble-sounding replies of 'No, Mr. Preston,' could just about be heard.

'I want them back. If you took one home, bring it back. Tomorrow!'

Good luck with that, Lauren thought, tomorrow is Saturday.

Reminded by Joanna that not everyone had told their news, the session continued. Joanna's news featured holiday plans, including parental disagreement. Her mum was fed up of camping and wanted to sleep in a proper bed without creepy crawlies getting into the sleeping bag with her.

Sally was anxious to tell the class about the new member of her household. 'She's called Loo chee ah and she's an oh pair. She's helping mum look after our Billy and we have to help her learn to speak English really well. Loo chee ah likes it when I teach her pop songs, but mum says I have to teach her proper words as well because she gets muddled all the time. She says sheep for animals and sheeps for big boats, exactly the same. She doesn't like our food but she does like Horlicks. Loo chee ah calls it Frolics and she sometimes has her Frolics in bed. Dad says there's a song about Loo chee ah but mum won't let him sing it.'

As usual Milly's piano lesson ended with a duet – a march this time. Listening behind the door, waiting for the lesson to finish so it would be cake time, Adam and Santa came in and marched round the room in time to the music.

A very large, sticky-looking chocolate cake stood on the kitchen table. The two Mr. Gregorys, Donna Jones and two other women studied the Fete chart on the kitchen wall.

Three slices of cake swiftly dispensed, the children disappeared into the garden.

Donna Jones beamed at Lauren. 'Hello again, Miss Massey, you really had my feet tapping with that march – I was all but saluting. We're starting the countdown for the Fete. Michael told me you and Miss Bates, is it? would be happy to run the bric-a-brac stall, is that right?'

'Yes, we thought it would be fun.'

'I imagine it will be. You wouldn't believe the assortment of stuff we've accumulated.'

'Yes, in my garage,' one of the women added.

'Miss Massey, meet Annabel Mason and this is Sandra Webster.'

Annabel Mason was one of those people so pale as to seem transparent. Her light blonde hair was not bleached – it just looked faded and her large, pale grey eyes looked … unfinished, they still needed a bit of colouring in, a bit more body to them.

Donna Jones turned to Lauren, 'Annabel and I wondered if you and Miss Bates would like to help us sort out the goods for your stall. There's no obligation … of course … '

So on Saturday morning, at ten on the dot, Lauren and Fiona turned up at a neat semi-detached house, to be greeted by Annabel Mason. Somewhere a button was pressed, a garage door slid up and out of sight, revealing tables and benches covered in overflowing cardboard boxes; the floor no longer visible.

Lauren gasped. Fiona burst out laughing. 'I love it, where do we begin?'

'Come in and have some coffee and we can decide

how to set about it. I've recruited some more helpers. I think we're going to need them.'

Through the kitchen window Lauren recognised a pair of twins from school, now wearing bathing costumes, squirting each with water pistols, sliding around on sodden grass.

'That stuff in the garage ranges from really good costume jewellery and crockery to absolute junk, only fit for the dump with just about every other category in between,' Annabel said. 'Freddie, my husband, is putting some trestle tables out and there are lots of black bags for the rubbish. There's such a lot of stuff we can't get too picky. I suggest we stick to three categories: really good stuff, just about saleable and rubbish.'

'Yes,' Fiona said, 'Treasure, also ran, and dump.'

'Right, table one will be labelled "Treasure". What about the other one?'

'Goods – good stuff,' Lauren said.

'I'll get the scribe to make the labels.'

'What about pricing?' Fiona asked.

'Apart from a couple of "everything here for 10p" trays, I really wouldn't bother, just turn on the charm and ask, "What will you give me for this elegant object?" Even if we only got 10p for everything in there, we'd make a fortune.'

The sorting began. For ten minutes the furthest table, designated 'treasure', bore a solitary teapot, soon to be joined by an only-very-slightly-peeling pearl necklace, jet bead dangly earrings, with a good three inch dangle to them and a set of faintly scented, lace place mats, done up in a violet ribbon.

Broken or incomplete items began filling the black

refuse sacks under the tables. Decisions started slowly. Lauren held up a tin tray depicting three white kittens attempting to bat a butterfly, so twee it made her teeth ache. About to put it in a sack, she remembered the picture on Charmaine's pencil case. The kittens went on to the sellable table.

As the heady sensation of power grew, decisions speeded up. It had been agreed, everyone's decision was final – no arguments.

Early on sub-categories became necessary: toys, cosmetics and clothes. Apparently most items of clothing were being housed in yet another garage. But some garments had strayed into the bric-a-brac boxes; the top half of an orange bikini came Lauren's way, and a blouse, whose buttons had been carefully removed. She picked up a pink knitted item adorned with a clumsily crocheted poppy. Judging by the shape it could be a hat, or maybe a tea cosy. Lauren tried it on. It fitted, therefore hat.

Annabel Mason held up a single blue suede sandal, sighed, said, 'pity' and put it in a refuse sack. Within half an hour Fiona was festooned with a genuine feather boa, Annabel Mason wore dark glasses with the price label hanging down and Sandra Webster had a beaded and tasselled evening bag slung over her t-shirt. Lauren had forgotten to take off the hat, although she was still in two minds about it. The object had a slit in it, seam come undone or deliberate? Perhaps for the teapot spout?

The trestle tables had been laid out in the front drive, the scene occasionally gathering little knots of neighbours at the gate. Seeing the tables getting dangerously full, Sandra Webster took it upon herself to start packing the loot into boxes. Yards of bubble wrap cushioned the 'treasures'. Mere 'goods' would have to take their chances.

Going into the kitchen for a drink of water, Lauren spotted a Sports Day certificate, pinned to the fridge with a fridge magnet. Lauren remembered the Mason twins winning their egg and spoon race. This was the first reminder that the Fete was for the school. No one had mentioned school, Sports Day, Mrs. M, or Mr. P.

Lauren and Fiona joined the lunchtime picnic in the back garden. Plates of ham, tinned salmon and cucumber sandwiches were passed round, together with Scotch eggs and pork pies. A cool bag held cans of beer and coke. There was much talk about Freddie.

'Freddie is going to give every stall a float of £3 in small change,' Annabel said. Lauren had gathered that Freddie was treasurer. 'Using outrageous bribery we've enlisted the children as runners. In pairs, in shifts they'll go from stall to stall asking if the stallholders need anything, so if you run out of change they can bring it. Don't ask what the bribery consists of Miss Massey.'

'I hope you've made it worth their while,' Fiona said.

Annabel's face lit up. 'Ah here's Freddie.'

Lauren turned to see a man, so round he could have been a ball, coming towards them. If he tripped, he would surely roll and roll ... Lauren was reminded of Tweedledum and Tweedledee in her 'Alice in Wonderland book'. Freddie wore a yellow t-shirt. Red braces held up his khaki trousers. Without the braces … well you might as well expect an apple to keep up a pair of trousers. Freddie's feet seemed to be small, but it was hard to tell, the rest of him sort of overhung them. Eventually Lauren noticed wavy black hair and a small black moustache over gleaming white teeth.

'I've got them, darling,' he said to Annabel, putting his hand on her shoulder. Annabel reached for his hand and held it.

Lauren and Fiona, who had been trying hard not to stare, were introduced to Freddie.

'You wouldn't believe the stuff we've sorted, Freddie. We've nearly finished,' Annabel said.

'I'll come and help you,' he said, 'then perhaps I can have my garage back.'

They made their way back to the tables and dragged the last few, slightly musty-smelling boxes tucked in the corner of the garage, out into the sunshine.

The sorting continued.

'Look what I've found.' Freddie held up something in front of him. With the sun in her eyes Lauren couldn't make out what it was. She went closer. It was a garment of some sort with hooks and eyes and lacing and whale bones. It was of an indeterminate grey with faintly rusty patches. It could once have been white, or maybe pink … possibly even apricot coloured… fraying, showing signs of wear … Lauren recognised it as a corset.

'I think she only ever had the one,' Freddie said.

Chapter 45

With Mrs. M still in purdah, Mr. P's tirade during morning assembly made it very clear that the coloured bands were still missing and this simply would not do. The bands must be returned. His tetchy monologue completely washed over the children.

From her vantage point at the piano, Lauren watched several girls fiddling with the hair of the girl in front of them. Boys tested the velcro fastening on their trainers or studied the cards in their pockets, weighing up which ones they might consider swapping, and there was at least one football game being planned. A boy gestured first to himself, then, using both hands demonstrated the goal. Nods of approval from lads further down the line indicated they'd got it. He'd be goalie. Mr. P rumbled on regardless.

At break time Lauren asked Fiona, 'Do you know where you can buy those coloured bands, like the Sports Day ones?'

Fiona nearly dropped her coffee, 'You're not thinking of replacing them, are you?'

'I am, but Mr. P is so sure there are two missing, what would happen if three bands were to be discovered and returned,' Lauren said, 'what then?'

Fiona thought for a moment. 'Too cruel. It would mean a nervous break down at the very least.'

Apart from Mr. P's reign of terror, school went on much as usual, as if nothing was happening 'out there'. Lauren reckoned she and Fiona were the only people aware of the activity going on in the streets surrounding the school.

Lauren discovered there was at least one other person

in the know: Mr. Beamish, the caretaker. He came into Lauren's classroom one afternoon as she was packing away. Mrs. Montgomery insisted that all adults on the premises must be addressed by their titles at all times. Lauren knew Mr. Beamish was Ken, but Ken had been placed out of bounds.

'Miss Massey. Freddie Mason told me if I had any messages for the Fete committee and couldn't get anyone on the phone, you are in touch with Mrs. Jones, is that right?'

'Yes, Mr. Beamish. Of course you must know all about it, too.'

'Have you noticed, Miss Massey, that my car has been on the road these last two weeks? I've got three portable barbecues, a child's paddling pool, some free standing umbrellas and all sorts in my garage.'

'It's very good of you Mr. Beamish, I hope it's not putting you out.'

'I can't remember when I've enjoyed myself so much. If you could get a message to Freddie or Mrs. Jones?'

'Of course. Will tomorrow do?'

'Yes, that's fine. Could you tell them the ducks have arrived.'

'The ducks?'

'Yes, rubber ducks. They'll be swimming in the paddling pool and Joe Public has to try and bag one, ring it with a hoop, oh and please tell them the hose does reach. I tried it out.'

Lauren felt like a conspirator and decided she quite enjoyed it. For a few seconds she considered retraining and becoming a spy.

With Open Evening looming, lessons took a different

turn. Would whatever they were doing look good on Open Evening? If not, don't bother. Favourite stories became illustrated books. Using a large needle and assorted scraps of wool, Lauren spent a great deal of time book-binding, sewing the assorted pages together.

Maps for geography and a time-line for history spoke for themselves. Progress in mathematics was more difficult to demonstrate – neat lines of sums, were just that … and signified very little. Lauren remembered the flip chart where she'd written, 'The answer is 16, what is the question?' Underneath she'd written the children's names and their questions. Everyone had contributed. Some questions, though correct, were predictable; Graham's 'what's fourteen and two more?' and George's 'just only one less than seventeen?' But Sally had ventured 'how old do you have to be to get married?' and Adam asked 'when should you start learning to drive so that you can pass your test on your next birthday?' These might more accurately come under the general knowledge heading, but… the flip chart page would go up anyway.

The classroom walls, a blaze of colour, showed the children walking through the school year. Every child had lain, full stretch, on a very large piece of sugar paper. Accompanied by a great deal of wriggling and giggling, Lauren drew round each child with chalk. Spencer's deep voice didn't extend to his giggle, which was way up there with the high sopranos, and being almost unbearably ticklish, his giggles began with the chalk still several feet away. The figures, then cut out and given an identity, with paint and felt tips, now adorned the walls illustrating every event; pride of place going to Kew Gardens. The children were life sized, the guinea pigs on what might be called the 'heroic scale,' of a size guaranteed to terrify any passing cat.

Lauren wondered how much the children in her class knew about the Fete and whether they'd been told not to mention it. Santa and Adam must be hearing about it all the time. If they'd been told not to talk about it at school, what reason had been given? One playtime Lauren had overheard Joanna say 'my mum's going to do makeup.' Lauren expected the Fete to come up at news time. It never did.

Kylie, having just discovered the word, suffered two agonies that week. The first agony, in her foot, could be explained by too-small plimsolls. The cause of the second agony, round the tummy area, was less clear. It could have had something to do with a minor tiff with Louisa about the swap, (or not) of a purple plastic troll with abundant orange hair, designed to sit on the end of a pencil. The troll's seating arrangement looked very painful to Lauren.

At break Brenda Cunningham came up to Lauren and Fiona and whispered, conspiratorially, 'It's ridiculous, isn't it? The world and his wife will be descending on the school on Saturday and in here ... by the way, what time will you two be getting here?'

Hearing about the bric-a-brac stall Brenda said, 'Do let me join you. You'll want two people manning the stall while the third roams around eating candy floss and burgers. You can't be stuck behind the shop counter all the time.'

'I hadn't thought of that,' Lauren said, 'Yes, please do join us ... we've got the most amazing tat to sell. One of us can wander and two of us sell stuff.'

'Did you notice any clocks in amongst the treasures?'

'Yes,' Fiona said, 'I came across a carriage clock with

no back to it and a couple of watches, one really old one. Why do you ask?'

'My old man will descend on them like an eagle on a rabbit. He picks up watches and clocks then cannibalizes them to mend other clocks and watches. Would we be allowed to hide them under the counter for him?'

'I think we could do that,' Fiona said. 'I've got my eye on a very small Buddha, for which I shall offer a good pound of my well-earned money. What are you coveting, Lauren?'

'I'm torn between a pink hat, which just might be a tea cosy and a tray with three kittens on it, doing their best to bat a butterfly.'

'I think you two had better keep in with me,' Brenda said, 'I do believe one of my dads is treasurer.'

'Freddie Mason?' Lauren asked.

'You've met him? The Mason twins are in my class. He's a lovely man, everyone knows our Mr. Mason. He's been trying to get a Parent Teacher's Association going for years, and he wants to raise funds for the school, but Mrs. Montgomery has not been keen. I don't know how she agreed to let this Fete happen. There must be someone out there who is even more persuasive than Freddie Mason.'

Yes there certainly is, Lauren thought.

Chapter 46

At half past nine on Saturday morning the hum of activity could be heard two blocks away. Fiona parked well away, not knowing if the staff car park was available. It might have been turned into a barbecue station or shooting gallery. The noise got louder as Lauren and Fiona approached the school.

On the railings, to the side of the gate a large banner read, SPRINGMEADOW SCHOOL FETE, SATURDAY 10th JULY 10:30 to 4:00.

Two tables funnelled visitors into the school. For ten pence visitors could not only enter the premises but were rewarded with a pink programme listing the stalls, times of events and the names of the local shops which had so generously supported the school. And the number on the programme also automatically entered the bearer in a raffle.

The man selling the programmes looked up as Fiona and Lauren arrived. 'Ah, Miss Massey and Miss Bates. No, no you don't pay an entrance fee. You wear one of these.' He handed each of them an enamel badge labelled 'stall holder.'

Slightly puzzled that the man knew who they were, Lauren realised that probably most parents knew who all the teachers were; an odd thought as she only knew the parents of children in her class, and wouldn't even like to be tested on those.

As Lauren and Fiona walked onto the field they were greeted by waves from parents and excited children. The scene reminded Lauren of one of those medieval paintings so crammed with busy people it was hard to know where to focus.

'Do you know what this reminds me of?' Fiona asked. 'Those pictures where you have to find Wally. Where's Wally?'

From a corner of the field Annabel Mason waved both arms and jumped up and down to catch their attention. She stood in front of two long trestle tables, behind one a large sign read, TREASURE, behind the other GOODS, GOOD GOODS. Cardboard boxes under the tables bore the letters T or G.

'I thought these might be useful, save you saying "how much will you give me?" over and over again.' Annabel produced two signs that would stand on the tables, each read, 'What's your best offer?'

'Would you like me to help you unpack?' Annabel asked.

'I think we can manage, thank you,' Lauren said. 'Brenda Cunningham is coming to help us.'

'That's lovely, the twins will be pleased. You're sure now?'

By some unspoken agreement Fiona became keeper of 'Treasure' with Lauren unpacking 'Goods'. Santa and Adam appeared, each carrying a plastic chair.

'For you and Miss Bates, in case you get tired, dad said.'

'Thank you, Adam, thank you Santa.'

'My dad's doing instant portraits,' Adam said, 'he's got a tent all to himself.'

'My mum and dad are on the cake stall,' Santa said. 'Mum told me to tell you to get in quick because everyone wants to buy cakes. We'll bring you some carrier bags and the small money. What's it called Adam?'

'The float,' Adam said.

Two large tins stood on the as-yet bare tables. With luck, by mid afternoon they would be overflowing with coins and perhaps even the odd note or two. A tearing sound cut through the general murmur; someone trying out a loudspeaker system.

Lauren and Fiona unpacked. Lauren remembered Kim's game which they played at Brownies. In one minute you had to memorise twenty assorted objects on a tray. She'd been quite good at it – another attribute a spy might need. From time to time, Fiona or Lauren went round to the front of the table to see how it looked, then they'd move an object; the photo frames from which half-remembered matinée idols leered, could stand at the back.

Brenda Cunningham appeared, 'Wow! I see what you mean … what an extraordinary array of … stuff. Fiona, Lauren, this is Geoff, my husband.'

A pleasant-looking man, wearing a linen cloth cap, striped t-shirt and jeans, shook hands with them.

'I believe you're saving some contraband, under-the-counter stuff for me.' He looked round conspiratorially.

Fiona produced the clock and watches.

'Splendid, yes please I'll have these. Will a fiver cover it?'

'That's far too much,' Fiona said.

'If it's for the school … and I'm not likely to buy anything else. If this Fete turns out to be like the Scout ones, you'll get a rush at the beginning. I can help here for the first hour if you like.'

With so much going on it was hard to tell the exact moment when the Fete started, but quite suddenly a surge of people headed for their stall. Geoff and Fiona dispensed treasure and Brenda and Lauren handed over goods in exchange for smaller money.

The tray with the kittens was the first thing to go.

A woman picked it up and said, 'Vera will love this. A quid all right, dear?'
Familiar faces began appearing.

Sally, holding 'our Billy's' hand, said, 'Hello Miss Massey, this is Loo chee ah.' A beautiful dark-haired young woman held our Billy's other hand.

The young woman smiled, 'How do I say? Please I meet you.'

'I'm pleased to meet you, too,' Lauren said. She could understand why Sally's mum was not too keen to have Sally's dad serenading Lucia.

Young Billy's attention had been caught by a magnifying glass among the treasures. With the sun likely to shine steadily all day, a magnifying glass could become a lethal weapon. Lauren needn't have worried. Billy abandoned the magnifying glass preferring a necklace of shells, which, within seconds of purchase, went over his head and hung down well below belly button area.

Business kept them so busy for the first hour or so that Lauren was only half aware of the children in her class and their parents, all of whom bought something from the 'Goods' side of the stall.

Geoff, prepared to haggle over prices, proved to be a superb salesman. When the crush subsided to a trickle, he announced that he'd have to go to pick up an order from the garden centre. Giving Brenda a peck on the cheek he left with clock and watches tucked into a Sainsbury's carrier bag.

'Lauren, why don't you have a look round now, Fiona

and I can manage.'

'You're sure?'

'Go on and be sure you get something to eat.'

A tune from an old musical played in the background. Smoke from the barbecues drifted towards her, almost masking the smell of burgers. From time to time someone announced over the loudspeaker that there were still valuable prizes to be won on the tombola stand, and 'if you want your portrait done, get in there quickly, the queue is getting longer … '

Two tiger-faced creatures, wearing dresses, approached: only just recognisably – Maria and Suzanna. 'Hello Miss Massey, my mum is helping Joanna's mum with the makeup. Have you seen Col?'

Trade in the cake tent had not subsided; delicious-smelling supplies still arriving on tea-towel-covered trays.

Donna Jones greeted Lauren with a smile and a wave.

'Oh good, I've saved you some goodies. I hope you approve. There's a box for you and one for Miss Bates … and no, you're not to pay for it. Here you are. Thank you for all you're doing.'

She's thanking me, Lauren thought. I'll benefit from the Fete; she doesn't have to do any of this. Glancing in the box Lauren saw, among the brownies and cupcakes, two pork pies. Clearly among her many qualities, Donna Jones was also clairvoyant.

Wandering round, Lauren came across an open tent. Concentrating on the woman in front of him, Michael Gregory sat on a chair holding a drawing board and a piece of charcoal. The woman, head held high, stared haughtily into the middle distance.

And here was Col; eye-patched and moustachioed,

with an evil-looking scar running across his cheek. 'I'm a pirate, Miss,' he said running off to show someone else his terrifying visage.

Lauren recognised the swagger coming towards her.

'Miss Massey,' Mr. Hawkins said. 'This is going well … really well, should be a nice little earner. What's it for? I mean, what's the cash for?'

'I'm not sure, Mr. Hawkins. I think the reception class could do with some smaller furniture and someone mentioned a video camera.'

'Video camera? Every school should 'ave one of them. I can get one, rock bottom price. Promise me, Miss Massey, if the school's buying a video camera you come to me. You won't regret it, Miss Massey. If it's for the school I can get you the best deal – the whole package. You won't get a better one, you tell 'em Miss.'

Turning to go back to the stall Lauren bumped into Annabel Mason.

'We're raking in the money. Freddie and Alan are in Ken's House. Two dads, who are policemen, said it would be wise if they were somewhere secluded. There are five people in there just counting the money as it pours in. Here are some envelopes. If you want to, when you reach £20 you can send the runners back to the treasurer with the envelopes. Be sure to label the envelopes bric-a-brac.'

Back behind the stall, Lauren was suddenly aware of a change in the general hubbub. Somewhere, in one corner, everyone had fallen silent. The silence spread … people turned searching for the cause …

And there they were: Mrs. Montgomery and Hugo Preston. Hugo Preston in his Sports Day outfit: too-small panama hat and rust coloured shirt. Mrs. Montgomery, carrying her mushroom hat, wearing a voluminous kaftan of blue and green.

For a few seconds no one moved. Lauren thought, here is the empress of all she surveys, yet just now she's on alien territory. Had Mrs. M and Mr P decided to come together, or was this just a coincidence?

As Lauren watched, Donna Jones went up to Mrs. Montgomery and led her into the tea tent. People began chattering again.

Hands behind his back, doing his best to bounce jauntily, Hugo Preston made his way around the grounds.

Reaching their stall Mr. P said, 'And what have we here, ladies?' Although in ho ho mode, Hugo P was clearly lost for words. Lauren dearly wished two coloured bands would materialise on her stall. He moved on.

The wind changed direction, blowing the smoke from the barbecues towards the bric-a-brac stall. Things began winding down. People ambled up to the stall, glanced absent-mindedly at the remaining objects, and moved on.

The loudspeaker announced the winners of the 'guess the number of Smarties' competition, the 'location of the treasure on the map' and the winning number on the entry programme.

'Ladies, gentlemen, children thank you for your support. I'm sure you'll all agree we've had a splendid time – and there are so many people to thank, I'd be here all afternoon. But I must mention one person, without whom this Fete would not have been possible. He's given us his time, his help and considerable expertise and this afternoon he's even given us his house. Ken Beamish, where are you? Thank you Ken.'

A huge cheer arose from the crowd. An overcome Ken

Beamish waved shyly.

'Joe Public' began drifting away. Parents with refuse bags scoured the field picking up paper plates, raffle tickets and discarded pink programmes. Trestle tables were flattened, plastic chairs stacked in fives and still-burning coals on the barbecues dampened down.

Lauren went over to the cake tent.

'Mrs. Jones, what should we do with the left over bric-a-brac?'

'Could you pack it into boxes? Someone will take it to a charity shop. I'm told there's not much left.' Donna Jones laughed, 'How you managed to shift some of that stuff I'll never know. Did you speak to Mrs. Montgomery?'

'No, I saw her arrive. Mr. Preston came to our stall.'

Donna Jones looked at Lauren for a moment. 'Mrs. Montgomery didn't stay very long but I'm really glad she came. It can't have been easy for her.'

What was it Michael Gregory had said about Donna? 'She should be running the country.'

She should. At the very least, Lauren thought, Donna Jones should be put in charge of the diplomatic service.

Chapter 47

On Monday morning a solitary pink programme, stuck under a bush, was the only trace of Saturday's Fete.

'Staff Notice Monday, 12th July (The Daily Shout)

'Reports are to be taken home today. Please ensure that the envelopes are addressed to the child's parent or guardian and that the envelope is <u>firmly</u> sealed. The report of any child absent from school today must be given to Mrs. Dawkins as soon as possible. These reports will be posted to the children's homes.

It has been brought to my notice that some school property, in use on Sports Day, is still missing. It is character-forming for the children to understand that they are responsible for school property in addition to their own possessions. Please ensure that the children in your class are aware of this. I expect everyone to do everything they can to see that the missing items are found and returned before the end of term.

The fund raising Fete on Saturday proved successful. The parents on the Fete Committee have asked me how the school will be using the sum raised. The Reception Class is in need of new furniture. A video camera was mentioned at a staff meeting, but I fail to see how a video camera could enhance the children's education in any way. If you have any suggestions for the use of funds please give them to Mrs. Dawkins, in writing. Use of funds will be an item on the agenda for the staff meeting on Thursday.

(signed) Squiggle omery'

The guinea pigs returned – all five of them, brought

back by Michael and Alan Gregory. The three newcomers had swelled so much they were barely recognisable. Such was the constant activity, there seemed to be more than five of them. The guinea pigs bumped into each other, pushed, shoved and vented their general dissatisfaction with high pitched squeaks. The guinea pigs were disgruntled. When there were only two of them they had been peacefully gruntled at all times. Lauren wondered if they took turns in sleeping in the comfiest place and didn't always agree about whose turn it was. There was always one, not-best-pleased, guinea pig on view.

Santa arrived with a letter.

'Dear Miss Massey,

Thank you for your contribution to the success of the Fete. I'm writing to Miss Bates and Mrs. Cunningham to thank them, too. Freddie Jones hasn't got the final figure yet because not everyone has sent in their expenses, but he thinks well over three thousand pounds was raised.

There is another reason I'm writing to you. With Santa's birthday on Christmas Day he loses out on parties. We would like to invite everyone in Class 3M to a picnic in the park next Saturday. Everyone in Class 3M, of course includes you. Santa very much wants you to come and I think, if I put on the invitation that you will be present, parents who don't know us will know that their children will be well looked after.

Please say you'll come and you – and the rest of the class will get an invitation tomorrow.

Sincerely, Donna'

Staring at the letter, Lauren felt a strange sensation

somewhere in the tummy area: that phrase 'parents will know that their children will be well looked after.'

Just before home time on Monday reports were given out with instructions to hand them to parents immediately. They'd all been signed by Mrs. M but Lauren wondered if she'd actually read them. Lauren thought perhaps she should have written a line of 'rhubarb, rhubarb rhubarb' on someone's report, just to see if Mrs. M reacted. Maybe next year ...

On Tuesday Santa arrived with 25 envelopes. Lauren opened hers:

'Dear Miss Massey,

You are invited to a class picnic in the park on Saturday 17th of July, starting at 3 p.m. We will be providing food, drink and games. Please wear clothing suitable for hide and seek and rolling down hills. We are very happy to let you know that Miss Massey will be with us.

This is not a birthday party so no presents, please ... just your presence.

We hope you will be able to come.

(signed) Santa Jones'

'Why don' you want presents, Santa? It's your birthday, innit?' Col asked.

'Course it's not 'is birthday, Dumbo,' Bradley said. "e's called Santa Claus because he was born on Christmas Day, 21st of December, dum dum.'

'My birthday is on the 25th of December,' Santa said. 'We thought a picnic would be fun, no other reason.'

'We might not be able to come,' Ash said, 'because ...'

Pritti butted in, 'I'll talk to Auntie ... I think she'll let us, if I tell her ...'

'It would be really lovely if everyone could come,' Lauren said.

Final touches for the Open Day display were made; objects placed 'just here' and not to be moved. Nothing messy could be contemplated. Powder paints, lids firmly in place, stood well to the back of the store cupboard, water pots and paint brushes banished to the highest shelf. The class played Lauren's skittles game, where she knocked children off their desks if they couldn't answer a spelling or mental arithmetic question. Extra stories were read, neat lines of sums frowned over ... whatever they did, it didn't matter what, as long as it was tidy.

Suddenly aware that the Fete had come and gone with almost no acknowledgement, Lauren decided this was completely ridiculous. She said, 'Hands up if you came to the Fete.'

Every hand went up.

'Good. In whatever way you like, writing or drawing – colouring with crayons or felt pens, write or make something you can remember the Fete by. You can work together if you want to. Think about it for a minute. Let me know if you need any words.'

'Barbecue', 'amazing', 'tombola' and 'scrumptious' appeared on the blackboard.

Several children conferred. Soon Chang and George, heads together, were in deep discussion. George came up and asked if they could have some of that 'thicker paper.'

'Card?'

'Yes, but not too thick, please.'

Opening their arms wide, Adam and Santa

demonstrated that they needed 'one of those really big sheets', as they were making a plan of the stalls, Pritti asked for the wax crayons so she could draw some of the made-up faces, Kirsty and Arabella made a list of all the things you could eat at the Fete and Charmaine drew some of the baby clothes on sale at the Craft Stall.

George said he and Chang needed some glue. Glue equalled mess. Lauren only hesitated for a moment before giving it to them.

When the playtime bell sounded Chang came up to her desk.

'Miss Massey, may George and I stay in this playtime and finish something?'

Less than two weeks to the end of term and Chang had come to ask her something. For the first time.

'Yes, you may. I'll go and get my coffee. If anyone comes in tell them Miss Massey is coming back.'

Explaining to Fiona why she was heading back to the classroom, Fiona said, 'I'm getting my class to write letters to the Fete Committee to thank them. The whole school should be doing it, really.'

Deciding not to get involved in what Chang and George were doing, Lauren looked at some marking. Concentrating, the boys didn't speak much; the understanding between them made speech unnecessary. Chang handed George the scissors, indicating where the paper should be cut, then drew some more lines. They reminded Lauren of the concentrated silence in an operating theatre.

George and Change stood back looking at two small tents; the teepee one Michael Gregory had occupied, and the longer one which held the cake stall.

As the children filed back in, they immediately surrounded the tents for a better look.

'That's brilliant!' from Charmaine, 'Did you make them Chang?'

'And George,' Chang said.

Lauren realised she'd have to tweak the Open Evening display.

'End-of-termitis' felt to Lauren as if everything lurched from one headline to the next – with nothing in small print: Fete, staff meeting, Open Evening, class picnic. Somehow she couldn't visualise the biggest headline of all – the last day of term.

On Thursday morning Lauren handed Rose Dawkins a note headed 'possible use of Fete Funds: A set of tuned bells.'

A cheeky suggestion, the bells were shockingly expensive but … Lauren remembered what Sally said when she first heard the sounds accompanying the 'ding' and 'dong' for their carol.

'That's just magic, Miss Massey.'

Chapter 48

With everyone crammed into the staffroom, more air was needed than the feeble breeze now wafting through the one, oddly-placed window.

Mrs. Montgomery made her entrance; late enough to ensure everyone's full attention, early enough to allow time to get through the agenda. Wearing a flimsy, loose-fitting maroon jacket, Mrs. M took several seconds to sink into the chair, the jacket floated a little before it, too, settled. The effect was of a maroon sphere with a head on it. Lauren was reminded of an ancient terra cotta statue dug up from an Inca burial site. With her permanent frown and sharp nose, Mrs. M could stand in for the Inca goddess of thunder.

Next year's classes had been assigned; Lauren inheriting Amanda Scott's lot, Brenda Cunningham inheriting Lauren's.

Mrs. M seemed dithery and out of sorts, more petulant than her default mode: rank disapproval. Mr. P glared round, no doubt searching for the missing arm bands, or maybe for a clue as to who had taken possession of them: a badly disguised smirk, perhaps, someone tapping a pocket, or looking furtively into a handbag ... Mr. P took the missing bands personally, their absence a deliberate slight directed at him.

Lauren's mind wandered during the first few items on the agenda; predictable whinges about 'slipping standards', 'the school year not yet over', 'children getting careless', 'the playground a disgrace', 'chewing gum', (twice) 'unsuitable foot wear,' and 'teachers must be vigilant because a parent had complained that her child was learning swear words at school.'

Where else, Lauren wondered. That's where she'd learned to swear. Jason was definitely the best swearer, instructing the whole class, and being specific about of the exact degree of outrage each word would meet. But he got carried away by his success and had persuaded her that 'district nurse' was really, really rude.

Lauren's attention roused itself when she heard the word 'recorders.' Someone suggested that school funds should be spent on buying recorders for an entire class.

Lauren cleared her throat and put up her hand. 'Who would be teaching the recorder, Mrs. Montgomery?'

Everyone turned towards her.

Mrs. Montgomery replied, 'As teacher with responsibility for music, Miss Massey, that would be part of your … duties.'

'If we are trying to help children appreciate music there are better ways of doing it than with recorders. The screeching sounds could put some children off music for life.'

Lauren winced at the memory of trying to teach the P.E. students the recorder at college. Just the thought still made the insides of her ears feel tender.

Mrs. Montgomery stared at her. Glancing down at her notes she said, 'I see you have made a request for tuned bells.'

Brenda Cunningham butted in.

'I would certainly second that, Mrs. Montgomery. Tuned bells would be a great asset to the children's musical education. We could do with some other musical instruments, too.'

Amanda Scott added, 'They could be used during

assemblies, too.'

Tuned bells was carried by a unanimous vote.

'And now, would someone give me an explanation as to how a video camera would enhance the children's education.' Mrs. Montgomery shuffled a little and leant back in her chair.

Lauren decided to sit this one out. Attempts were made: to make records of lessons, to film school activities, school outings, scientific experiments.

Mrs. M remained unconvinced. 'It is as I thought. The mere recording of something is not, of itself, educational. A video camera is not necessary.'

So school funds would be spent on: furniture for the reception class, ready-mixed paint, which Brenda persuaded Mrs. M would be less messy and less wasteful than powder paint, tuned bells and some new plants for the front of the school, even a tree if the funds ran to it.

The item, 'upholding the standards of Springmeadow this evening' and 'ensuring that an essential formality when dealing with parents is maintained at all times', wound up the staff meeting.

The guinea pigs were objecting. Usually evenings were theirs alone. Now the noisy comings and goings caused a disturbance and someone had had the temerity to move their cage.

Lauren waited for the first parents to arrive: Mr. and Mrs. Hernandez. They must have found a way to sort the 'sifts'. They were coming together.

She glanced round the classroom and decided not to touch anything. Lauren wondered about the purpose of this evening. Would the conversations centre on the reports? Not a lot could be changed in five remaining working days.

Every flat surface now held maps, pictures, objects made by the children, the tents and the big Kew scrapbook. Most desks displayed open exercise books and drawings. On top of the plan of the Fete, two little piles stood on Santa and Adam's desk. Having discovered the joy of book making, the boys had churned out volumes and pamphlets, both fiction and non-fiction, starting with 'How to look after guinea pigs,' and finishing with the adventures of the very small flying dragon inspired by the dragon fly at Kew.

Parents came in, greeting each other with easy familiarity, studying the classroom walls with delight. The main topic of conversation – the Fete. 'What would we have done if it rained?' The guinea pigs also received attention. 'That was a bit of a surprise, the guinea pigs producing babies. Out of sight were they? Pity that, they could have usefully illustrated the "birds and the bees talk".' 'I understand Toffee and Chips are going up a year with the children, to Mrs. Cunningham.' 'Am I right Robert is having the two female babies, with the male one going to the pet shop?'

When parents sat beside her desk, what transpired was like a cosy chat, 'Behaving himself, is he?' 'She likes your skittles game, Miss Massey.'

This evening, Lauren decided, was the beginning of the winding down, the first in a line of farewells; almost, but not quite the full stop.

Then only four people remained. They stood studying the tents Chang and George had made: the two Mr. Gregorys and Donna and Leo Jones.

'Did the boys make these without a pattern?' Michael

Gregory asked. 'Pretty impressive. They left just the right amount on the tabs to hold the glue.'

Had she done this deliberately, Lauren asked herself, given Michael Gregory and the Joneses the last slots? No – there had been a request for a late appointment from Michael Gregory. In case there had been any problems she wanted the evening to end with these people.

There hadn't been any problems. Mr. Hawkins's insistence that the car she needed was, even now awaiting her in a nearby garage, could hardly be described as a problem. Lauren decided to withhold the school's decision regarding a video camera from Mr. Hawkins. He needn't know that they would not be needing his services acquiring one just yet.

'Christine wants to photograph the classroom,' Donna Jones said, 'did she ask you?'

'She's coming tomorrow morning. She'll take some photos before the children arrive, then some with them in the classroom.' Mrs. M had not been consulted.

'How are you feeling, Miss Massey?' Donna asked. 'Relieved? You should be pleased.'

How am I feeling? Lauren wondered. How long have you got?

Smiling, Alan Gregory said, 'I expect Miss Massey would like to get home. Thank you.'

'By the way,' Donna Jones said, 'all the class will be coming to the picnic. Isn't that lovely? We'll see you on Saturday.'

Chapter 49

'You look ... jaunty ... dapper.'

Fiona looked up as Lauren came into the Apollo cafe.

'Hang on, Fee. Those are words reserved for sprightly old gentlemen. I have never had an invitation with such a specific dress code. Am I suitably attired to play hide and seek and roll down hills?'

'Spot on. Judging by what you're wearing I would have known, immediately, exactly what you were about to do. Black jeans, red blouse, red sandals ... and the little strawberry earrings giving it the final "tah rah". So what are you going to do at this picnic?'

'Be there. I just have to be there. My attendance, apparently, makes the whole thing respectable.'

Fiona nearly choked on her sandwich.

'You realise, Lauren, that this time next week ...'

'I do. But time is doing funny things. Sometimes, in class, I think the clock has stopped, then whoops, Open Evening has come and gone.'

'I hope,' Fiona said, 'that you remembered to tell the parents that their once thick children are now finely-tuned founts of all knowledge, thanks to your brilliant teaching.'

'Oh, they already knew that,' Lauren said, 'they were much more interested in the guinea pigs.'

Starting late, Lauren managed to spin out lunch until it was time to head for the park.

Two benches, forming a right angle, under the trees in the far corner of the park, had become the picnic HQ. The two Mr. Gregorys and Mr. and Mrs. Jones greeted children heading in their direction. Lauren glanced at her watch: 2:55. A cloud suddenly obscured the sun. The deep shadows vanished. Lauren wondered whether there was a plan B in case of rain. But just as suddenly as it had disappeared, the rays of sunlight coming through trees picked out the outlines of leaves, making them look like dark freckles on the lime-green grass.

Several children ran towards Lauren.

'There's a treasure 'unt, Miss,' Col said. 'I never done one of those. Bet I find it, Miss.'

The children seemed to be doing something between bouncing and milling, occasionally grabbing each other. It reminded Lauren of a just-landed flock of birds, jostling for territory.

Pritti and Ash approached, watched by two women in saris, standing a little distance away: Ash's mother and Pritti's aunt. Lauren wasn't sure how it all worked, but it very clearly did. Lauren started to wave, realised that could seem dismissive, so she walked over to them. The women made a slight bow, to Lauren and, hands together, gave her the *namaste* greeting.

'Good afternoon,' Lauren said, 'I'm so glad Pritti and Ashok were able to come. Thank you.'

'Miss Massey,' Auntie said, 'we may be a little late fetching the children. I am concerned …'

Lauren butted in, 'Please don't worry, Mrs. Patel, I will stay here until all the children have been collected.'

Donna Jones made a head count: 25. Number 25, being smaller, was not immediately visible, then Millie burst out of the throng to give Lauren a hug round the middle.

Pairs, and one threesome, set off with a clue to the whereabouts of the treasure.

Bradley's method was to run in every direction, covering as much ground as possible in the hope of spotting the treasure. He had misunderstood the instructions: find the answer to clue number one, then come and get clue number two.

Stopping by the notice board with the map of the park on it, Suzanna pointed and conferred with Maria. The girls raced back to the grownups to get the next clue. They had been seen. Other pairs went over to the notice board. Word got around. A queue formed for clue number two. Eventually, Suzanna and Maria, having found the final answer, strolled back nonchalantly, so no one would guess what they'd done. The prize was theirs.

Alan Gregory said, 'Santa wants to teach everyone how to play kick the can. Santa can be on guard first. This patch here is the prison. Anyone Santa catches has to stay in here, until someone sets them free, by kicking the can. If Santa catches them first, they are put in prison, here. To start with, if someone can kick the can before there are any prisoners and before Santa catches them, they become keeper and Santa is their prisoner. Off you go … run away and hide.'

A carefully washed empty tin of Heinz baked beans was placed by the side of 'the prison'. It didn't take long for Santa to nab seven prisoners. The 'cell' got crowded.

From the corner of her eye Lauren saw George emerge from some bushes and crouch behind the bench where she and Leo Jones were sitting; Santa's concentration entirely on the opposite direction.

George emerged and gave the tin a swift kick. Whooping with joy, hissing "Yesss" the prisoners escaped.

Santa laughed, 'I was sure it was going to be Ash … '

Picnic tea came in individual, named boxes. Lauren noticed Pritti glance at the contents of her box, smile, and nod to Ash. Lauren's box contained a box of apple juice, dainty cucumber sandwiches, a brownie and a small pork pie. Uncanny.

Empty boxes collected, several girls started doing cartwheels and handstands. The boys jumped on each others' backs and were piggybacked for a few steps before collapsing into untidy heaps. Some of the heaps stayed where they were. The seemingly boundless energy began to flag. The children sat on the grass, some back to back, one or two absent-mindedly pulling up little tufts of grass. Kylie searched for daisies to make a chain, but as three didn't quite do it, she tossed the flowers aside in disgust.

Donna Jones leaned forward. 'Just before you go home, there's another little box for each of you, so don't forget to collect it before you go. Now ... Mr. Gregory has written a story, specially for you.'

Michael Gregory opened a folder, took out some sheets of paper and looked around.

'Are you sitting comfortably?', was greeted with giggles. 'Then I'll begin. This is a story about some ... creatures in Kew Gardens.

A wicked wizard found an old book about magic creatures. He read that two creatures, possessing magic powers, were hiding in Kew Gardens. But the page saying exactly what these creatures were, was missing. The wizard thought that if could capture the creatures (whoever they were), and put them in a very small cage, he would be able to force them to hand over their magic. When he caught them, he planned to keep them without food or water and he'd make horrible loud noises with his trumpet all night long so that they could never sleep. And he would go on doing this until they gave him their magic.

The problem was that the wizard, clever as he was, only knew that they were creatures. They could have been tigers, ladybirds, rhinoceroses, grasshoppers, monkeys or gnus. He had no idea what they were.

The wizard's assistant, who didn't like his master one little bit, managed to get a message to Santa Jones.' (At this point in the story, little gasps escaped from the children. Santa got a pat from both sides.)

Michael G's deep voice and the story had the audience hypnotised. 'Santa recruited the whole of his class to creep into Kew Gardens one dark night to rescue the creatures. The iron gates were locked with a great big, rusty padlock. Searching around the children found a gap in a hedge and one, by one, they crept through. The wizard's problem – not knowing what the magic creatures were – was also the children's problem. The wizard's assistant said, "please try, I'm sure you'll know them when you see them."'

In their quest to find the creatures Michael Gregory mentioned every child's name. Jonathan had noticed a low vine which they could all have tripped over, Graham caught a plant pot which would have set off a burglar alarm, Inga held back the branches as everyone climbed through. As his or her name was mentioned, the child wriggled with delight, smiled shyly or gave themselves a little hug.

'Just as the search was about to be called off Pritti noticed a rustling under the bushes. She shone her torch. "It's not magic creatures," she said, "just two little guinea pigs. We'd better rescue them, I think they must be hungry."

Creeping back through the hole in the hedge, the children took the guinea pigs home. Santa reported to the

307

Wizard's assistant on the telephone, "We tried, we really did," he said, "but we didn't find any magical creatures, we just rescued two hungry guinea pigs."

For a moment the Wizard's assistant was silent. Then he said, "You've done it! You've rescued the creatures with magical powers and if ever you meet a Wizard, please don't tell him you have the guinea pigs or where you found them. Never, ever give that information to a Wizard. Promise me you won't."'

No one noticed that some of the parents now stood behind the children, listening to the end of the story.

Graham asked, 'Is that true, Mr. Gregory, that Toffee and Chips are sort of magic?'

'Toffee and Chips are magic,' Louisa said, 'so the babies must be magic, too, they must be mustn't they because if their mummy and daddy have magic, the little ones are as well.'

Still a little dazed, the children began thanking Mr. and Mrs. Jones and collecting their 'take away' boxes. Col, seeing his mum, flew across the field only to be sent flying back to say thank you for having me.

Ash and Pritti spotted Ash's Mum. Pritti turned to Michael G.

'That was brilliant, Mr. Gregory. Would you lend me the story so I can copy it?'

'I'll give you a copy, Pritti. Adam will bring it on Monday.'

Of course, Michael G was an author, made his living writing children's books, but this...

'That story,' Lauren said. 'The children loved it. It was ... absolutely perfect. You went to so much trouble.'

Michael G laughed. 'I'm sorry, Lauren, I don't mean to

be rude, laughing at you. It's just <u>you</u> saying to <u>me</u>, that I've gone to a lot of trouble.'

Adam, Santa and Millie lay on the grass some way off, finding engines, dragons and currant buns in the clouds.

The four adults sat on the benches in the, still warm, sun. Holding on to the moment, savouring the afternoon, no one spoke. There was absolutely no need.

Chapter 50

The sound level rose. Mr. P, patrolling the premises, made perfunctory attempts at restoring discipline; wasted breath. As there was no tomorrow here, there could be no sanctions, no punishments. Anarchy ruled.

Everyone was 'demob happy'. With bare walls and overflowing waste paper baskets, Lauren's classroom resembled a junk yard. Piles of rubbish had to be separated from someone's 'essential possessions' to be taken home at the end of the day. Trying to get pictures off the wall, torn ones were confined to rubbish sacks; surviving pictures claimed and argued over. Exercise books, identified as having more than five blank pages, had already gone up to the classroom that would become 4C.

The children played games, wandered around, sat on each other's desks and fidgeted. Everyone marked time until that final bell.

Surveying the pile of presents and cards on her desk, Lauren surrendered to her exhaustion. For the next few days she'd set the alarm for the delicious pleasure of turning it off and rolling over for another hour or two's sleep.

The class register, here on her desk, was now a historical document. Lauren had seen the old registers, covers fading, piled up on a high shelf in the storeroom. Perhaps some day, someone doing research would refer to one, blow off the dust and search for a name...

The summer holiday stretched ahead, already glowing in the sunshine of Fiona and Ben's wedding. Solemnly declaring that she would not be walking up the aisle masquerading as an exploding meringue, nor would she promise to obey Ben, Fiona had persuaded Lauren that her chief bridesmaids dress of apricot silk would be most suitable for 'future balls'. Miles was to be Ben's best man.

On several days in August, according to her diary, Lauren would be going to Michael Gregory's home to collaborate on his new book. He had assured Lauren that she would get equal billing. Greg hoped it would make a series ... three or four books following the antics that the Finks, Kelses, Nuffs and their mates got up to in the classroom at night.

Lauren thought of the children who had just walked out of the door. She'd see them again, of course she would, but they would no longer be hers. They were growing up fast; already taller, more solid and confident than they'd been last September. Soon they'd be out there, doing jobs – possibly not as politicians nor captains of industry, maybe not even making headlines as famous pop stars. But Lauren knew they'd be doing the really important things, the jobs that make other people's lives possible, the ones that keep the world turning.

Kirsty and Arabella, who spent a great deal of time plaiting each other's hair would, no doubt, be raising people's spirits in a hairdressing salon. Charmaine was determined to be a carer like her mum, Adam and Santa, having got the bug, would churn out instruction pamphlets. Pritti had decided to be a teacher and George would have grown enough so he could see out of the window to drive an underground train.

In too few years Class 3M would be running the world. And the world would be in good hands.

Printed in Great Britain
by Amazon